Master Thorn and the Red Bean Princess

A Minimus Mu Adventure

Pattison Telford

eBook ISBN: **978-1-7781240-1-3**
Paperback ISBN: **978-1-7781240-2-0**
Hardcover ISBN: **978-1-7781240-3-7**

For Sarah, who said she'd only read the book if it was dedicated to her.

Acknowledgements

Thank you to my early readers: Samuel Alfrey, Norman Finlayson, Mary O'Neil

Impeccable editing by vickybrewstereditor.com

Cover illustration by Audrey Jacques
Cover design by Darin Morrison-Beer

Minimus Mu Adventures

You can find out more at www.pattisontelford.com

Master Thorn and the Red Bean Princess

Books by Pattison Telford

Redferne Family Series (Contemporary Fantasy)
Sky Lanterns Over Nether Ides
Shadow Over Loch Ghuil
Whispers Under Middle Ides

Minimus Mu Adventures
Master Thorn and the Red Bean Princess
Master Thorn and the Mothers of Midnight (Forthcoming)

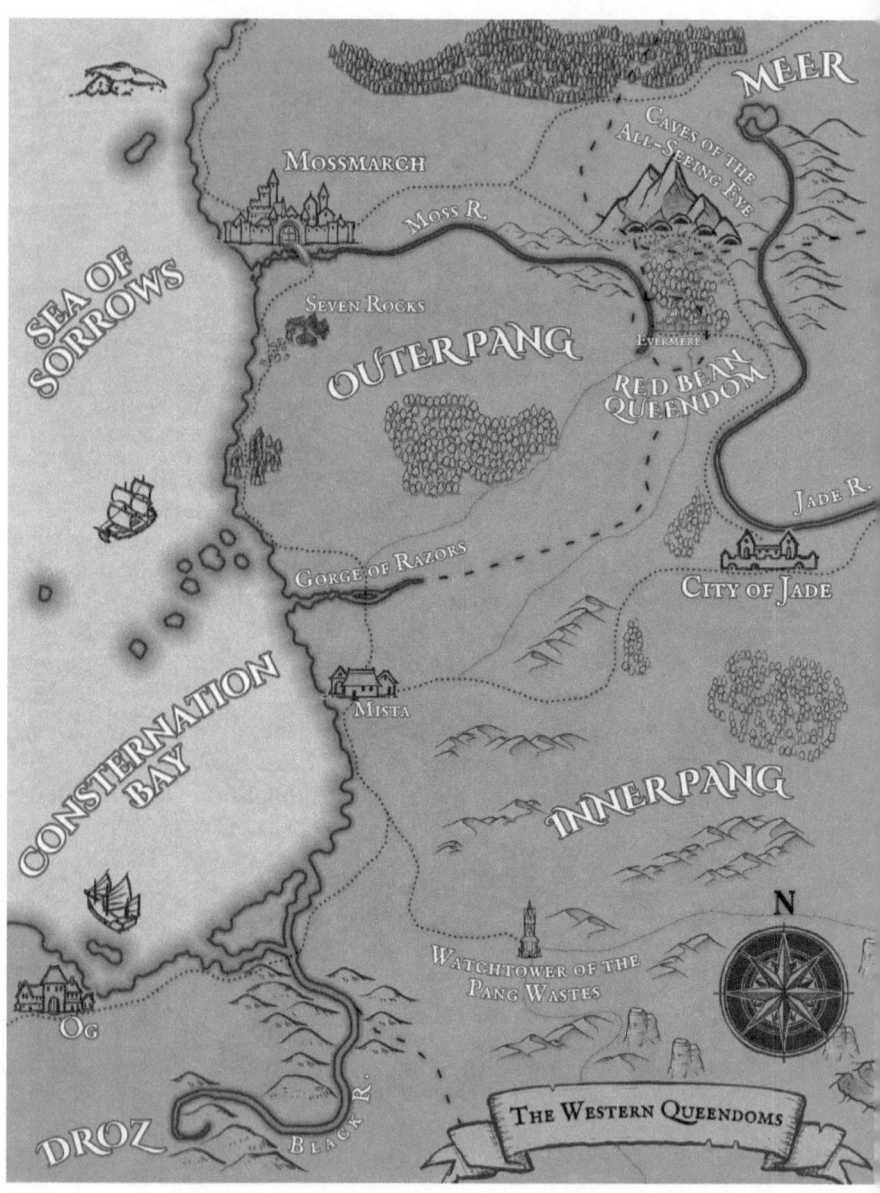

CHAPTER 1 - GORGE OF RAZORS

Sugarday of Moon, Year 127

As I hoisted the burdened cart overhead and teetered across the swaying rope bridge, a single pan from Master Thorn's collection fell clattering into the unseen depths of the Gorge of Razors. Master Thorn, atop the cart's higgledy-piggledy tower of goods, informed me in graphic detail of the thrashing he would deliver once I hauled us across. Jing Jing tightened the clasp of his grasping tail around the cart's spokes and chattered beside my ear in animated monkey tones. Straining, with every knuckle white, I couldn't shoo him away.

The wispy point of Master Thorn's daggerish silver beard preceded his face with its hooked nose and fabulous eyebrows as he leaned out, threatening to topple the cart. "Minimus, stop here! I'll catch us a gorge cod for supper," he said.

I didn't bother to ask myself whether he was serious. Master Thorn was always serious. I lurched forward a step as one of the bridge's rotten boards snapped underfoot and braced myself in as comfortable a position as could be expected, with the weight of a cutlery merchant's every worldly possession pressed upon me.

A mottled purple mushroom whizzed to my left, hooked on a glinting thread that Master Thorn spooled past my nose. It descended in an endless blur toward the waters hemmed in far below by the chasm walls. Strain turned to pain in my aching thighs and shoulders as the line jinked, seeking to tease the gorge cod with its payload. I tried to think of something, anything, beyond my overloaded muscles and turned my mind to a favorite subject: my misfortunes.

Master Thorn often treated me as nothing more than a workhorse. Indeed, I took the place of a workhorse, pulling his cutlery cart from town to town. It made sense, I guess. Although Master Thorn tells me I still have much growing ahead, I had been as strong as five normal orphans combined for as far back as I could remember. Even longer, as Master Thorn had assured me, grinning as he remembered the quantities of boiled oatmeal I'd wolfed down as an infant. It was no wonder my mother had abandoned me. Despite the grind of work as a spoonwright's apprentice, I was grateful he'd scooped up my swaddled, crying form from that grimy alley and trundled me off in his rickety cart.

But enough of my complaints. With Master Thorn shouting, "Got one!" and the fishing line reeling up in a series of jerks, I coaxed my cramping legs into motion. With cautious steps, keen to avoid the planks in the worst state of disrepair, I advanced across the rope bridge.

Even with this extra care, my colossal cargo nearly dropped. A vision crept unbidden into my mind—of a cartload of apparatus bouncing between the gorge walls to bob in the waters below, where the river surged to froth against ocean tide, exposing the sharp rocks that gave the gorge its name.

My right foot dipped toward a solid-looking plank when my eyes tracked the flapping, cawing progress of a coal rayvn that swooped below the bridge. Its characteristic puffs of fine black powder gusted with each powerful flap, leaving a vague dotted line littering its flight path. With a screech, it passed below the rope bridge, halting my descending foot as I realized a cloud of rayvn dust permeated the intended board, revealing its weakness; if rayvn dust wafted both around *and through* the wooden slat, it wasn't safe enough to withstand my weight and the crushing mass of the cart overhead.

I corrected myself and avoided that board, finding safe purchase on its neighbor. The coal rayvn flew three silent circles around me as I completed the crossing, wheeling away as I angled my aching back forward to let the cart roll onto firm ground. Jing Jing, clad in his tiny leather jerkin, swung free and pranced on the rocky slab beneath the cart's iron-shod wheels, excited at Master Thorn's catch.

"Look at the size of this fella!" Master Thorn said. The gorge cod dangled, magnificent. Its scales scintillated in the slanting afternoon light, and its proud tailfin, twice the height of its body, shed the last few drops of river water. "Your beatings will have to wait, Minimus. We must eat this beauty immediately. Prepare a fire."

I guess other orphans' misfortunes were more serious than mine. Threats of punishment for being too clumsy, too strong, or not smart enough often concluded this way, unfulfilled. Master Thorn likely wouldn't discipline me once our bellies stretched, full of gorge cod seasoned with spices from a tiny drawer secreted deep within the cart. One time, Master Thorn flogged me with a stringy noodle. Another, he lashed with a blade of long grass on my palms, more tickle than viciousness. Maybe a lesson lay buried in his threats. But was the moral to have more respect for kitchenware? Don't become an orphan? Avoid the rope bridge across the Gorge of Razors? Steal a donkey so I could glide atop the cart with Master Thorn and Jing Jing? I'd never learn.

I assembled a ring of small stones while the knee-high monkey scrabbled for twigs and tinder. Soon, the three of us snacked on snakefruit pulp, while its stripped rind segments smoldered into wisps of aromatic smoke, cuddled up to the blue-white gorge cod flesh. Master Thorn's elegant, thin-hammered pan was the best vessel for cooking the meal at hand, and I wiped a trace of drool from my chin.

I'd have preferred to complete the second stage of crossing the Gorge of Razors before settling in to dine, but we'd negotiated the longer bridge and paused on the aptly named Island in the Sky, a flat-topped pillar of rock that rose from the gorge and offered a place of respite in neither the queendom of Inner Pang nor Outer Pang. We squatted in a purgatory, mid-gorge, grateful for the slanting afternoon sunshine's warmth. It would take only ten minutes of cart-pulling to cross to the next, shorter bridge. The scrubby bushes and pebbled soil clumps that clung to this improbable pillar cared neither for queens nor cutlery artisans, ignorant to the fact that they salted an unruled territory. Or maybe a secret earth-wish acted—the Island in the Sky huddled closer to Outer Pang, with its farms, plains, and red sand beaches, and further from Inner Pang, with its untamed, dusty wastes. Perhaps the slab we'd settled on secretly crept from Inner to Outer Pang, so slowly that nobody noticed.

Just as Master Thorn, poised with a narrow-slotted spatula, prepared to slide a steaming slice of gorge cod onto my gorgeous, polished brass plate inlaid with a spidery ivory pattern, a meek, high-pitched voice interrupted my anticipation.

"I hope you'll excuse me, but might we dine with you three?" the voice said.

Master Thorn looked around, as confused as I about the source of the voice, but Jing Jing's ears twitched as his gaze settled on a bloated, half-eaten gourd that lay discarded beneath a nearby bush. As I peered, a pair of tiny human heads peeked through the jagged opening in the gourd's lumpen orange skin. Rich red curls framed the first face, chin resting on finely boned, alabaster fingers that clung to the gourd's punctured skin. The opening obscured the rest of her body, but I glimpsed a ruffle of lace and the hint of an embroidered top. The second impossibly small person's long hair burnt an even deeper red and fell like a cascade of water. I saw only half of her face, the rest obscured behind her curly-haired companion. I was toothstruck; something about the shape of her fine nose and the radiance of her uneven smile stirred memories deep within me.

I'm not even sure if people use the term *toothstruck* across all nineteen queendoms. Or are there only seventeen? Master Thorn once said he thought a twentieth queendom might lie hidden behind the Quartz Mountains, wherever they lurked. But if you aren't familiar with being toothstruck, it means *pleasantly surprised*. As if a drifting tooth from a hovering goat hit your face unexpectedly. Especially if it was a molar, because they are worth ten front teeth at the currency exchanges. This tiny girl toothstruck me like a molar.

None of us replied, so the closer of the two gourd-lurkers slipped free of the husk, revealing herself to be a little taller than two hand spans. The scarlet top I'd noticed earlier dovetailed into a quilted floor-length dress, and glossy black shoes scuffed at the dusty ground as she spoke again.

"I don't mean to be rude, but might we have some food?" she asked.

Something glittered among the gourd's seeds and pulp, but the tiny woman's companion stepping through the rough-skinned fruit's opening distracted me. She fussed behind her companion, brushing specks of detritus from her padded shoulders. Meanwhile, the first woman regarded our open-mouthed stares with a hint of amusement, idly twirling a shoulder-length curl.

Interruptions perpetually distracted me from important matters, and it would have saved me significant wear and tear on my leather sandals if only I'd investigated the glittering object. I promptly forgot it as the girl leaned from behind her mistress, smiling at me and gesturing with one hand that someone should respond to the question.

Words failed me, and even Jing Jing fell uncharacteristically silent. Master Thorn, ever a stickler for manners and potential sales, bowed low. "Of course, you may, my ladies. The surroundings are scenic, the gorge cod exquisite, and you may even find our company amusing."

He spun to the cart and pinched the knobby handle of a narrow drawer in the bank of hodgepodge cabinetry, squeaking it open with a slight jiggle to overcome the minor warp. With a flourish, he produced a pair of tiny silver platters and fished out two five-piece sets of miniature cutlery. Had he expected such miniscule guests, or had he worked these wondrous items for a royal doll's house? I'd never know the answer; Master Thorn would confound me with mumbles, elisions, or a side story about the shrinking woman of the Jade River if I bothered to ask.

"Dinner is served!" he said. "Join us, ladies."

The young woman and her attendant strode toward the sizzling pan, their footsteps a little too urgent to hide the losing battle between hunger and manners. The girl smiled in relief, but the elegant woman spoke, her vowels ripe and pleasant to the ear.

"Noble sir, our thanks given. We were riven by hunger and fear. We know no one around here."

She curtsied as she approached the campfire and settled to a cross-legged position, dusty dress hem concealing her feet. Master Thorn prised the juiciest-looking morsels from the pan and slid them elegantly onto the silver platters, offering them with a flourish to our guests before serving Jing Jing and me. I got my favorite bronze plate and Jing Jing, a more rudimentary, pounded steel circle that we often used while traveling. Master Thorn gave himself the last portion on his preferred plate, a thin and inconceivably worn copper oval that he often said his great-grandfather fabricated.

"The sight of your food put me in a good mood," the woman began. "I am Tasha of Evermere, and this is Rayne, here. We'd no plans to roam this far from home, but took a chicane. I'll let my handmaid explain."

Chicane should have been my middle name—it seemed every road I hauled us along objected to straightness, finding virtue in each meandering. The girl took up the story, eyeing her waiting plate as her mistress dug into the gorge cod. The name *Rayne* reminded me of stormy weather, but her voice drifted to us like sunshine.

"Technically, we're not supposed to venture beyond the walls of Evermere, but my lady enjoys sneaking out from time to time. I told her she hadn't dressed properly, but it seemed harmless to climb into the hollowed-out gourd there."

"Evermere?" Master Thorn asked. "Are you from the Red Bean Queendom? I've visited only once, when young. That explains your ... um ... stature."

Our guests both nodded. Crossing the delicate cutlery on

her half-finished plate, Tasha replied. "Kind sir, you may not look the part, but you too remain young, like your heart."

Master Thorn had often told me he never blushes, flinches, or stammers. He'd probably say he wasn't blushing now, but Rayne spared him from saying anything by continuing the story.

"It's wild boars and lightning snakes you'd normally worry about outside the walls. Even so, dangerous wildlife encounters rarely happen. Nevertheless, the prin—I mean, Tasha—her mother doesn't approve of such wanderings. And who'd've thought a drift goose could cause so much trouble?"

The clink of cutlery on plates accompanied the rest of the tale about the snatched gourd's voyage from the Red Bean Queendom across the width of Outer Pang. I imagined thermals lifting the drift goose's broad wingspan. The young woman and her enchanting handmaid had snatched glorious but nervous views of the landscape as they bobbed to the wingbeats, hands sinking into the gourd's flesh for stability. Just as suddenly as the goose snatched them up, the honking flyer had deposited them here, on the Island in the Sky, taking only a few lazy pecks at the gourd before flapping away on some other inscrutable mission. The pair had cowered for two days, gnawing bits of gourd and drinking dew before we'd arrived.

Leaning back against a still-warm stone that restrained the campfire's embers, our little lady guest hesitantly asked a question we'd all been considering.

"I know it's not your task, and perhaps too much to ask, but might we hop aboard here and influence you toward Evermere? There'd be a reward."

With the sun setting, Master Thorn declared that we'd cross from the Island in the Sky to Outer Pang tomorrow morning, setting our sights on Mossmarch, the capital city of Outer Pang. From there, we could hop a barge up the Moss River to Evermere in the Red Bean Queendom.

As I staked the flaps of our nightly below-cart shelter, I realized we'd embarked on a quest. Or an adventure. Or maybe a mission. Whatever it was, we had a purpose beyond making and selling cooking equipment. And the promise of a reward. What an offer!

I heard the faint exhalations of our new travelling companions as I lay awake, many wonderings meandering through my mind while Tasha and Rayne slept.

CHAPTER 2 - ISLAND IN THE SKY

Pepperday of Moon, Year 127

Master Thorn had a philosophy about education that was not, to my knowledge, shared by any school, tutor, or palace of learning. He believed that I should absorb all understanding of the world through the medium of puppetry. Each day began with felt figures cavorting about a miniature curtained stage that Master Thorn plopped on the cart's rear ledge, and it seemed we would not break this daily ritual on account of our visitors. The messages of these little performances varied from life guidance, through philosophy, to zoology, and accounting. Many were inscrutable, but all were enthralling, accompanied by Master Thorn's endless selection of voices and occasional interludes of discordant playing of homemade musical instruments. I assumed my traditional position, seated cross-legged on the ground behind the cart, just as I'd done since I had run around bare-chested in a cloth diaper. Tasha and Rayne joined me, exchanging quizzical glances at the unusual spectacle.

Today, Master Thorn used marionettes, his hands scrunching and tugging at the threads of two worn wooden figures with felt clothing. One wore a golden crown, and the other had a shock of white hair and a pair of glassless spectacles attached to its featureless wooden head. The scholarly-looking one held a book between its two hands, and Master Thorn worked his expert fingers to open and close the book as the person addressed the queen.

"Behold, your majesty! I have brought forth a copy of the *Catalog of Lands, Waters, and Beasts* from the Royal Library," the scholar said.

"Lord of the Lakes, it's such a fancy-looking book!" said the queen's voice, sounding less regal and more like an old man attempting to imitate a woman. "Whatever can be written inside?"

"Your majesty! This part contains maps and lists of all the

world's rivers, mountains, and forests. The back section contains a description of every known beast, complete with sketches. Which one might you like to see?"

I would never dare to heckle a puppet performance, but our guests didn't know the protocol and probably didn't care. "Drift goose!" Rayne called out.

There was a pause in the puppetry before Master Thorn took up the scholarly voice again, jinking the strings to close and open the puppet's book. "Indeed, here it is, your majesty. The drift goose. Known to inhabit the western queendoms, it can fly long distances. It may occasionally seize upon young ladies and fly them across the width of a queendom."

* * *

Our tiny new companions sat atop the cart on a pair of delicate silk beanbags that Master Thorn normally used to weigh down the corners of the stall's tablecloth when we set up in town. Jing Jing capered ahead, impatient with my plodding pace as I pulled the cart. He was as eager as I to cross the stubby bridge from the Island in the Sky to Outer Pang proper, but the monkey didn't have to drag a vondabeast's weight of possessions behind him.

As I approached a clump of shrubs around which the path bent, Jing Jing appeared from his advanced scouting position and skidded to a stop in a low cloud of dust, gibbering and gesturing at the way ahead. I ignored him and tried to imagine what a finer pair of sandals would feel like on my calloused feet.

As I rounded the shrub, I halted, lowering the cart arms to the stone pathway with the gentlest bump so as not to dislodge any of its riders, despite my astonished despair. The path straightened and revealed that the short bridge was gone. Ten cartlengths ahead, only the wooden posts staking each end remained.

"By the great hairy beard of the Soup King!" Master Thorn exclaimed. "What's happened here?"

The path ahead ended in a slight ramp, where the wooden plank bridge formerly began. Its meander continued, a shade lower, after the brief interruption of the Gorge of Razors' northern channel. What was normally an easy cart pull now posed a problem.

Master Thorn dismounted and offered a palm to each lady, lowering them to the ground. We approached the gorge lip as a team.

"Hmmm," Master Thorn said. After a pause, he added, "I have a plan."

I knew full well that whenever he said this, he never had a plan. It foretold improvisation. After much experience, I had learned to accept this approach, because somehow, his impromptu actions tended to work out. Like the time we ended up rolling the cart backwards down a steep hill, my legs freewheeling as I clung to its up-thrust handles. We escaped the pursuing city guards and ended up matching speed and blending in with the departing caravan of the Iron Merchants' Guild. Not only did we stock up on raw materials, but our cutlery sales came fast and easy as the guildsters marveled at Master Thorn's handiwork. I became temporarily famous for repairing the bent and twisted tools and implements of the caravanners, owing to my uncommonly powerful hands and lack of other hobbies or prospects.

But this time, I wouldn't trust some vague daydream of Master Thorn's that he'd doubtless bring to life. After sizing up the gap, inspiration fizzled in my head. I figured I could impress Rayne, so I spoke up.

"Wait, Master Thorn, I know what we can do," I said. "Look how narrow the gorge is. I can easily jump across!"

Despite a little shriek from the red-headed woman, I showed how easily I could clear the deep gorge, taking only a two-step run up.

"See? Easy!" I called from the other side. The gap was barely as wide as I was tall. I jumped back again.

"What about the cart, smarty pants?" Master Thorn asked. "You can't make that jump with the cart on your back."

I shook my head but smiled. "True. But look—over there it's lower. If I get a good run up, the cart's momentum will take it clear across."

Master Thorn pulled a short ruler from a back pocket in his knee-length robe and made a great show of measuring the height of the ramp that led to the former bridge. He flicked through a series of impenetrable finger calculations and let out a sigh. "I think you are right, Minimus. This is quite close to my original plan. Let me tie down everything on the cart, and then you can jump it across the gap. We'll wait to one side here, so we can congratulate you on your success without the risk of sharing in your failure."

Congratulations came only occasionally and begrudgingly from Master Thorn's lips, so I looked forward to the possibility. I wouldn't fail. Rayne flashed a smile at me over her lady's shoulder, and I felt a surge of pride course through my cheeks and chest.

With every clanking and swinging item on the cart tied or strapped down for what was likely to be a hard and bouncy landing, I swiveled the vehicle on its sturdy wheels to face the other direction. Now I could use the handles to push the cart toward the gap, allowing me to lean in and propel it with all my strength rather than dragging it behind me. I wiped my grimy palms on even grimier trousers and gripped the wooden handles with knuckle-bulging familiarity.

"Stay clear!" I called.

The replies consisted mostly of monkey chatter, but I heard Rayne's tinkle of a voice urge me to be careful.

My first four steps coaxed the heavy cart into motion, sandals slipping before they gained traction on less dusty sections of the rocky path. The next four were all acceleration, and the final four steps after that were a breeze—simple adjustments to the cart's course so it would hit the ramp square on.

I was airborne—or *prayerborne,* as Master Thorn likely would have said—flying across the gap and praying I had thrust enough speed into the clattering mass of the cart. The cool, wafting breeze from the gorge waters far below fluttered across my flying form before I came to a shuddering stop as the cart's wheels landed and stuck in some unnoticed rut on the chasm's far side.

My plan was mostly a success. The cart cleared easily. But I had expected a further roll along the path, dragging me along to safety. Not stranding me, dangling by only two fingers of a single hand, above a drop that would give me plenty of time to consider my miscalculation before I hit the bottom. If the cart wriggled free from the rut, the handle I clung to would dip, and I'd slide to my doom. The weight of a piccolo bird landing in the wrong place could spell disaster.

"Minimus!" my three human companions called, almost in unison. Only Master Thorn offered advice, though.

"Grab on with your other hand," he shouted. Not a particularly insightful morsel of guidance, but I was glad to hear encouragement rather than scolding.

I often amused the children of shoppers at Master Thorn's cart by demonstrating a one-fingered chin-up. I knew I could lift my entire body weight using a single finger, but I normally showed off on a narrow bamboo bar. Two fingers—two nervous, sweaty fingers—on something as thick as the cart handle might be too much, even for my prodigious grip strength. Far more inspiring than my master's voice was the ill-advised glance down at my swaying feet. A glint of sunlight from the distant bay showed me how far I'd drop if my grip failed.

Straining, with sweat droplets falling from my eyelashes to sting the corners of my narrowed eyes, fingers three and four eventually joined the original two, followed by my free hand. I swung myself to the gorge lip, teetering between the cart handles. A few graceless arm circles saved me from losing my balance and toppling backwards into the Gorge of Razors.

I turned and tried to look as casual as possible, dusting myself off with shaking hands. "See? The cart is across. No problem," I said.

There was a chorus of applause from the other side of the

vanished bridge, and it heartened me to see that Master Thorn clapped with enough vigor to waggle his beard. Was that dust or a tear that he wiped from the corner of his eye?

Rounding the cart, I squatted and pulled the right-hand wheel from its rut, then rolled the cart a short distance along the path, clearing a better landing area. I prepared for the easy leap back across, but Master Thorn held up a palm. "Bring that spare suspension spring when you come, Minimus," he said. "We may need it."

I grabbed the spring from a compartment beneath the cart's wheel arch, a coiled metal shape that I was often ordered to spitz with olive oil. I wasn't sure why we'd need it, but as usual, I followed Master Thorn's instructions without question. Hefting the large spring, I made the return jump.

Our two tiny companions ran to me and hugged either side of one leg while Jing Jing climbed knee-high on the other.

"What a jump! And a bump—I was sure you would fall," Tasha said. "But I'm so relieved you've returned to us all."

"You're so brave, Minimus Mu," Rayne added, her smile wider than ever before.

"Okay, thanks, everyone. I'm all good. Although, I must admit that two-fingered pull-up had me worried for a second. Now, should I jump everyone together, or will you take it in turns?" I asked.

"Jump? Holding us? No, no, my boy," Master Thorn said. "That's so uncouth. If you simply lean across and grab the far lip, we can cross using your back. Much more proper. That's why my plan needs the spring."

I hoped the flush I felt at Master Thorn's criticism of my manners didn't show. I also remained unclear about the spring's purpose. Yes, I could stretch across the span, with toes on one side and fingers gripping the rocky ledge on the other, but how was that more proper than being carried across?

Tasha and Rayne objected, saying they had no problem being carried across. "We let a drift goose carry us across the width of Outer Pang. I'm sure one little jump won't besmirch my lady's good name," Rayne said.

But Master Thorn was having none of it. With the intricacies of his code of honor, there was no point in arguing. I soon faced the depths of the Gorge of Razors once again, this time suspended by only my fingertips and toes.

Jing Jing sprang across first, only a single landing on my lower back before I heard his chatter from the far side. Tasha and Rayne crossed my calves and hamstrings with careful footfalls, one on each side. I imagined them holding hands as they made their way up my back and then edged their way along my triceps and forearms. They were safely across.

Master Thorn came last. He was not particularly heavy, often referring to his state as *slimbo*—desirous of being stronger but trapped in his skinny body. My fingers, wrists, and core muscles burned with the strain of preventing my body from dipping. Anything less than full extension would mean a nasty drop to certain death. But he crossed swiftly and light-footed.

It was only then I realized we had a problem. I could lean across and support myself in the bridge's former position, but there was no way I could get myself upright again. Moving my toes even a fraction would mean one end or the other of my fully extended body would clutch nothing more than cool air. Master Thorn hadn't the strength to pull me up, and Jing Jing and our two new companions were as good as useless against my bulk. My only choice was whether to let go of my fingers or my toes. Did I want to dive into the gorge, or plummet feet-first?

A quiver of fear colored my voice. "Uh, Master Thorn? I'm kind of stuck. Any ideas?"

"Of course I have an idea, boy," he said. "Why do you think I made you attach that spring to your belt?"

I thought it odd that he'd stuck the hook at the spring's end through a belt hole at the back of my belt, but it was just another in a series of his odd behaviors, so I'd given it no further thought. No ordinary belt would encircle me, so mine was composed of two belts, linked. The spring attached just shy of where the belts joined at the small of my back.

"Let me tie the rope from the spring onto this tree over here," I heard him call. "Then we'll follow the plan. You can let go, and the spring will bounce you back up."

Master Thorn sounded confident, but then he excelled at over-optimism. This still sounded like a poor plan to me.

"What if my belt breaks?" I asked.

"Breaks? Impossible! Don't worry. It's made from the toughest ox hide. My great-grandfather passed it down to me. Don't you remember the story of how he used it in the fighting pits of Droz to hold back the mighty Lion of Og?"

I knew that story well. It was one of his favorites, and I was sure he'd regale Tasha and Rayne with the full version soon. I gave a silent prayer that I, too, would hear it at least once more. "But Master Thorn, what about the *other* belt? The one you attached to the tougher-than-dragonhide one your great-grandfather gave you so that it would fit my waist?" I asked.

"Let's not think about that right now. I'll check its strength once you stop fooling around and join us up here."

There was no arguing against that kind of logic. In fact, there was no logic at work to argue against. Master Thorn called that he'd secured the rope from the end of my belt-spring, and that I should continue with the next part of the plan.

I held my breath and counted slowly down from ten while I tried to imagine what my mother's face might look like. I made it to three before Jing Jing kicked my fingers from their tenuous grip on the rocks at the gorge's edge, and I plummeted head-first into the depths.

CHAPTER 3 - FOREST OF DAGGERS

The Same Day

I forgave Jing Jing as my fingernails scraped the gorge wall in vain, even before my toes lost purchase on the Island in the Sky. I knew in my heart that I would have counted down to zero and still clung on. Probably started from ten again. And again. Until my fingers or abdominals lost their strength, and I folded into free fall. The monkey had done me a favor.

I extended my arms overhead, as I'd seen divers do as they sprung from the smooth overhanging rock at the beach on Consternation Bay. Less graceful than those professionals, I was about to be bounced like a discarded snakefruit from wall to wall as I sped into the dim depths of the gorge. Had Master Thorn used the wrong knot? Or maybe failed to tie the rope's other end onto my spring? I seemed to fall further than his so-called plan would have suggested. But at least I hadn't hit the gorge wall yet.

And then I did. The rope screamed tight, and the pair of belts dug into my waist as the giant spring yawed open, pinned between my back and the rough chasm wall. Upside-down, my heels hit the stone hard, the impact absorbed by the mass of calluses that clustered there. Luckily, the spin kept my head from striking anything. I heard the belts creak but not snap, and the spring lengthened until I decelerated to a momentary pause. My pant legs slid toward my knees, and my tunic crumpled to bare my chest.

With an ascending whine, the spring snapped tight again, and I shot upwards. Spinning in slow rotation, head over heels, my eyes closed involuntarily as my head crested the gorge lip and sunlight graced my face. Then my hips cleared the clifftop and, finally, my feet. I'd sprung back to the right height and in an upright position. Master Thorn's unlikely plan had worked. I smiled as I made an even more graceful landing than I had on the cart jump, shrugging my shoulders to release a bulge of pinched skin where the spring had closed as it contracted. I could feel that the spring had clamped onto my tunic in several places, and my heels throbbed from the impact with the gorge wall, but I was overjoyed to be alive.

"I think this other belt could have held off the Lion of Og, too, Master Thorn," I said. "Can someone please pull this spring off the back of my tunic?"

Relieved laughter reached my ears as Jing Jing scrabbled up my side and wrapped furry paws around my neck.

* * *

I padded along the path, happy in the morning warmth to resume my normal duties without the threat of certain death looming under me. Master Thorn answered many questions during the unavoidable recounting of his great-grandfather's encounter with the Lion of Og. I smiled, listening to the lilt of the two young women's musical voices.

Eventually, conversation on the cart turned to other matters.

"Master Thorn, may I ask you something?" Tasha said. "Where did you find your friend here, Jing Jing?"

I heard Master Thorn's low chuckle and could picture him stroking his beard. "We got Jing Jing when Minimus was only five years old. Do you remember that, my boy?"

Of course, I remembered it. I remembered the shackle binding the little monkey's emaciated leg to a greasy rubbish bin behind the fish processing warehouse. How, even at that age, my hands were muscular enough to bend the shackle and pry him free. How I smuggled him under my vest back to the cart and asked Master Thorn if we could keep him.

"And did you know we named him Jing Jing after the rattle of goat teeth in a rich man's pockets? There's nothing more appealing to our little friend than relieving such pockets of their ill-deserved money," Master Thorn said.

He did not mention that he had a specially crafted pouch of his own with individual felt-lined crevices for each goat tooth to avoid unnecessary temptation for our miniature companion.

I, of course, never had two teeth to rub together and had to settle for rubbing one tooth against accumulated pocket lint during the rare periods between being granted a tooth and spotting a frozen zingberry peddler where I could spend it.

I noticed the slight change in modulation as Master Thorn asked his next question. It would have gone unnoticed by anyone who hadn't spent a lifetime in his presence, but I could tell from the first three words that he was asking something a little uncomfortable but important. I turned to look.

"Lady Tasha," he said. "I have heard that, in the Red Bean Queendom, the royal family always speaks in rhyming language."

Rayne opened her mouth to answer on her lady's behalf but stopped as she noticed Tasha's subtle hand-raise. "What you've heard is true. It's this thing we do."

Tasha stopped there, letting her silence answer the unspoken question.

"Wait!" I said. "So you're a ..."

Rayne nodded at me, raising an eyebrow.

"... queen?"

"Princess, actually," Tasha said. "Don't treat me in any way new. I'm not different from you."

She clearly differed from me. Smaller, certainly. Better dressed. She had a handmaiden. And money. She probably had access to a nearly uncountable number of goat teeth. That explained the reward she could promise. She was both someone whose rescue was worth rewarding and a person with access to reward money. I'd thought of our mission to the Red Bean Queendom as an interesting detour, but the extra responsibility of escorting a princess added precision to my steps. We could ill afford a sprained ankle along the road to Mossmarch.

The cart rumbled on as we all considered the implications of this fresh information. Jing Jing unscrewed the lid of a water canteen and chugged away, vocalizing each gulp. The morning sun was not scorching, but I looked forward to the cool walk through the approaching forest.

"Master Thorn?" I asked. "Maybe after we get to the Red Bean Queendom, we could keep going. To other queendoms, instead of crawling back and forth across Inner and Outer Pang."

Rayne nodded as I looked over my shoulder to judge Master Thorn's mood. "Good idea!" she said. "You could follow the Jade River into Meer. They brew fireroot tea there that is so good you might never leave. Better even than the red-leaf tea from Mista. But if you go to Meer, you could sail across to Oceanplat. We'll travel a few months hence, right, m'lady?"

Tasha nodded in Rayne's direction, her finely boned chin a pale contrast against the powder-blue and cloudless sky. "True! I'm supposed to renew our trade treaty with their new queen. Maybe after, you can ask our drift goose to fly us back to Red Bean, Rayne."

Surely, if anything could sway Master Thorn's route planning, it would be the advice of a princess. He paused for a moment, twisting his icicle of a beard around a crooked pointer finger. I plodded on, partly turned, as I waited for his response. Shivering leaves at the edge of the ancient forest that bracketed this section of the path to Mossmarch cast shadow-play upon his face, emphasizing his nose, brows, lips, and ears in turn as they moved from darkness to light. But before his answer formed, a gruff voice called from the undergrowth on the left.

"I don't want your wares, only your money. Empty your pockets, and nobody gets hurt."

One thing I've learned from our too-common misadventures is that if Master Thorn springs into action, I should, too. No point in being caught open-mouthed trying to figure out what's going on. It's better to fail at doing *something* than fail to do *anything*. Jing Jing's instincts lent themselves naturally to this philosophy, too.

Master Thorn was in motion even before the unidentified voice finished its threat. He sprang to his feet and turned his back to the voice, using his body as a shield for the Red Bean Princess and Rayne. A glance and an eyebrow twitch in my direction gave me my cue.

As Jing Jing leapt from the wagon carrying Tasha, I vaulted across the cart arm, snatching Rayne as gently as I could. Master Thorn joined us on the cart's right side via an elegant somersault dismount. With the voice sounding on our left, the cart should offer us some protection from whatever might happen next. We scanned for the voice's source, eyes scouting for additional threats. Jing Jing released Tasha, who sprang onto my squatting thigh and then scaled my sleeve to cling to some errant wisps of hair at my shoulder. I opened my palm so Rayne could perch on the other shoulder.

A whoosh of air preceded a sound like a jostled spring. A dagger quivered in the bark of a tree that filled the thin gap between Master Thorn and me. It must have narrowly missed Tasha. Arriving at high velocity, I couldn't discern whether someone had thrown the knife over the cart, under the cart, or through some chink in the mountain of fabrication equipment filling the rear bed. But it definitely came from the cart's far side, so we were nominally cowering on the correct side. The Red Bean Princess slid herself into my breast pocket. It was large enough to hold three princesses or a medium-sized ferret. Holding all four together would have created an ill-advised mixture. Rayne remained latched onto my right shoulder. At least this way, if a flying dagger killed Tasha, it would also pierce my heart, saving me the disgrace of surviving my failure to protect her.

"Amazing that it hit the tree. It could have been the end of me," she murmured, voice quivering.

Master Thorn was calm and philosophical in the face of this surprise attack. "That throw would need to be exceedingly accurate to pick you off, my lady. You're no bigger than—my earlobe!" His voice lost its calmness toward his statement's end.

"Well, your earlobes are rather large," I said. "Bordering on legendary. But they are not quite as tall as Lady Tasha. I'm very familiar with them because you always make me rub them for good luck, just like your cousin, the other Master Thorn, used to do before that yak train trampled him to death."

"No, no! My earlobe, you oaf! It's bleeding! That rogue's dagger-toss nicked it."

Master Thorn's drooping lobe sported an already congealing arc of blood around its lower margin, resembling the jeweled ear-clasp of a Xondarian scarf-dancer.

"Master, if he'd thrown but inches to either side, the dagger could have killed one of us!"

Dabbing at his ear, Master Thorn turned to inspect the dagger. "Nonsense, my child. Look at the blade's poor quality. It lacks the sharpness, and dare I say, elegance, of even my most basic set of cutlery. That dagger stabbing you'd be no worse than a gongo bird feather's tickle."

Still, he dabbed his ear again. "But I will concede that the handle shows some potential. It seems a waste to add a touch of style with that ornate leatherwork to such an inferior implement. But let's take it, anyway. Pry it loose."

Unsure of when or where the next attack might come from, Jing Jing and I grabbed several pans from the cart to act as makeshift armor in case we needed extra protection. As I'd demonstrated on many previous occasions, a stout iron pan was a pretty serviceable weapon when wielded correctly. I fancied my chances with a sturdy pan and a fire poker against a sword-wielder any day. But as I made a grab for more protective cookware, a second thrown dagger toppled an object from higher up the tower of stacked goods. The displaced object bounced and rolled to our feet.

"My pewter decanter! Oh, they're going to pay for that!"

"Master Thorn, I hardly think they will stump up the eighteen teeth you normally charge."

"No, you oaf, not *pay* pay. I'm going to get prevenge on them."

"Uh, don't you mean *revenge?*"

"No—prevenge. I'm gonna get them before they get us. Prevenge. It's really quite simple."

The gravelly voice called again. "There'll be no prevenge *or* revenge occurring here, boys. Those were warning shots. Allow me to prove you aren't getting out of here without surrendering your money. It's goat's teeth or your lives, I'm afraid. Old man—open your palm."

I saw a quivering bush that seemed to move contrary to the light breeze's eddies, but there was no way to charge over there without ending up like a dagger-filled pincushion.

"Wanna see something amazing? Move your hand a shade to the right," the voice said. Not normally one to take orders from a thief, Master Thorn was a sucker for spectacle. Against my hopes, he obeyed. I held a pan in either hand to protect each of my small companions from attack, and Jing Jing and Master Thorn had their own array of makeshift armor deployed.

A quiet snick followed the sound of a tumbling dagger warping the air along its flight path. A thud marked an impact high in the tree above us. A moment later, an acorn dropped from a high branch into the center of Master Thorn's palm.

Closing his shaking fist around the acorn, Master Thorn cleared his throat. "Okay, okay. Point taken. Seems like prevenge isn't the best plan if you can make an incredible throw like that. But I have a better idea. How about we make a trade?"

The bush I'd eyeballed shook slightly as a laugh floated to us. "Trade? Like trading your lives for a measly bit of money? Sounds like I've offered the best possible deal."

"Not even close!" Master Thorn said. "You clearly don't want to kill us, or we'd be dead already." I kept my pans raised, although now I was dubious about their protection against the prowess of this knife-thrower. "Look at one of *my* daggers, and you'll change your mind. We'll trade each of your average ones for a knife so fine you might waste away from hunger while admiring its beauty. My assistant here will bring you a sample. We won't disappoint you."

I hoped he meant Jing Jing, but knew my hopes would fail me once again. I let the Red Bean Princess and Rayne position themselves on either palm, and they alighted to cower behind one of Jing Jing's pans as I straightened, brushed away the wrinkles in my tunic, and stepped toward the cart.

"The bone-handled throwing knife, Master Thorn?" I asked.

"Yes, yes, boy. Good choice. Take the one he stuck into the tree here for comparison."

With both knives in hand, I peeked around the cart, still unsure whether I'd end up as part of an eyeball kebab as soon as our attacker got a full glimpse of me.

"Come along then, big fella," the voice said. The bush I'd seen twitching earlier parted, a clutch of scraggly branches pushed back by a weathered forearm. The man's eyes squinted despite the shade of a wide-brimmed, moss-colored hat. His scowl was puckered as if he sucked on an invisible lemonroot tendril.

I took steps toward the bush that were as tentative as my bulk would allow, proffering the two knives as I advanced. I extended them, handle-first, at full arm's length, trying to show I meant no harm and was not clutching some concealed weapon.

"M-Master Th-Thorn made this one using his secret amalgam of steel and other metals found deep in the P-Pang Wastes," I stammered.

Even before my hands reached the fringe of the bush, his eyes widened, and his scowl softened into an expression that I wouldn't call a smile, but one less likely to make a child cry or a dog growl at him. He stood, revealing his full gangly height, with wiry limbs only partly hidden by a mottled cloak. Greasy tufts of hair, clearly self-trimmed without the use of a mirror, escaped from beneath his hat.

"By the blood of my forefathers! Your master makes these knives?"

From one of many sheaths along his right leg, a dagger appeared in his hand so quickly its motion wasn't so much blurred as instantaneous. I don't know what offense I'd caused, but knew defending myself against someone that quick would be impossible. I took a moment to wish I'd complimented Rayne on her magical voice before my death. Another wasted opportunity.

But just as quickly as he'd drawn it, the dagger whirled through a rotation and a half, and he offered me its hilt, its blade now held between his scarred finger and stubby thumb. "Look. Same hallmark stamped here, above the hilt," he said, gesturing for me to take the dagger from him. "My uncle won this in a high-stakes game of roll-the-bones. It's my most prized possession. And your master made it, too, right?"

I traded the bone-handled knife for his dagger and inspected the markings. Although I'd never seen this knife, I had spent enough hours etching Master Thorn's insignia onto his wares with an acid dropper to recognize it instantly as his work.

I didn't even have to answer as the stranger inspected our knife. "Yes! Same inscription!" He called loudly, so his voice could be heard on the cart's opposite side. "If you have even three such knives, you've got yourself a deal."

Master Thorn replied without hesitation. "Make it five. And we'll throw in lunch as long as you build the fire."

"Deal," the stranger called back.

As we swapped daggers once more, I held out a pinky finger. "My name is Minimus Mu," I said.

Swiping my pinky with his own in the traditional Pangan greeting, he smiled. Crooked, but a proper smile. He tipped his hat with a sleek hand gesture. "Sala Doon's mine. Pleased to meet you, Minimus Mu."

Master Thorn and the Red Bean Princess

CHAPTER 4 - SCARLET SAND BEACH

Saltday of Moon, Year 127

Master Thorn conducted the morning's puppet show as he lay supine in the cart and thrust his hands into three finger-puppets that cavorted around the stage. One was a bird, the second a fish, and the third one I supposed was another animal, but appeared as a nondescript and worn felt flap. My gaze flitted between Sala Doon's belt bristling with knives, Tasha's rapt face, and Rayne's fingers expertly re-braiding her mistress's hair. There was a moral to the story—something about making a deal instead of fighting amongst one another, but my distraction drained all meaning from the tale.

* * *

Sala Doon walked us to the forest's far edge, warning off a pair of greasy-looking brothers with flattened noses who blocked the path at one point. Two of his new daggers flashed into his hands at the brothers' appearance, and he held them upright, fingers clasping the blades with wrists cocked to throw. The brothers muttered but dissolved into the bushes, glancing over their shoulders as they scuttled out of sight. It was nice to have someone to ease our passage and even nicer to know that they carried Master Thorn's best blades. I knew Sala Doon could split a blade of grass at twenty paces with such weapons. He'd waved us off as we'd left the shade of the woods and followed the road into the coastal plains and farmland of central Outer Pang.

Wary from the recent threats along the road, I'd pulled the cart into the lee of a grassy hill when we set up camp for the night. Master Thorn and I took turns keeping watch, but nothing approached us more threatening than a mother Pangan lemur and her three babies, strung in a hands-to-tail line. Tips of the mother's wiry fur glowed with rippling blue light, creating a pool of turquoise grass beneath her. The babies were too young to possess their own glow yet, relying on the mother's magic to light their way and warn off any predators lest the glow turn to angry lightning.

With dawn, we packed, and I trudged onward. The road here was better-kept, allowing space for carts to pass without leaving the roadway. This was a luxury rarely found in Inner Pang, but the increased traffic between villages in the farmlands of Outer Pang meant more civilized amenities. I found myself jealous of a donkey as Master Thorn negotiated a trade with a farmer heading in the other direction on a dray laden with cucumbers and tomatoes. I rested, shaking out my aching shoulders and legs while the farmer's donkey seemed content, chewing on fallen bits of hay as he waited for the nudge that would once more urge him along his way. Rayne pointed her toes as she balanced her way along the sloping cart handle and sat on its weathered wood beside me. She swung her legs as I squatted to stretch my back.

"If you didn't have to pull this cart from market to market and instead chose something you've always dreamed about doing, what would it be?" she asked.

"I'd board a sailboat and look for sea monsters," I said without a pause for thought. "One with lots of tasty food and other kids our age. Friendly ones that wouldn't laugh at me."

Her brows knit. "Why would anyone laugh at you?"

I scuffed a foot in the dust and looked away. "Because I'm so big. Because I have no mother or father."

"That's no reason to laugh," Rayne said. "Look at me! I'm as small as you are tall. And my mother died after bearing me. But the Queen is like my mother now. I'm no princess, but I live in Castle Evermere, and she's ever so kind to me. And look at you—Master Thorn is pretty much your father. Even better than a father because he saved baby-you when nobody else looked twice."

I took up Rayne's offer to look at her. She was right. *Her* size didn't matter, so why should mine? It was part of her mystique. And I'd noticed boys with fathers who did much worse to them than Master Thorn did with me. I was never hungry, never really beaten, and knew he wouldn't cast me aside if I broke a leg or became infected with feverchill.

"You're right," I said. "With all those nice snacks on board, the other kids wouldn't be mean. I've never even been on a boat, let alone a sailing ship."

"Maybe Lady Tasha will ask the Queen if you can come to Oceanplat with our delegation. I'm sure some fine cutlery would make a splendid gift to kick off the negotiations. The Queen of Meer lets us borrow her flagship for missions like this. I've sailed twice already—it's amazing, with the salt spray on your face and the waves of the Forgotten Sea as far as you can see."

Master Thorn had finished packing the bartered vegetables onto our cart. "Up, up, boy!" he called. He gestured toward the coast that we'd left to cross the Gorge of Razors. Unseen, we could all sense the tang of salt air that proved its nearness. "We'll take the Low Road across Scarlet Sand Beach."

"Can't we rest another five minutes?" I asked. "My shoulders are sore."

"You have my shrimpathy," Master Thorn said. "But we need to push on if we hope to reach Mossmarch tomorrow."

I didn't know as many words as Thorn, but this one sounded—well, fishy. "Don't you mean *sympathy*?" I asked.

"It's *like* sympathy," he replied with a faint grin, "but smaller. Much smaller. Shrimpathy."

* * *

The road forked, and taking the left-hand branch eased my strain as we descended the meandering slope, surrounded by blue-tinged fields of lavender. The way straightened once we were within sight of the beach. I'd seen it before, but Tasha and Rayne could barely contain their enthusiasm over the last ten minutes as we rolled to sea level. The shallow crescent of blazing red sand scintillated in the afternoon sunlight, stretching before us like an over-colored dreamscape. Waves curled ashore, spending themselves on the sand in pink-tinged froth.

Tasha pointed and momentarily struggled for words, her arm suspended mid-gesture like a marionette animated by an absent-minded puppeteer. "Rayne, look! It's like the picture in the book Mama read to me as a child. Such brilliant red, but weird and wild."

"It is, m'lady. It certainly is," Rayne murmured. I looked at the spectacle with fresh eyes, their excitement contagious. It was an amazing sight, putting every other beach to shame. Squinting into the Sea of Sorrows, I saw a few distant sailboats, spinnakers billowing in the sea breezes. Maybe they had snacks. And friendly children dozing in swinging hammocks.

Jing Jing scuttled from the cart along the handle closest to the beach to perch on my shoulder. He gave a long, impassioned, and untranslatable speech with frequent gestures toward the waves. Could other monkeys understand these squawks, or were they meaningless? I could understand the emotion behind the sounds; maybe the message was pure emotion.

"Yes, Jing Jing," Master Thorn said. "Let's leave the road and let our guests take in the full experience. Minimus! Hard left!"

The easy jaunt down the sloping road ended. The dry sand was a powder finer than flour, squeaky underfoot as each footfall submerged my toes in a wash of cascading red dust. My calves and hamstrings strained as the cart wheels met the shifting sand, only easing once we reached the packed scarlet undulations formed by the waves' furthest reaches. When wet, the fine sand hardened, making a surface as smooth and firm as any road in Outer Pang.

Dropping the cart handles once I'd reached the waves' furthest lappings, I scooped our two traveling companions from their perches and lowered them to the sand. They tittered and skittered across the sand, teasing the lapping waves with their bare feet. I threw my sandals into the cart and joined them, Jing Jing springing alongside. Master Thorn squatted next to the cart. When I glanced back, I may have seen a smile forming below the wisps of his snowy mustache.

"Lift us, Minimus!" Rayne called. "Carry us out deeper!"

How could I refuse such a command? Soon Tasha and Rayne perched in what were becoming their standard positions. It was almost like my shoulder muscles had been custom-built to seat people of their stature, legs dangling in comfortable freedom to my collarbone, their hands twined in the creases of my tunic for balance. I strode with confidence into the waves, relishing the slaps on my thighs and the resulting spray. An involuntary laugh escaped my lips, and my passengers echoed it a couple of octaves higher. Gulls wheeled and added their own voices to our glee, but dispersed as a coal rayvn skimmed the waves and banked in a tight circle around us, close enough for a cloud of its wing powder to dust my face. It circled twice and broke off in a barrel roll toward shore, then repeated the maneuver when it noticed we were not following.

Tasha pointed at the circling creature; it was mostly bird-like but had four glossy black feather-covered legs instead of two. Coal rayvns could travel at speed on land or in the air. "It's like the story Daddy told, about the orphanage when you were two years old. Coal rayvns flapping round your bed, two at the footrail, and one by your head."

Rayne giggled on my other side. "Maybe I could secretly speak bird, and they were my only friends," she said.

I didn't speak bird, but I could tell the coal rayvn's urgings told us to leave the water. When I turned to trudge from the waves toward Master Thorn, he was no longer watching us frolic in the waves, and his smile had faded. His gaze fixed on a group of riders advancing from the north, clods of colorful sand arcing behind them as their horses' bright and ornamental caparisons flapped as they cantered. They carried sheathed swords, the dark leather armor of the flanking riders a contrast to the lead rider's flamboyant, flapping robe and feathered flat cap. To merchants scraping a meager existence from their trade, riders in fancy clothes normally meant only one thing: trouble. Having the money or the power to own horses and command the attention of a tailor generally accompanied a lack of respect for those beneath you in the carrion pile of life.

While the coal rayvn cawed in agitation, I waded back to the cart as the riders slowed to a trot and looked down their noses at Master Thorn. I expected little sympathy. Probably not even shrimpathy.

Master Thorn gave a stiff bow as the lead rider reined in his horse, stopping short of our cart.

The bow drew no response or recognition, not even a brief pinch of the hat brim. Silence reigned for a moment while the man regarded Master Thorn. His eyes were too close-set to call him handsome, and hawkish features presided over a well-manicured mustache and gray-tinged, close-cropped beard. His mouth hung open for a full second before he spoke. "It's true that not even rabble like yourselves require permission from Queen Jada of Mossmarch to travel Scarlet Beach, but it's customary to ask for leave from Lord Vendark, no?"

I could tell from the flourish of his right wrist that he referred to himself with this remark.

Master Thorn straightened, and the wrinkles gathered at his temples as his gaze turned to glare. I figured some regrettable turn of phrase was about to pass his lips, so I jumped in. "By your leave, my lord, we mean to pause here but a moment, and we'll be up the track in a few minutes more. We meant no disrespect to your queendom's fine beach. Or to you."

"Silence, boy!" Lord Vendark thundered, cutting me off with a slicing motion of his gloved hand. "If I wanted to hear from a child, it would be from a silver-tongued songster, not some grubby tinker."

I felt anger well up within me, sure that Lady Tasha and Rayne would detect the rising temperature in my shoulders. Tasha raised an arm tipped by an accusatory, pointed finger. But before she could say anything, Lord Vendark continued.

"And don't you start, you tiny waste of space. I'd call you an animal, but you lack any magic, so I know not what you are, other than unfit to associate even with these foul-smelling, grimy merchants. At least they're proper humans."

The four other riders chuckled at their leader's insults. One said, "And soon they'll lose their queendom, too."

Vendark nodded. "That, indeed. Eighteen queendoms seems quite enough. If my father could see my hand in this expansion of Outer Pang, maybe he'd be proud of me. For once."

Rayne had enticed Lady Tasha's arm to half-mast by leaning across the back of my neck and running a hand down the princess's outstretched biceps. The calming touch had been working until the suggested threat to the Red Bean Queendom slid from Vendark's lips. It was a revelation he'd not have dared speak aloud in the presence of anyone he thought had a scrap of influence or power, but uttered in our presence as if we were nothing. What could scum like us possibly do? Request an audience with the Red Bean Court?

Lady Tasha's voice rang out with an authority and force I hadn't heard before. Nor did it seem possible for such a commanding tone to come from such a slight person. "How *dare* you—"

This time it was not Lord Vendark that cut her off. It was chaos. It was a sun-drenched day at the beach turned to nightmare. A giant tentacle bristling with sea-stench slapped against leather armor as it yanked the rearmost rider from his horse and dragged him, furrowing the sand, toward the surf. Its progress paused for a moment. A ring of inward-pointing, jagged teeth flashed at the bulbous end of the sucker-encrusted blue tentacle as the jaw opened and expanded its grip on the rider. The initial attack had latched onto his forearm and elbow, and now the tentacle surged up to swallow the entire arm and engulf a shoulder. The riderless horse reared and fled the water's edge, neighing in fear.

Every head turned toward the threat. The rider screamed as the fanglimb hauled him into the Sea of Sorrows, his sudden silence interrupted only once as he resurfaced for a moment a good fifty paces into the waves. Only the fizzing surf and squawking birds that had taken flight en masse from the sands punctuated the silence during our moment of indecision.

"Fanglimb!" Master Thorn shouted. "Run, Minimus!"

Everyone scattered. The horsemen wheeled, two riders bolting across the sand directly away from the water's edge while Lord Vendark and the other remaining rider galloped along the shoreline in the direction from which they'd come. The horse with the vacant saddle ran alongside Vendark's.

Rayne and Tasha clung to the collar of my tunic as I lifted the cart handles and turned to pull us across the sand to the road and the safety of the hills.

Shadows flickered across us as four more obscene fanglimb tentacles rose from the waves. The first one crashed into the sand between Lord Vendark and the rider ahead of him. Without breaking stride, his horse showed its years of training and leapt the beached tentacle, pulling up its forelegs in graceful synchronization. A normal jump could not have cleared an obstacle as daunting as the fanglimb's searching appendage, but the horse's natural magic blazed into involuntary action. Hooves trailing tendrils of golden fire, the horse flew higher than any natural leap. It was like an invisible hand boosted the horse from behind, an adult tossing a laughing toddler into the air.

Vendark's windswept hair framed his face as he craned his neck to survey the bedlam behind him. "Why me? What do I do to deserve such abuse? Circumstance makes me abandon *everyone*."

While Vendark's horse sailed, the oozing jaws of the next two fanglimb appendages latched onto the other two fleeing guardsmen. The heavy horses became bogged down in the dry sand as they left the biggest waves' reach. One tentacle knocked the rider from his sprawling horse. I saw eyestalks extend from the gums of the terrible jaw and identify their prey before the tentacle reoriented itself and swallowed the fallen rider's helmeted head. The next tentacle speared the other horse's haunch. It dragged a rider and horse seaward as the remaining horse and dismounted rider slogged with panic-stricken steps over the sand to the crimson dunes.

I knew full well the position of the final fanglimb jaws.

Overhead. The cart was in full shadow, and I'd barely moved. I zigged, hoping to avoid being crushed or snared by the descending limb. My intention was to make a slight course change, avoid the falling tentacle, and then complete my sprint across the sand to the road's fringes. But even as dripping seawater and bubbling saliva splattered around us from the descending strike, I realized this was a mistake. If my feet and the cart's wheels sank into the dry sand, we'd suffer the same fate as the two spooked riders. Instead of zagging after my zig, I knew I must remain on the wet, wave-packed sand and sprint along the beach, hoping the Fanglimb would busy itself with its three other prey.

I had built up enough speed to avoid the thudding impact as the tentacle slammed into the sand behind the cart. The wheels rose on a sand wave that coursed from the craterous whack. Pans rattled. Master Thorn rose into the air and slammed back to his seat. Rayne slid down my back, but I felt the reassuring tug of her hands on my collar and hair as she scrambled back to cling to my unruly mop.

Looking back over my shoulder as I picked up speed on the hard sand, I saw Jing Jing, airborne. He landed atop the squirming tentacle. Grabbing the reopening jaw's top lip, he regained his balance.

I ran as fast as my legs allowed, not daring to turn the unwieldy cart to head back the way we'd arrived. I was almost to the ruts left by the rapid journey of the dragged rider and horse into the shallows. But it would not be enough. The fanglimb tentacle was too long. How far out to sea was the thing's body, anyway? If it spotted us and reoriented, two hundred paces would not be sufficient to outstrip its infernal reach. Five hundred, maybe, if the whole fanglimb wasn't repositioning itself to chase us. But there wasn't enough time to distance myself before the second strike fell.

There was also the tentacle that Lord Vendark had eluded. Its tip turned in our direction, and an array of eyeballs emerged from beneath the lips, scanning and orienting on our position. We were trapped between two jaws, each wide enough to swallow a horse, gaping with concentric circles of dagger-sharp fangs and oozing with malevolent slime. It seemed only fair, after eating fish my whole life, that I would end as this sea creature's next meal.

Like all land animals, but sadly not humans, Jing Jing possessed his own innate magical power. Like Vendark's horse's hooves, Jing Jing's delicate fingers took on a golden glow when his magic rose from within. His power was to move those hands with outlandish speed and dexterity. I'd seen him strip a nobleman's pockets of their currency with nothing more than a small leap and a golden blur. I knew his hands must be riffling and probing pockets and belt pouches, but they moved too fast for my eye to follow. It was only when he came dancing back with a collection of goat's teeth and a pocket watch that I could comprehend exactly what he'd accomplished.

Atop the slithering tentacle, Jing Jing's magic was in evidence. Four eyestalks extruded from the gumline at the jaw's highest point. The mucous-lined stalks, pink against the blue lips encircling the fanglimb's tip, flexed muscle-clad tendons and pointed toward our fleeing cart. I dared not look away, even to check on the other tentacle.

One eyeball squirmed in Jing Jing's grasp, its stalk torn from the gums that the monkey held back with his other hand. Comically, the dismembered eyestalk rotated, so the eyeball stared Jing Jing in the face, as if to express outrage at its severer. In a golden blur of monkey hands, the other three eyestalks were in his grip, amputated in an instant of magic-assisted savagery. He held them like an obscene, limp bouquet, the stalks squirming momentarily before the eyeballs drooped over his clenched fist.

Both visible fanglimb tentacles recoiled, like worms nudged by a booted foot. The motion threw Jing Jing to the sand, and he capered away as the tentacles convulsed and contracted. Dragging across the beach, the ooze-filled suckers collected dollops of red sand. The tentacles rose before thrashing into the sea.

Lord Vendark and his accompanying rider looked like toys in the distance. The men-at-arms galloped to catch up to their master, whose back remained turned to them. The nearer horseless rider perched atop a scarlet dune, staring at us, wild-eyed, and speaking to himself in muted tones. Just over the dune's peak, the riderless horse chewed at tufts of long-bladed, red-tinged grass. It munched away, trappings fluttering in the breeze, either oblivious or having forgotten the recent peril.

I turned from the hard beach, glad to avoid the rutted furrows left by the fanglimb's attacks, and began the trudge through the softer sand to the muttering soldier.

Jing Jing circled the cart three times, calling in high-pitched animation and showing me his grisly bouquet of droopy-lidded eyeballs. Master Thorn persuaded him onto the cart after the third cycle, saying, "Come, Jing Jing. Let's plop those eyestalks into this bottle of brine. I'm sure they'll fetch an unbelievable price with the potion master of Mossmarch."

* * *

If Master Thorn had taught me one thing, it was to never miss an opportunity. I had aimed the cart at the traumatized associate of Lord Vendark, but the whole time I was thinking about the horse. Once I had pulled us to the roadway's hard-packed earth skirting the foothills backing the beach, I lowered the handles and asked the others to wait for me while I trudged up the low dune.

When I reached the man, he continued to chatter away to himself, staring out to sea.

"She was nineteen when I last saw her, but she'll be twenty now. Passed close but never allowed to stop. I swear I could smell one of her mother's fruit pies, couldn't I?" He rambled on.

I approached slowly, and the young man didn't even glance at me. I settled beside him, shoulder to shoulder, and scanned the sea. With the sun glinting off the slow-rolling waves and the occasional froth of a distant whitecap, I couldn't believe a peril like the fanglimb lurked beneath in the dimness.

I listened to the stream of words for a while longer; mentions of camaraderie among his fellow guardsmen, a younger brother whose leg had withered from some childhood disease, and how delightful it would be to feast on river trout and fried potatoes. There was a whispered diatribe about Lord Vendark, how he swung from moments of charity to unpredictable venom at any hint of disapproval. He sounded like a traumatized child, lashing out to protect unseen wounds. Eventually, I turned my head to look at the muttering guardsman and spoke, placing a tanned hand on his leather-clad shoulder.

"I'm Minimus. What's your name?"

His lips closed, and he turned his head in a theatrically slow swivel to face me. "Huh?" was all he could muster, surprising in its brevity after his extended monologue.

"Minimus Mu. That's me. And I can't very well call you 'Lord Vendark's ceremonial guardsman number three' if you're going to ride with us, now, can I?"

He shook his head, and his eyes finally focused on me. A hint of color seeped into his blanched and whiskerless face. He'd looked like a grown man in his leathers and perched on his commanding horse, but now I could see he favored the young part of the 'young man' description. He was probably only seventeen. "No, no. Of course not. You can call me Sang. Sang of Seven Rocks."

"Oh, Seven Rocks! We've been there before. It's between here and Mossmarch, yes? And I heard you mention pies. You must be talking about Madame Zhang's pie shop."

"You know it?" Sang asked. "I am promised to her daughter, Elda. Next year, when I'm permitted a week's leave from my service to the court, I will return and marry her. Did you have the zazzberry pie? It's the most delicious food in the whole queendom."

"Hmm, no," I said. "We had apple and anise. I guess we'll have to go back, although maybe she saves the best pies for her favorites, like you."

Soon, I stood and hoisted him from the sand. We both brushed off the drying cakes of scarlet, and I motioned to the horse. It had moved on from munching the sparse grass and was stripping a bush of its tiny purple berries at the roadside. "How about I hitch up that horse to our cart? We can drop you off at Seven Rocks on our way to Mossmarch. As far as Lord Vendark knows, the fanglimb dragged you off. Nobody will notice you took a few days of rest before your miraculous return."

Sang of Seven Rocks stared into my eyes, and for a moment, I thought outrage was about to bloom. His right hand caressed his sword's pommel. But then the corners of his mouth twitched, his smile broadening and gaze softening. "I like the way you think, Minimus Mu. I like it very much. I'm sure Miss Elda will, too."

New experiences drew me like a magnet—especially when they included riding in the cart instead of pulling it. Maybe there was even a slice of zazzberry pie in my near future. Or two.

Master Thorn and the Red Bean Princess

CHAPTER 5 - PARTS UNKNOWN

Spiceday of Sun, Year 112 (Fifteen Years Earlier)

The witch Alianthe was not human. Nor could she be. Humans had magic taken from them in a time before time, leaving the vast powers of nature to hoof and claw, paw and mandible. But she observed humans with relentless purpose.

She watched from on high as the sabreclaw tore out the exhausted woman's throat and dragged her deeper into the forest without a second sniff at the crying newborn left behind.

She debated whether to wait for the inevitable; a human infant, unguarded, would not last long amongst the woods' nocturnal perils. But premonition scorched across her vision. This was Alianthe's witchpower, compelling her to arrive at the right place at the anointed time to mold the future.

This child could not die here alone. There was an important future ahead, a role in saving magic itself.

Alianthe swept darkness over the newborn, providing concealment from predators and soothing its cries to avoid unwanted attention. Soon, the witch's kin would arrive and carry the child to safety. Soon.

CHAPTER 6 - SEVEN ROCKS

Milkday of Moon, Year 127

The Giant was Master Thorn's biggest, most detailed, and scariest marionette. Rayne and Tasha sat cross-legged to either side of me while Jing Jing perched on Sang's knee, eyeing the soldier's gear and pockets while the puppetry played out on the tiny stage.

The giant always spoke in Master Thorn's deepest tones and was known—at least to me—to emit exclamations that were either imagined on the spot or beyond my language lessons' scope. "Guhdinggy! What's for lunch?" Giant said.

The marionette stomped back and forth across the stage with accompanying booming sound effects created by the puppet master.

"Ka-zow! I'm sure I had a gold coin here somewhere." The giant patted his thighs with exuberant comical slaps of his hands, fingers nearly as long as his calves.

The curtains closed for what I knew was the inevitable narration and possible morality statement. Sure enough, Master Thorn's normal voice returned from behind the stage curtains.

"And that's how the seven rocks became scattered here. They were but pebbles to the giant and sprinkled from his out-turned pocket. The village of Seven Rocks sprang up when rumors circulated of a massive buried golden coin. Mining caravans arrived, convinced the giant's coin could provide a hundred miners with their fortunes. Sadly, the mining turned up nothing more than roots and more rocks, but the village remains, a quaint stop along the road to Mossmarch.

* * *

The next morning, Sang of Seven Rocks pointed out an ever-increasing array of local landmarks after we'd left the Mossmarch road to veer toward his home village. The horse's clopping hooves were music to my ears as I lay on a lumpen sack toward the cart's rear and gazed at wisps of high cloud. Rayne lay beside my ear, using a tuft of my still-salty hair as a pillow, while Tasha sat up front with Master Thorn, Jing Jing, and our armed escort.

Tasha's voice trailed back to us. "Sang, I heard your master say the Red Bean Queendom would be gone one day. That's our home, so I wondered what you'd say. Is there some plot underway? Should I return without delay?"

"I don't rightly know much," Sang said, "but Lord Vendark's hinted at some plans. And our training exercises have ramped up over the last month. Something's afoot. I don't know any details, though. Doesn't seem fair, does it? Even a smaller soldier like me could easily take on ten fighters your size. No offense meant, m'lady."

"None taken, Sang. Your soldiers would overrun Red Bean. But invasion's unthinkable—who's behind it? Your queen?"

Sang laughed deep in his throat. "I've only ever seen Queen Jada on a distant balcony. I know nothing of what she commands, but I can't see Lord Vendark acting alone. He'd lose his head as surely as the sky is blue. He swings between over-protective and vicious with his guardsmen, but he's forever seeking approval from the other lords and the Queen. He's broken, somehow, but would never embark on something this big on his own."

As the road's final chicane led us past the sixth of the seven granite boulders that gave the village its name, I smelled baking. Warning Rayne first, so she wouldn't lose her position as I moved my mop of hair, I sat up. Sure enough, the first ramshackle, bamboo-framed village huts peeked above the next rise. Seven Rocks was about to receive its wayward son, not to mention a sales pitch from the most fabulous cutlery master in either Pang.

* * *

The return of Sang to Seven Rocks brought much rejoicing.

Elda ran barefoot in a cornflower-blue shift across the hardened earth of the village square, snaking her way around typical obstacles—discarded fruit rinds, wandering dogs, droppings from pack animals, and an occasional playing child. Sang barely had time to alight from the cart before villagers were shouting friendly greetings, and he'd advanced only a few paces before Elda sprang, flinging herself onto him and clamping on for a heartwarming embrace.

Amid the sea of questions that flooded Sang, I led the horse to a spot beside the only other merchant vehicle in town and unhitched him from our cart. Taking his reins, I led him to the water trough beside the central hitching post, where he drank deeply. I rubbed his mane and forelock, mumbling thanks for the distance he'd spared my journey-worn feet. I plucked a handful of hay from a half-plundered bale beside the trough and offered it as an after-drink snack.

As the horse munched, his jaws mulching the hay into digestible pulp, I wondered whether I was feeding a beast that would one day invade the Red Bean Queendom. Hopefully, that whole unsavory business was but idle chatter among Lord Vendark's guardsmen. Some ploy to heighten their morale. Or maybe a way for Vendark to show off and get the approval that Song thought his battered ego needed. I hadn't even known what war *was* until Master Thorn described the battles that split Wraithwatch from the Queendom of Astella, across the Fading Sea. That happened two hundred years ago, and the queens of the time gathered and pledged to avoid any such unpleasantness in the future. Despite life seeming to comprise a series of disagreements between people, no queendoms had fought battles or wars since.

Back at the cart, Master Thorn was unfolding the tables of our stall, their clever hidden hinges clicking as legs snapped into position. I wrestled the awning into place to offer enticing shade for any prospective customers. Setup was quicker than normal; Rayne and Princess Tasha skipped across the tabletops, laughing as they arranged the cutlery, cookware, and knives into fans and arrays more artful than anything Master

Thorn or I had ever conceived.

With the excitement of Sang's return, the villagers largely ignored us. But our first visitor brought payment without purchasing anything. A jolly-faced woman with red ringlets spilling from a bonnet approached us, bearing a plain wooden tray.

"I understands you saved my daughter's man from a sea monster. I justs wanted to give me thanks. It's been whiles since a smile that big has flashed in Seven Rocks." Her smile was wide, too, as she held the tray at full stretch toward Master Thorn.

Ever the gracious receiver of compliments and gifts, Master Thorn responded with a graceful bow and replied, "It's all part of the duties of a traveling artisan, young lady. I'll gladly accept your pie as a token of thanks, but if you ever need saving from some ferocious beast, you know who to call upon. I am Master Thorn, and this is my, um, associate, Minimus Mu. And these two lovely ladies are from the Red Bean Queendom. We are escorting them home."

Elda's mother, the famous baker Madam Zhang of Seven Rocks, flashed a smile in my direction. "There's a natural born pie-eater if my eyes don't deceives me," she said.

She wasn't wrong. Was I drooling already? "Is it zazzberry?" I asked. "Sang wouldn't stop talking about your famous pies all the way here from Scarlet Beach."

Lady Tasha glided across the tabletop, carrying a finely serrated knife half her size, and offered it to our visitor. "Would you honor us by cutting the first slice? And if you like the knife, I'm sure Master Thorn will give you the best price."

There was nothing like fine dining to show off Master Thorn's wares. The pleasant lump in my belly and the purple stain in the margin of Master Thorn's beard were unexpected but delicious elements of our promotional activity.

* * *

Despite the small size and relative impoverishment of Seven

Rocks, Master Thorn sold several sets of his most practical kitchenwares and a few knives. Madame Zhang bought some pie plates at a steep discount, a dusty hooded traveler in many-buckled brown boots bought one of Master Thorn's famous daggers, and the showman setting up his tent to our left swapped some construction tools for a set of pans. Master Thorn's pouch was considerably lighter than when we arrived, filled with several new goat's teeth.

It should be no surprise that only the most barbaric or most desperate among us hunt and eat the queendoms' land animals. Risking magical retribution was not something to be taken lightly. You'd think hovering goats would be especially vulnerable, what with their mouths full of currency, but their magic was undeniable. They drifted wherever they pleased, free to munch on third-story flower boxes and food stall rubbish undisturbed, safe because of tales of woe that every child in every queendom could recite. Their magic was to impart bad luck upon any predator. *Terrible* luck. I'd seen a street beggar in the City of Jade pry loose a tooth from a goat that was unwell but still alive. Still smiling at his prize, a molar held aloft in front of his mud-streaked face, the beggar was killed by a metal bedpan, accidentally dropped, brimming full, from a window high above. Jing Jing had wasted no time, and plucked the molar from the twitching hand, somehow sure of his immunity to second-hand bad luck. But thank the gods fish lacked magic, otherwise Master Thorn and I would starve.

As we packed our wares for the night, the other merchant swung into operation beside us. Where we offered goods, he offered entertainment. His cart was double the length of ours, encumbered with shrouded bamboo cages, and pulled by a pair of draft horses. Two! I guess he was short of orphans.

Poles twice the height of a man propped up the jute panels of his impressive tent and gave the tired village square an air of faded majesty. The front of the closed-in tent was decorated with worn paintings of fabulous creatures. Winged, dog-like figures, a lizard with uncountable legs, and even a close-up of a fanglimb's ichor-dripping mouth that had far more telescopic eyestalks than we'd witnessed at close range only yesterday. The entry flaps had a realistic drawing of the proprietor above the name of his traveling show. The picture showed a leather band holding back a mane of flowing, frost-white hair, an accompanying thick beard, snowy save for the icicle of remaining black pointing to his broad chest. Beside the glossy black ibis perched on his shoulder, gold-limned lettering pronounced him as *Vik Gaard, Beastmaster.*

It surprised many people we encountered on our journeys that a foundling could read. And write! Master Thorn was proud of the fact we were both as educated as circumstances allowed, and I often took solace in the fond memories of him reading to me in the flickering campfire from his limited book collection. He often traded books when we stopped and set up our stall, and I admit it helped pass the hours of plodding when he read to me as I dragged us from town to town. But I suspect he had an ulterior motive when teaching me these skills. I was now the sole bookkeeper for his traveling enterprise, noting the items we'd sold or traded, tracking the number of goat's teeth held in his reserve as a reference to be consulted whenever there were questions about Jing Jing's penchant for theft, and identifying trends to help decide which items to fabricate next. The more you learned, the more people expected from you.

After we'd settled onto the stained camp blanket, full of dinner and the remaining zazzberry pie, I broached the ever-sensitive topic of payment for my services with Master Thorn.

"Master, might I have one tooth, so Rayne and I can see Vik Gaard's show? He said he'd let us both in for the price of one, seeing as how Rayne is smaller than his usual customers."

"He should let us *all* in for one tooth!" Master Thorn said. "But then again, if it was my show, I'd let Rayne in for free and charge you double. It's only fair, based on your size. Other children would weep as they strained their necks behind your massive head, unable to see whatever charlatanry his show involves. On the other hand, he should pay *you* to see Jing Jing's fanglimb eyeballs. But best not show them around. People might get jealous or steal them as an ingredient for some cockamamie potion."

I examined my calloused feet and worn sandals, not daring to look Master Thorn in the eyes. "I'll take that as a *no*, then?"

"Listen, Minimus, there's a shrimple solution that costs zero teeth. Sneak around the back of Vik's tent, where you and Rayne can peek under the hem and get a free look at the supposed mythical beasts' backsides."

"Shrimple?" I asked, raising my gaze. "Does that mean small but simple? Sort of like shrimpathy?"

"No, you fool! There's no such word as *shrimple*. I simply misspoke. Now stop asking silly questions and shoo off to the back of the tent. You'll need to rest up for the road to Mossmarch tomorrow, now that we're deprived of horse."

I felt that was the only deal Rayne and I would get, so I offered her my hand—as a conveyance, as it would require a back-swizzling bend on my part for us to stroll hand-in-hand—and we idled toward the village square's margin, sidling behind the tent as surreptitiously as my bulk would allow. The show was about to start, and the chatter of the crowd inside hushed as Vik Gaard introduced himself in a booming entertainer's voice before proceeding in oddly quiet tones that were too low to be intelligible from outside the tent.

At its rear, stakes held the tent panels to the hard ground, but a pair of vertical rips provided the easiest peephole. I'd need to pry one peg loose, and could then raise a small rectangular section. We'd have an observation hole about Rayne's height, and I'd be able to kneel and get a good view. Rayne stood to my left as I pulled the peg, and two grimy children jockeyed for a suitable position to my right. Heavy footfalls paced the stage inside the tent; the audience had dropped into eerie silence. Maybe the flying dogs required absolute quiet to achieve lift-off.

I peeled up the strip of tent as gently as I could. The four of us stuck our noses into the newly revealed view port. That was a mistake. Screams of terror ensued. Rayne jumped back, and the two kids tumbled over each other in their recoil from the flap. My face went numb. It seemed the only mobility left in my body was whatever muscles powered my eyebrows. They rose higher up on my forehead than seemed healthy, but I was too scared to otherwise move.

Strings of spittle criss-crossed my face as a pointed set of wolf teeth lunged from only inches away. The teeth, as you'd expect, were capped with inflamed red gums and attached to a snarling, wild-eyed gray wolf. Neck straining, the wolf snapped its jaws shut. I felt the short spikes of fur surrounding its lips scratch the end of my nose as the teeth clacked together a fraction short of my face. I noted the restraining rope limiting the wolf's range as a second set of jaws on a second wolf's head lashed toward me. The second head sprang from the same body, and it, too, snarled without having enough slack in the leash to rip my slack-jawed face to shreds.

At least three people screamed at the flap. Possibly four, as I wasn't sure what my own vocal cords were doing. After a moment of shock, I jerked backward, too, still holding the flap open upon the spectacle of the two-headed wolf. Then I heard the laughter. An entire audience laughing.

Vik Gaard's chiding voice bellowed over the uproar from the audience. "I told you, I told you!" he said, arms wide to the crowd. A glossy ibis towered on his broad shoulder, adding its caws to the general uproar. "Works every time, in every village, town, and city. There's always someone wants a free pass to the show, so I tie up Tessa here right by that booby-trap flap to scare the pants off 'em. C'mere, Tessa."

Both heads ceased their vicious snarls, and the she-wolf padded over to Vik, who nuzzled her behind each of her four ears. Rayne had stopped shrieking and cowered at my shoulder. The two children were long gone, their footsteps fading as they sprinted around the tent's far corner. My heart slowed a little, and I dampened my tunic's shoulder, wiping away the saliva that dripped from my cheek.

The beastmaster Vik Gaard waved us away from the flap with a backhanded gesture. "Shoo, now, you lot. If you go around front and pay admission, you can watch the rest."

CHAPTER 7 - ROAD TO MOSSMARCH

Creamday of Moon, Year 127

Master Thorn packed our cart early the next morning, and I limbered up for a long day's pull toward Mossmarch. Vik Gaard's tent emitted subtle growls that sounded like one of Tessa's heads warned the other to keep an impossible distance. Eerie avian warbles accompanied the ruckus like the background music of a spooky puppet tragedy. But despite our early preparations, Seven Rocks' finest baker must have been up half the night. Madame Zhang hustled over as I lifted the cart's arms and prepared to haul us away from the village. She bore two glorious fruit pies, steam wafting from pastry slits into the cool morning air.

"Yous stop in a'whenever passing Seven Rocks, ya hear?" she said. "Yesterday were the happiest day of the year 'round our way, and we's owes it to you. Safe travels, little ladies!"

The lacy trailings of her bonnet strings swayed as she waved us on our way, and I admit the scentful teases of warm fruit pie made a plodding pull along an uneven road more tolerable. I considered Sang of Seven Rocks as we left him, his village, and most tragically, his horse behind. Was his situation much different from mine? He had a master, Lord Vendark, who he was honor-bound to follow. Poor pay. No input into the direction or duration of his travels.

Rayne must have read my mind, or at least been pondering Sang, too. She took dainty steps along the cart handle, balancing against the judders as she made her way to perch as usual on my shoulder.

"Did you notice how that ugly Lord Vendark abandoned Sang of Seven Rocks when the fanglimb attacked?" she asked. "Galloped off to save his own melon without so much as a backward glance. Didn't even return for Sang after Jing Jing made the monster retreat. What kind of leader is that?"

I probably wasn't paying attention to the most important part of what she said, but it seemed odd that she called

Vendark ugly. I'd thought he was handsome, with his well-brushed hair, fancy robes, and muscular steed. Maybe Rayne's eyes didn't see the impressive and looked deeper. Interesting.

I realized she was correct. Leadership included responsibility, both for your own safety and the well-being of any followers in your wake.

"Master Thorn wouldn't have left *you* on the beach," I said.

I felt Rayne nod vigorously as her hair brushed against my earlobe. "Exactly! Or you! You should have seen his gaze snapping between you and the approaching fanglimb jaws. I thought he might will the cart into flight, such was his determination to keep you from the monster's clutches."

There was a lot to think about. Was I Master Thorn's servant? Friend? Son? Or just an *associate*, as he had proclaimed me yesterday? But too much thinking was bad for business, as he'd oft repeated. It apparently produced forehead wrinkles that appealed to customers no more than a surprise squirt from a musk-lemur.

But I knew exactly how to escape serious thoughts. The sloping path down to the Mossmarch Road from Seven Rocks was the perfect opportunity to show Rayne how to conserve leg power. "Get ready," I said to her, not warning her exactly what was in store.

I gripped the cart arms, the muscles in my hands and forearms bulging like roughened marine ropes as I eased into a front plank, my legs lifting from the road and extending back between the cartwheels. I repositioned myself gradually, both so Rayne could negotiate a new position astride my mountainous shoulder, and so I could distribute my weight to balance the cart.

At first, we rolled at my normal walking pace, but soon the rhythm of the wheels picked up, and it wasn't long before Jing Jing expressed his chattering opinion. He sounded his excitement at our acceleration down the gentle slope, then scampered along my taut legs and back. I swung my weight to either side to keep us on track and enjoyed the simple pleasure of the wind in my hair, Rayne's tightening grip on my collar, and the tinkle of laughter from Master Thorn and the Red Bean Princess behind me.

* * *

Master Thorn spoke loud enough for me to hear, too, given I was not beside him like Tasha and Rayne. I also had to contend with the rumble of traffic and the blood of exertion pumping in my ears. I'd heard the tales of the gem hens before, so I only half listened.

Master Thorn cleared his throat before speaking, a signal that an extended story was knocking on the backside of his lips. "The Meeran gem hen produces a gemstone much like a normal hen lays an egg, but much less frequently and only under very specific conditions. They are extremely fussy about where they lay—it's thought that each one and its descendants will lay only in one location. If the nest site gets contaminated or the hen is driven out, they will never produce a gem again.

"The gemstones emerge cut with light-catching precision only the finest jewelers can reproduce. And different hens lay different gemstones. Emeralds, rubies, sapphires—the Royal Palace of Meer has a resident gem hen that produces an occasional diamond on a velvet cushion underneath the throne. And did you know that each hen also creates a unique, shadowy structure at their gem's center? You can tell, for example, if the famous Gem Hen of Magnificent Bay produced a sapphire because of the seven-pointed star embedded deep within."

Rayne asked an insightful question. "If they lay gemstones, how are new gem hens produced? Will a chick hatch from a ruby?"

"Nobody knows," Master Thorn replied. "But they have outrageous lifespans. The palace hen in Meer has been alive for over four hundred years. And their magic is crazy powerful. Legend has it that a thief tried to smuggle it from the palace, and the resulting magical eruption blew the dome from high above the throne room into a neighboring courtyard. The thief's scorched head was seen bouncing down the palace steps a good bowshot away!"

"The only such stone I've ever been near," Princess Tasha said, "is in my mother's tiara—a present from Meer."

"Would you like to see another?" Master Thorn asked. "I have a small ruby blessed with an inner pyramid awaiting its future life as a dagger pommel."

* * *

Traffic in both directions increased as we neared Mossmarch. I plodded to the right as various oncoming vehicles laden with fish, clattering crates of tools, and bundles of finished construction materials radiated from the capital city of Outer Pang to the queendom's towns and villages. Riders overtook us, their horses ignoring my envious glances. Picnicking families gawked from the roadside as we passed; I was unsure whether they stared at my unusual strength, our two tiny companions, the suited monkey, or the roguish splendor of our laden cart.

People are like animals in many respects, aside from our lack of magic. We follow instincts most of the time, which serve us well when conscious thoughts might paralyze us. Fish don't leap from the water to snatch a look at the skies. Drift geese don't think, *Gods below, my wings are tired today—maybe I'll walk to the next forest.* And we're the same. We look left and right, maybe down at a patch of treacherous ground so we avoid a stumble. We might reserve half an eye for threats charging at us, but we hardly have the worries of the lowly field mouse under constant threat of attack from behind, ahead, beneath, or above. It takes something pretty unusual to make a person look up. Maybe a majestic mountain, a castle keep peeking over city walls, or a peal of thunder. Definitely, the shadow of a swooping abomination bird.

That's what I feared as the shadow passed over us: an abomination bird attack. I wished I'd had my slice of pie during our mid-morning break—it would be a shame to die leaving it uneaten. I'd seen an abomination bird twice before. The first time, scything talons snatched a donkey from a farmer's field and flapped away with its braying cargo. This sight was so confounding that I couldn't choose whether to flee, chase, or cheer. Instead, I stared open-mouthed at the contraption that floated above.

But the thing that cast the shadow was less ragged than expected. Mostly oval, with no sign of the six beating wings I'd feared. No dark protrusion suggesting a viciously hooked beak straining at the end of a crooked neck. And I heard an unfamiliar noise instead of the screech of four lungs; it sounded like a violent rush of air, like crashing waves in a sea cave's depths.

Rayne and I craned our necks in unison, squinting through the sunlight to discern what oddity passed overhead. Our eyes locked onto a spectacle.

An enormous basket dangled from a man-made device I'd never seen or heard mentioned in any puppet show. It was woven from reeds and jute, although it was clearly far larger than the laundry baskets I'd seen servant-folk lug from palace to river. A curious head poked over its lip and glared down through red-lensed goggles. The basket hung in the air overhead, higher than the tip of the tallest possible tree and wide enough to hold six or eight adults.

The rope that dangled from the basket's lip and left a line in the dust where it dragged across our path was also mundane. Vik Gaard's tent was held upright by several woven ropes of a similar gauge.

But the spectacular components above the basket held our gazes in thrall. A great sack, formed from stitched-together swathes of deep purple fabric, billowed above and dwarfed the suspended basket. A lattice of ropes enwrapped the floating sack, lines running down to fasten into metal loops ringing the basket slung below. It looked like an airborne puffer fish doll trapped in a form-fitting net. I peered through the sack's opening, and it looked completely empty inside. No floating goats cavorted inside the sack, which was the only way I could imagine it remained airborne. Some other invisible force operated.

The maniacal face disappeared over the basket's lip as the rushing air roared again briefly. It stopped before the curious man peered down again.

His hair shot from beneath a helmet that looked like he'd constructed it from a pearly sea shell, its chin strap dividing tousled bunches of curls that strained to vacate the vicinity of his head. He snapped the goggles to his forehead to squint at his own version of a spectacle—a person immune to the awe-inspiring sight of his floating contraption.

Well, a person and a monkey. The trailing rope cleared the roadway and dragged in occasional jerks across the grassy field. Jing Jing, perhaps detecting the clink of valuables in the airborne vehicle, had already ascended a quarter of the dangling rope, scrambling hand over hand. A tint of magic limned his hands as he rose ever faster.

Master Thorn was the only traveler unfazed by this unexpected encounter. He raged and shook a fist at the man overhead. "Get your infernal device away from here, you madman! You bring disgrace on your family and bad luck to ours, tempting the gods to swat you from the sky! Don't you know traveling by air is unnatural and punishable by death?"

As he paused for breath, Master Thorn moved his eyes hard to the left under slitted eyelids, then pursed his lips and looked down at Princess Tasha. "Well, not if you're carried by a drift goose, obviously," he said in a stage whisper.

"Maybe keep an open mind," she replied, "lest your rage leave you behind. Imagine *flying* across the sea! No seasick mission for Rayne and me."

If I'd contradicted him like that, Master Thorn would probably have made me spend an extra hour pumping the bellows as he worked cutlery in our portable furnace, but suggestions somehow sound more friendly coming from a princess.

"Hmmm," he said. "That could work for Minimus and me. We'd *fly* wares across the Fading Sea."

Rayne tittered and whispered in my ear, "Now even Thorn is rhyming. Think he's got some secret royal blood in his veins?"

My smile was only half-formed before the goggled man's reply drifted to us. He sighed, as if repeating himself for the ninety-eighth time. "It's science, old man. Nothing infernal happening here. Only science, you poor fool."

Then I heard a sound that always meant trouble—somebody shouting at a prattling Jing Jing. He'd ascended the rope and was up to his usual hijinks.

With one furry hand held aloft, clenching a metal trinket, the monkey used his other three limbs and tail to whirl around the drifting basket's perimeter, pursued by the crazy-haired man. By the time the pilot finished shouting, "Give that back, you rapscallion, or I'll not find my way home!" Jing Jing had negotiated a leap to the drag rope and was making his way back to the ground.

As the floating craft and its accompanying shadow drifted further and further from the road, the irate calls of the man aboard faded, and the gawkers returned to their terrestrial activities one by one. It appeared that science was no match for a light breeze, and traffic resumed on the Mossmarch Road.

Jing Jing showed me his new possession, a hollow sphere of steel that fit nicely into my palm, formed from three circlets overlapping at its poles. Inside, on a fine cross-beam, a slender metal arrow rotated of its own volition whenever I turned the sphere. It always pointed in the direction we were heading, north toward Mossmarch.

I offered it to Master Thorn, who scrutinized it and watched the arrow inside as he spun it in a series of experiments. After a few grunts and two tugs on his beard, he spat sideways into the dust. "Yes, Princess Tasha, it would be easier to fly to our destination, but I still don't trust this *science*. Nice workmanship, though. You keep it, Minimus."

I pocketed the strange device and trudged onward, hoping the Moss River and the facades of Mossmarch beyond would appear over the next rise.

Master Thorn and the Red Bean Princess

CHAPTER 8 - MOSSMARCH

Beanday of Moon, Year 127

As with every visit to the capital, we had pitched camp at the foot of the bridge that crossed the Moss River where it pierced the towering gray walls of Mossmarch, veined with ivy trails. I'm not sure how he had timed our arrival, what with the stop at Seven Rocks, but Master Thorn was an uncanny master of the calendar. Beanday was market day in the Mossmarch city square, and we'd make enough profit in a single day to pay for a barge-drover, more provisions, and hopefully a hearty feed. I was hoping for striped river trout but knew the meal decision lay somewhere between Master Thorn and what the food stalls had to offer. Maybe a quiet word with Tasha could swing the menu in my favor.

Shoulder to jowl with the surge of other traders, we crossed the bridge's graceful arch shortly after dawn. The Moss River's banks were high enough here that the bridge needed little extra elevation to allow even the tallest boats to pass beneath. I kept my head turned toward the outer harbor in the west as I hauled the cart over the worn cobblestones. Tiny-looking sails punctuated the harbor cove I knew would dwarf us up close.

We endured the usual squeeze through the imposing steel gates and then jostled into a prime trading spot where we set out our stall. Tasha and Rayne outdid themselves this time; no passerby could resist at least a peruse of Master Thorn's most attractive goods.

Business was brisk as the morning rushed past. The clank of blacksmiths re-shoeing horses echoed across the market as egg vendors packed shells of every color and size into straw-filled bowls. A chef dressed in royal livery moved through an astonished but parting crowd, cradling a speckled red egg the size of a cow's head. Grimy children ducked through the throng, chasing each other's laughter or nudging a hovering goat that had drifted too low back into the open air above the stalls. I kept a vigilant eye on our table from my usual position at its front corner; it wouldn't be the first time I'd needed to buttonhole a thief with a firm hand gripping their collar, and no doubt it wouldn't be the last. In the rowdiest markets, I often made an early show of heaving the first suspicious-looking person into the dust as a warning to further potential burglars.

Master Thorn exchanged knives, cups, and pewter trays for goat's teeth, and a full set of the finest cutlery left the stall in return for a small bag of gemstones. I knew they would be both currency and raw materials for some artisanal future working, maybe a jewel-hilted dagger or inlaid into a fancy serving dish. Jing Jing couldn't help himself and edged closer to Master Thorn as he returned the thoroughly inspected gems to the worn sack and slipped them into an inner jacket pocket. A sharp glance from Master Thorn warned the monkey against any stealthy attempt, and Jing Jing turned his back with a harrumph before slinking off. He disappeared for an hour, which was unusual for him on a market day; his habit was to stay at Master Thorn's side and alert us to any shady activity.

It was possibly our most successful trading day ever, and by early afternoon, with the hum of market activity fading, we began the regimented tear down of our stall. With half of our goods stowed, a last customer approached. His wavy brown hair touched his shoulders, more in the style of Inner Pang than Outer, and his style of dress suggested traveler more than city-dweller. A long, hooded jacket, cinched at the waist, reached almost to his well-worn but hardy-looking riding boots. The boot buckles, three per leg, seemed familiar, but I paid them little attention until later. His fine-boned hands and wrists made his cuffs seem cavernous.

A languid, liquid voice gave us all pause as he produced a pair of goat's teeth with a flourish. "Might this be enough for a set of basic travel cutlery?" he asked, a faint smile accompanying a raised eyebrow.

"More than enough, squire," replied Master Thorn. "How do a soup spoon, teaspoon, fish fork, veggie fork, and serrated knife sound? I'll even throw in this woven carrying bag."

"Lovely!" the man said. "Is it possible you might also have a spork somewhere in your collection? It would so remind me of home."

You'd have thought I'd be familiar with every piece of cutlery on the cart, but apparently, there were some esoteric and rarely requested implements that escaped even my awareness.

"A spork?" I asked, my voice rising until it broke. "Is that some sort of spoon and fork combination?"

"What? Don't be ridiculous," Master Thorn said. "I assume the gentleman here is from the Queendom of Golden Shores. A spork is a spoon made from cork, commonly used on the east coast for eating the hottest fish stew without overheating the spoon."

Our visitor nodded. "Indeed, indeed. It's been a long time since I've been home to Yinti, but I still carry my grandmother's recipe and prepare it whenever I can. Finding a replacement spork in Outer Pang has proved an impossibility."

"Until now!" Master Thorn replied. With an excited quickness in his step, he pulled out one drawer and then another before producing a long-handled but lightweight spoon. He presented it with both hands to our visitor, who pursed his lips, nodded, and ran its length under his nose.

"Hardened by steeping in honey, of course," Master Thorn said. "It is to your liking?"

"A masterpiece of cork workmanship. I love it!"

Sliding the two teeth across the tablecloth, where one rose slightly and threatened to drift away in the light breeze, the man continued, "I heard tales from my acquaintance, Sala Doon, of some throwing knives of unequaled quality."

"You know Sala Doon?" I asked. "He almost took Master Thorn's ear off before we all calmed down and engaged in honest trading."

The man chuckled. "Heh. Typical Sala. When I first met him, he wrestled me to the forest floor and had me at knifepoint before I realized I was not alone on the path. Start of a steadfast friendship, that was."

Master Thorn performed a bow that was closer to a token nod than anything else. "We are honored to have you at our stall, friend of Sala Doon. But I'm sure if he told you about my daggers, he must have mentioned their unmatched workmanship. We normally take a deposit before bringing them out. You know how it is in the big city, and I'm sure you'll want to check their balance and feel. Shall we say two molars?"

Our guest smiled, a crooked affair that emphasized two scars on his chin and revealed a chipped front tooth. "I get it, I certainly do. Can't be too careful! But two molars is not a problem."

His drooping cuff disappeared inside his jacket, where he finessed a woven palm-frond pouch from an obscure inner pocket. The molars tended to float away even more than the normal teeth, so Master Thorn slapped a steel mug overtop as our visitor placed them on our stall's tablecloth, shaking his hand to clear his sweeping cuff as he tapped the two goat's teeth on the surface.

Running an appraising eye over the man, Master Thorn freed three highly polished blades from their concealed sheaths at the back of his belt and placed them down with a practiced gesture that caught the best light. "These two have subtle curves, in the style of Wraithwatch dueling knives. And the third is a classic Inner Pangan throwing knife. I'm sure these are common in Golden Shores, too, yes?"

The visitor hefted one, finding its center of gravity before flicking it a quarter turn to balance it, point-down, on a calloused thumb. He recoiled and dropped the knife to the tabletop as a speck of blood blossomed on his thumb tip. "By goat, that's sharp! It takes a lot to poke through the callouses on these fingers."

He caressed the hilt once more before fully grasping it and thumping the pommel on the table between the other two knives. He fixed Master Thorn in his gaze. "I'll take it," he said. "How much?"

"Normally, two molars, but for a friend of Sala Doon, I'll let you have it for one and a half. Sheath included!" Master

Thorn replied after a moment's hesitation. I knew full well that one and a half molars was the usual price, but wasn't about to interrupt.

"You're a gentleman and an artist," the man replied. "Keep both molars, and no need for the sheath. I have other plans for the blade."

He pocketed the knife with a movement so fluid, I was unsure which of his many jacket compartments it filled. Glancing beneath our stall table, he smiled again and did a curious three-step dance, flicking heels and stomping included. Odd. Maybe dancing to show your thanks was a Golden Shores tradition that the morning puppet shows had yet to touch upon. The man looked me in the eye, and a wink accompanied his wide smile. "The dagger is of such fine quality I can't help but dance a wee jig."

He was already turning into the crowd and waved back to us, calling as he left, "It was most pleasurable doing business with you, Master Thorn!"

With our takings for the day already comforting his pouch, Master Thorn smiled at me. "Never hurts to make a last-minute sale, does it, boy?"

Fishing an additional purse from under his belt, he raised the upside-down cup from the stall to secure the two molars. Then he held the cup to one eye, peering inside. A noise somewhere between a panther roar and a strangled duck came from his mouth. His seething tongue momentarily allowed no room for words before he expressed his outrage. His beard quivered. "That fiend! Where are his two molars?"

"What?" I said. "I watched him put them right there on the table. Let me see the cup."

Master Thorn would not miss two goat molars inside a cup held so near his face, but incredulous, he handed me the cup.

While I examined it—no teeth—he flew into a further rage. "And where are the other two blades? Don't tell me he took them, too! Scoundrel! Rogue! Look, there he is!"

Tasha, Rayne, and I followed Master Thorn's shuddering index finger that angled up and away from the stall. Our visitor ambled atop the city walls' parapet. He broke his stride long enough to tip an imaginary hat toward us before cracking the smile of a man satisfied with his swindle. Then he turned and disappeared into the milling throng.

He was too distant to pursue, so I knew what came next. Master Thorn would need an outlet for his frustration, and that outlet was me.

"You useless buboon! Why didn't you catch him?" he shouted. A bubble of his spittle landed on the bridge of my nose. I had to restrain myself from either wiping it away or crossing my eyes to focus on the offending sputum. But then I made a mistake: I asked Master Thorn a question.

"Master Thorn, don't you mean BA-boon? You said BUH-boon."

"I say *exactly* what I mean, boy. A buboon is half baboon and half buffoon. Sums you up precisely! Ooh, I'll ... I'll—"

Rayne diffused the situation. I never discovered the terms of his threatened punishment.

"Ooh! Good one, Master Thorn," she said. "Or what about a buffaloon? Half buffoon, half buffalo. Or a clonkey?"

There was a pause before Master Thorn replied, hesitant. "Half clown, half donkey?"

Both Princess Tasha and Rayne tittered in unison. "Exactly! In the Red Bean Queendom, we *love* a good insult."

Master Thorn turned to me again, his cheeks a shade less puce. He spoke in a much-hushed voice, almost conspiratorial. "But you are part genius, too, my delightful clonkey boy. Remember when I said the idea of a spork was ridiculous? It's not. That's a brilliant concept. I didn't want anyone to overhear and steal the idea before I could make a few prototypes."

I smiled. Part genius! "What about a *runcible spork*?" I asked. "Like a spork with a serrated edge for cutting?"

Master Thorn shook his head and laughed, to the relief of us all. "Let's not get ahead of ourselves just yet, eh?"

As we finished packing our stall away and deciding where to dine, the broad-shouldered man with a face like a prize gourd who was taking down his linen goods stall, called across to us. "I see you fell foul of some professional sleight of hand there," he said. "That's Mirko Leatherfoot. Never done me any mischief, but he's a bit of a blighter. Looked like he nicked something from under your stall table, too, although the draped cloth blocked my view. Consider it a life lesson."

As if in response, Jing Jing threw a tantrum of his own, scrabbling in the dust where our table had been as if Mirko had stolen monkey treasure. Master Thorn cocked an already sky-reaching uproar of an eyebrow but knew that we kept nothing attractive to street urchins beneath the stall table. There was no accounting for the imaginings of a monkey.

Master Thorn and the Red Bean Princess

CHAPTER 9 - MOSS RIVER

Lettuceday of Moon, Year 127

The steel-hulled barge made slow progress upstream. It seemed the two hauling donkeys spent more time jostling and braying at each other on the towpath than pulling the boat. We rode in moderate style—sleeping on straw beds under a canopy that we rolled back on warmer nights for a view of the bejeweled sky. We spent our days tidying and re-organizing the cart's contents, or lazing atop makeshift sofas formed from our bedding and the many crates headed upstream. Each day we'd stop at riverside towns, offloading cargo and picking up fresh goods. It took six days to cross into the Red Bean Queendom, but the simple days passed pleasantly.

As we skirted the clustered trees of Applewood, Princess Tasha and Rayne pointed out the pathways and regaled us with tales of the unusual and often miniature places they led. They were describing the nearby emerald mines, when a troop of mounted riders startled the barge donkeys in their hasty pass. Their leader reined in his horse, and the remaining armored riders clustered around him. The horses' heavy breathing and the scuffle and stamp of hooves full of nervous energy became apparent once the donkeys ceased their abrasive braying.

A familiar voice called out from beneath a feathered cap. "I hear from my man Sang, here, that you fought off a fanglimb and saved his life at Scarlet Sand Beach. Is that a fact?"

Lord Vendark. I hadn't expected to encounter him again. To see him beyond Outer Pang's borders was a mild surprise. I viewed him with fresh eyes. Where before I saw snatches of majesty, now I beheld a greasy coward. It seemed a tincture brewed from Rayne's low opinion of Vendark had seeped into my being.

Master Thorn was ever the diplomat. "We sought only to save our own lives, my lord. Sparing Sang of Seven Rocks was merely a fortunate side effect."

Vendark stroked his beard. "Interesting. I'm glad you

helped Sang, he's like the son I never had, although I pray to the gods below that I'll treat him better than my own father would. But exactly how did you force a beast as ruthless as the fanglimb to retreat? I didn't fancy you as masters of weaponry when I saw you dragging that hapless cart through the sand. And your association with those undergrown slatterns suggests little in the way of class. I see you haven't rid yourselves of those parasites either."

At this comment, I rose, blood coursing throughout my limbs, readying me for any needed action. Rayne stood, too, beside me, but gave my taut thigh a restraining touch, cautioning me against whatever rash action I might imagine.

But it was Tasha that replied. "Sir, your senses must be as dull as your dinner parties. You should have stopped at Applewood's first trees. That was the start of Red Bean. I'm certain your queen would prefer to avoid a scene, so if you leave in haste, we'll not send word where you've been."

She delivered the message in a firm but relaxed tone that conveyed a total lack of fear and very little respect.

The man's face twitched and his eyes blazed at the disrespect. "You must address me as *my lord*, you insignificant wretch," Vendark barked.

Tasha placed her hands on her hips, unfazed. "If you *were* my lord, I'd call you such. But sir is enough, if not a bit much."

Vendark snorted like the pig Rayne considered him. "I'm on a personal mission from my queen, Jada of Mossmarch. I care little about a dividing line between queendoms that will soon cease to exist. And I care even less what you call me. You won't be alive much longer to call me anything."

Princess Tasha called out with even more commanding tones, playing on the insecurities Sang of Seven Rocks had pointed out. "I need call you nothing, you're a petulant child. You see *me* as tiny, but you're smaller inside."

The rasp as he pulled his sword from its scabbard repeated itself as another dozen weapons leapt from their sheaths. Despite our opinion of his leadership skills, it seemed he'd conditioned these men to follow his every whim. Even Sang of

Seven Rocks drew, although he looked to the side, unable to meet our gazes.

Vendark raged, his cheeks and ears flushed. With wild gestures of his sword he shrieked skyward, toward some unseen antagonist. "You see what they make me do? I don't care! Nobody can tell me what to do. Watch this!"

The sputtering lord spurred his horse into action, slicing viciously at the lead donkey's neck. Its head lolled at an unnatural angle after the attack, legs buckling even before the blood squirted into the rippling waters at the river's edge. Nobody dared move or even breathe as Vendark continued screaming. "See? I did it! Everyone tells me what to do. No more!"

Panicked at the sight and smell of his bellicose partner's blood, the second donkey reared and flailed its front hooves toward the cluster of soldiers. The hooves were worth avoiding, but as with all large animals, it was their magic that you needed to worry about. A torrential braying poured from the donkey's jaws, its mouth crackling with electric-blue fire as it opened unnaturally wide. It was loud to us on the barge, but a visible cone of rippling blue air erupted from the donkey's flapping lips toward Vendark and his closest soldiers. The pulse died out as it reached the forest's first gnarled apple branches, but not before inflicting a terrible toll.

The four men within the cone dropped their swords without a thought and clapped their hands to their ears. I could see blood seeping between Vendark's fingers as his eyes squinted with the pain. One soldier dropped from his saddle, unconscious. The rest of Vendark's men paused, slowing their horses.

Vendark must have known better than to kill an animal. Maybe frustration at his own lack of self-restraint was what fueled the man's howl of pain and rage. We stood paralyzed as the nobleman stumbled from his horse, losing his feathered hat. He spared a quick glance at his blood-splattered hand as he moved it from his ear to the pommel of his dagger. With two weaving steps and a sweeping slash, he tore out the second donkey's throat.

His voice slurred as he waved his men forward. "Kill them all. Wait, no—leave the bargeman. He's one of us."

It took a moment for the uninjured soldiers to muster up the courage to move forward, their horses' hooves clopping unsynchronized on the towpath.

Sang of Seven Rocks trotted ahead, then turned to block the path and called back to Lord Vendark. "My lord, why not let them go? They can drift back to Outer Pang on the current. They can't stop us now."

It proved difficult for Vendark's men to divine his response. He sank to donkey blood-spattered knees on the grass beside the path and murmured to himself. "Why do I keep doing this. You always make me do bad things," before his eyes rolled back, and he collapsed onto his side. I reached behind me and grabbed the still-hot pan we'd used for lunch in case the soldiers drew the wrong conclusion.

Our two groups remained motionless and stared at each other, but eventually, the current caught the barge, and we drifted away, back toward Mossmarch and Outer Pang.

Eventually, we relaxed as the bargemaster wrestled the boat into a safe line along the wide river's center. "Do they really mean to start a war with Red Bean, m'lady?" Rayne asked.

There was no rhyming response. Princess Tasha shook her head and replied with a simple, "Yes, Rayne. Yes."

Master Thorn spoke like he had a grand plan to avert war, prepare the queendom's largest feast, and manufacture enough runcible sporks to supply the continent twice over. "Bargemaster! Steer us back to the shore, please. Minimus— see the donkey ropes? You know what to do."

I'd pulled nothing as heavy as the boat before, but if two donkeys could do it, I'd meet the challenge. The hauling work would be an interesting change, but I didn't think Master Thorn's plan would be that shrimple.

CHAPTER 10 - EVERMERE

Lightningfruitday of Moon, Year 127

Two days later, legs exhausted, I released the barge rope for the last time, relinquishing it to a pair of stevedores who tethered the barge to a trio of massive cleats affixed to the dock at Port Evermere. The men looked at me with questions behind their surly exteriors, but their taciturn nature produced nothing more than grunts and narrow-eyed scans of my sweat-drenched form. I may be stronger than two donkeys, but I had a newfound respect for their endurance.

A combination of full-size people and Red Bean citizens populated the docks. It would have been unwieldy to operate the port with only locals; cargo from Outer Pang or further afield was packed and parceled at a scale that made it impractical for Red Beaners to maneuver. Some shipments' final destinations were elsewhere; longshoremen loaded wagon trains that would travel the quick trip to the Jade River, which emptied into the Fading Sea on the east coast, providing access to the queendoms beyond.

When Princess Tasha alighted from the barge, the commotion was palpable. It wasn't long before an ornate carriage approached at speed, pulled by two knee-high, six-legged ponies. A similar scale liveried coachman ushered her and Rayne inside. A miniature bowing footman held open the carved wooden carriage door. He wore a draped red jacket in what Master Thorn assured me was the Red Bean Queendom's royal colors. Judging by the carriage's size, it was clear our foursome would now part ways. Jing Jing could fit nicely into the small vehicle, but thieving monkeys and royal carriages were a combination best left unexplored.

I'd dreaded this moment since the first day we'd met Rayne. Although she had no more royal blood than I, her service to the princess bound her to the royal household, where Master Thorn and I would surely be unwelcome. I'd held some unspoken daydreams about being appointed royal cutlerers, but given I'd never heard of such a role, it seemed impossible. I squatted beside Rayne, my constant companion throughout the journey, and opened my mouth to spill my feelings, but a flash of princess Tasha's palm silenced everyone.

She spoke with a tone and elegance she hadn't used since we first met, directing her words at the footman. "My friends have brought us all this way, and I'll not move an inch without them today. Hurry, good sir, and prepare for their stay. Send another carriage right away."

The footman glanced fleetingly at the princess and raised an eyebrow, but the message was clear and seemingly not to be disputed. He spun on a heel and legged it across the docks, ducking up a lane between a ramshackle tavern and a nautical repair shop.

An awkward silence surrounded us while we waited. The morning sun beat down, and fresh rivulets of sweat descended my chest and back, replacing the dried traces from this morning's final barge pull. A stooped Red Bean woman with a shock of gray hair sidled up to Rayne and opened a parasol, motioning that Tasha required shade.

I felt a change. In the gourd, on the cart, and along the river, Tasha and Rayne had behaved like sisters, but here, among the princess's citizens, a decided separation of royalty and servant descended. Having seen Tasha at ease, I hoped and felt this was merely protocol, a show for the gawping citizens trying but failing to go about their usual business at the port. I vowed to ask Rayne about it later, now it seemed there would be a later.

It heartened me to find that when the larger carriage arrived, the four of us and Jing Jing traveled together, leaving the smaller carriage to travel empty in the wake of the cutlery cart bouncing in tow behind us.

* * *

The walls of Evermere were no less imposing than those of Mossmarch. I'd envisioned a fairy-tale city where I could clear the walls with a casual step and would find room for my feet in only the broadest of city streets.

"They built the outer city to accommodate both Red Beaners and outsiders," Rayne explained as we passed through the broad gates. "Up ahead, you can see the royal city, with its lower walls and gilded citadel. The royal lodgings you see to the left, there, abutting the lower walls? That's where the queen receives guests of your stature. It's a divided building, with the outer parts built to your scale and the inner parts passable only for people of our size. Or children. You'd barely fit an arm through some of our doors," she giggled.

Our carriage might have squeezed through the gates in the royal wall, but we detoured through an archway into an open stable area. Stable hands attended to several other posh-looking carriages, and two rushed out to take the reins from our driver, waiting for us to alight. It verged on comical to see two boys little taller than Rayne holding the reins of horses quadruple their height, but the beasts behaved well.

"I must find Mummy in haste," Princess Tasha said. "There's not a moment to waste with these plots swirling round—Vendark must be found."

"And put in irons in the city square," Rayne added. "I'll be the first to throw a rotten peach. Or better yet, Minimus, I'll have you chuck it on my behalf."

I was glad to see that Rayne was acting less constrained by rank now that we'd left the public eye. My laugh was unforced. Maybe Vendark had doubled back and returned to Mossmarch after the donkey attack. But that seemed unlikely; he would have taken the River Road, and one of us would have seen his band of mounted soldiers passing, even if it was during the night. Perhaps he was spying on the Red Bean Queendom, deciding how many soldiers it would require to assume control.

We followed Tasha to a door that led from the stables into the royal lodge. She would forge ahead to find her parents while Rayne would speak to the house manager and arrange our quarters. But before we could split up, the question of Vendark's whereabouts was answered in the least appealing way.

The man that strode from the doorway was an unkempt version of the Outer Pang lord we'd encountered twice before. In place of his feathered cap was lank and greasy hair. A loop of bandage wrapped tight around his ears, reaching from his forehead to the nape of his neck. A bundle of rosy-stained gauze covered each ear-hole, and Vendark's unshaven face sported a scowl that would frighten children at a hundred paces.

He gave Tasha and Rayne a wide berth but confronted Master Thorn at the railing dividing the sheltered walkway from the stable yard's packed ground. Adrenaline pumped through me at the unexpected arrival of the man who'd ordered our deaths, but I was too stunned to react in time.

Vendark pushed his palm into Master Thorn's chin and shoved him, bending him backward over the rail and toppling him into the brimming drinking trough beyond, startling the horses. Vendark shouted something slurred and only semi-intelligible. It might have been, "Back off, you bloodsucking peasant scum," but could just as easily have been, "Bake a huge brood of cooking, unpleasant scamp."

Either way, the message was obvious. He wanted to finish the job he'd commanded earlier. Jing Jing sprang from my shoulder and swung from the walkway's rafters, screeching. I lunged to my right to position myself between Vendark's throng of soldiers and Rayne, who scurried in front of Princess Tasha. My right fist closed, and I pulled that shoulder back—the strike on Vendark's ugly face would be like an anvil.

Two things stopped the blow from uncoiling. The first was the snick of swords being unsheathed as Vendark's soldiers surged forward to protect him. That alone wouldn't have stopped me—I could still land a powerful strike on Vendark's head before a thorough skewering. But Master Thorn's pained voice spluttered as he surfaced from the trough's shallows. "No, Minimus! Not now! Save it!"

Several swords pointed at various parts of my anatomy that I didn't care to have explored. The soldiers retreated a step, Vendark folding into their midst.

Princess Tasha pushed past my calf, and her voice rang with imperious command. "If you so much as poke the end of this boy's thumb, I will consider it an invasion of my queendom. The other queens will come down so hard on Outer Pang, you'll be lucky if you find a shard of rotten apple in your gruel bowl, hidden from sight in your prison hole."

Vendark didn't even look in Tasha's direction, but I don't think he could hear much from beneath the bandages. His men could, though. They lowered but did not sheath their swords, and ushered their lord toward the horses clad in Outer Pang's livery, glimpsed through an opening to a second stable area abutting our own. A career for me as a spy seemed unlikely—I'd failed to notice the sliver of Outer Pang colors earlier. If I'd only looked around instead of gaping slack-jawed at the towers of Evermere, we'd have been on high alert from the moment we left our carriage.

Behind Vendark's spitting, purplish face, I noticed Sang of Seven Rocks, who was the only guard who had not drawn a weapon. He shrugged as he mounted, directing an apologetic frown our way.

Horses whirled as the group turned and rode from the yard, their hooves thundering across the cobblestones beyond the gate. I figured this was not the last we'd see of that seething face. Maybe next time, it would suffer a flattening surprise beneath a swung frying pan.

* * *

Whenever I'd imagined meeting a queen, it was nothing like this. Queen Violet of Evermere and Tasha's father, Lord Alfred, descended the staircase from the inner city into the guest hall as we took the first steps up. I was carrying Master Thorn, whose teeth ground with the pain from his spasming back where Vendark had knocked him through a round of involuntary gymnastics over the rail into the trough. I sweated, and my rage had only half subsided. Jing Jing's tail encircled my wrist. He chattered and smoothed Master Thorn's hair as if that could heal him.

The staircase was divided, with three-quarters of its width composed of what I considered normal treads and the rest composed of Red Bean proportioned ones, with quadruple the steps. Tasha had raced ahead and was half-way up, with Rayne close behind, when her parents turned the corner at the next landing and began their descent.

"Mummy!" she cried, halting everyone on their current step. "You're letting that ill-mannered Lord Vendark of Outer Pang walk free? After his threats to our country?"

Queen Violet and Alfred of Evermere paused only a moment before rushing on pattering feet to their daughter. The Queen wore a cloak with a hue that matched her name, covering a sleek pair of trousers framed by tan boots and a tailored shirt. She looked more elegant than regal, but the sophistication and cut of her informal clothes hinted at her status. Alfred looked a decade her senior, wire-rimmed glasses framing inquisitive eyes and helping to restrain a flop of salt-and-pepper hair. They managed a joint embrace of Tasha before replying.

"I thought you were dead or maybe kidnapped," Alfred said. "Nobody has seen hide nor hair of you since you left the city gates on Nutday of Sun. Where did you go?"

Before Tasha could form her first word, Queen Violet cut in. "You know you're my only heir—how could you wander out there? And Rayne, too. I expect more of you."

I noticed Rayne examining the toes of her boots as Tasha answered; like me, she knew there was never reward in answering nuggets of your master's criticism. "Listen, Mummy, I'll explain everything—you'll see. These fine people rescued Rayne and me. More than once. The biggest one is Minimus Mu, the one being carried is Master Thorn and the little squeaking one is Jing Jing. But we need to talk about Outer Pang. What's Queen Jada threatening?"

I smiled and attempted a small wave with the hand supporting Master Thorn. Master Thorn managed an apology for our appearance through pain-gritted teeth. I liked Lord

Alfred's plain speaking and sent a smile his way before turning to the queen.

Queen Violet smiled back. "Then you are our honored guests. For Minimus, Thorn, and Jing Jing, only the best." She turned her focus to Tasha. "I gathered there was some threat he meant to deliver, but Lord Vendark was so discombobulated, I understood only a sliver. His men claimed a banshee attack at our western border and feared going back. Their story was tough to believe, but they pleaded for help so they could leave. I ordered poultices of fermented tea tree sap for their ears and let them rest for a day. After that, I sent them on their way. It's unseemly for foreign soldiers to be seen in Red Bean, but I feel that they said much less than they mean."

It was not my place to speak, but my tongue had its own ideas. "They're plotting to invade Red Bean! Vendark told us as much right before he tried to have us killed. If it wasn't for Sang of Seven Rocks, our bodies would be at the bottom of the Moss River."

Alfred's eyes widened, magnified by his glasses. "Is this true, honey? Outer Pang tried to kill you?"

"I'm afraid so, Papa. But they can't justify the affront they've made, and the other queendoms will come to our aid. Hopefully, Jada will send a less roguish lord or lady to our nation with an apology instead of an escalation."

Queen Violet's brow furrowed. "Worrying indeed. But at dinner, tell us all. Master Thorn and Minimus deserve a banquet, so we'll prepare the guest hall. Rayne, show them to a room where they may bathe and rest. Then return to the castle and help Tasha get dressed. By then, our guests will be hungry as well. You can return to fetch them when Cook rings the dinner bell."

Rayne replied in a more timid voice than I'd heard from her before. "And, m'lady, can I summon the royal doctor? Vendark's done in Master Thorn's back."

"Of course, Rayne. We can't have our guest in pain."

Alfred turned and ushered Tasha up the steps, draping a wiry arm across her shoulders. "And you, young lady, must be

83

exhausted. You could do with a salts bath and freshening up. Let's get you to your chambers and changed into proper banquet attire."

The same thought must have occurred to both Tasha and Rayne: they flicked their heads toward each other and locked eyes. I was watching Rayne as closely as ever, so I saw hers widen. "Oh no," she said.

Tasha covered her mouth with a quivering palm. "My tiara! I left it in the gourd!"

CHAPTER 11 - EASTERN OUTER PANG

Cheeseday of Moon, Year 127

It took but a few minutes for me to prepare myself for dinner. The talk of bathing, dressing, and jewelry made me realize I was at the fringes of a world I'd never considered. Folding my tunic to the waist and dousing myself with a ewer brimming with cool water pushed my normal limits of primping. A fine cotton cloth lay folded on the table beside the ewer, so I wiped the least ground-in grime from my palms as a further attempt to make myself presentable. I shook droplets from my hair, and they spattered around my sandals.

Familiar with Master Thorn's often cantankerous lower back, I tugged on both legs while he lay on the floor, hands clutching the door frame. He groaned a little as I upped the pressure, but grunting was his mother tongue, so it was hard to tell whether my therapy helped or hurt. I released his ankles when a musical voice called from outside the door to our allotted room.

Rayne's preparation for dinner was far more transformative than mine. Her hair was combed where mine was a hopeless field of tufts. An embroidered dress of delicate texture made my apprentice's tunic look like something to be discarded or burned. I thought I could smell flowers of a variety unknown in either Pang. And all this seemed effortless. She had returned to our section of the castle while the sun still rode high in the sky. I expected we could chat a while before dinner, so I left Master Thorn to sink into the white sheets of our bed and closed the door behind me. Rayne gestured me toward a two-seated bench, segmented to allow a Red Beaner and a full sized person to speak with their chins at the same level.

I considered our differences, which had faded from my mind since the Gorge of Razors. "When it's not just you and me riding on a cart, there's a lot to it, making things work for both your kind of people and mine," I said.

She looked me up and down, smiling. "We're all just *people*,

Min. There's no two *kinds*. Yes, staircase treads are shallower for people of my size, the castle is divided into tall and small zones, and the stable hands fuss over either full-size horses or ponykins, depending on the size of the person, but we've always made things work."

"I guess visiting Red Bean is a good way for people from other queendoms to not only dwell on the differences, but to really feel the things that make us the same," I said. "I've forgotten our different sizes these past days, but seeing you and the princess here, in court, brings home that we're from different worlds. Look at your dress. And you know what to expect, how to behave at dinner, and all I'm good for is pulling a heavy cart and drooling over an occasional gorge cod."

Rayne's brow furrowed, and she took advantage of being level with my head to hold my gaze and put both hands on my shoulder before she replied. "Don't be ridiculous, Min! You've helped Tasha and I more than anyone, ever. It's my turn to return the favor. And don't think it's all fancy dinners and dressing up for me. I normally eat at a table in the kitchens after trying to appear invisible but available during royal banquets. I'm as happy to be invited tonight as you."

It was reassuring to have a friend that could provide a rapid run-down of Red Bean royal etiquette. The conversation came as easily as ever, and Tasha talked about the ingenious ways that Evermere accommodated natives and visitors of all sizes, some of the local dishes that might be served, and reminiscences of small adventures she and Princess Tasha shared as children. I felt relaxed and more confident by the time a footman came to summon us to the dining chamber.

* * *

I paced my chewing so I'd be able to hear what everyone at the banquet table said. This was my first ever feast, a glorious opportunity to absorb every sight, sound, and especially flavor. I harbored worries that there was some limit on the number of poached quail's eggs one should scarf down, but Rayne's small nods of encouragement suggested I remained within polite bounds.

The staff had adjusted a clever set of table leaves that could rise or sink by turning a concealed crank. This allowed the Red Bean natives to perch on their higher chairs and sit at eye level with Master Thorn and me, with none of us stooping or looking awkward as we dined. I'd watched Rayne ascend the spiral steps built into her chair as she took her place at the table and felt a wave of embarrassment as I realized we'd only ever eaten crouched on the ground, sprawled on some rocky roadside perch or with my master and I leaning against the cart while they sat aboard it. Much more gallantry had been deserved, and I felt a flush creep up my neck as I pondered the thought.

"Vendark said he'd suffered an attack by banshees?" Tasha asked her parents. "But really, he'd killed our two loving donkeys. Their magic kicked in, and their braying, the din, deafened him and his soldiers, you see."

Alfred of Evermere shook his head and sighed. "I now regret having the poultice-maker see to their ears. Vendark seemed shifty, but I never imagined him such a scoundrel."

Talk of the rescue and the nebulous threats to the Red Bean Queendom swirled around the table while I took full advantage of the roasted vegetables, creamy sauces, and spiced fish. An impossibly large quantity of food appeared on a progression of silver platters, borne to the table by full-height waiting staff. I was sure the engineers who designed the table could have invented some concealed staircase that would allow Red Bean servers to appear through a trapdoor in the table's surface, delivering fresh dishes with a flourish of spotless sleeves, but having staff from Outer Pang, Inchin, or Meer seemed the sensible option. I considered the feast a challenge that I accepted without question: how much deliciousness could I send down my gullet without directing any down the fresh white cotton tunic that a footman had delivered to our room? The many unfamiliar vegetable and nut dishes did nothing to dampen my enthusiasm. I saw every dish, known and unknown, as a part of the experience to relish.

I noticed Master Thorn closely examining a three-tined fish fork. He held it by its butt, pointing it upward as he spoke into a lull in Tasha's storytelling. He addressed Queen Violet, "I should chat with your silversmith when the moment is right, but first, I want to thank you for your hospitality. As you can tell from the nearly empty state of Minimus's platter, we are unaccustomed to such delights. And although the beauty of your daughter and her handmaiden were apparent the moment they stepped from the battered gourd, to see them in court finery—what a stunning transformation."

There was no dispute from me. Rayne's splayed red hair tips peeked from where she'd slung her structured braids over the shoulder of an embroidered gown that made her look almost a different person. Princess Tasha radiated gleams of light from reflective threads woven into her frilly dress.

As usual, though, Master Thorn included me in a plan, unwarned. "As our way of saying thank you, Minimus will journey back to the Island in the Sky and retrieve Lady Tasha's tiara. Hopefully the gourd has not been disturbed since our departure. I would accompany him, but I can barely hobble with my back twisted after my fall, and time is of the essence. He can set off tomorrow."

All eyes swung toward me. It appeared they expected me to comment on the mission that was unknown to me only moments earlier. I swallowed, realizing I had only a couple of seconds to respond. Hopefully something impressive, brave, and insightful.

All I managed was, "Uh … what's a tiara?"

Rayne smiled at me. "It's a jeweled band you wear on your head. A crown open at the back. Like Queen Violet's."

I'd seen something similar before but had forgotten it in an instant of distraction. The sparkling item inside the gourd when we'd first met Rayne and Tasha. That must have been her tiara! But I couldn't admit that now—I'd look a right idiot.

"We can send our riders to escort Minimus, right?" asked

Rayne. "They can ride cross-country, along the border path between Inner and Outer Pang."

On reflection, there were two reasons I ended up setting off alone, but I'm not so sure my brain registered either at the time. The first was that I'd been with Master Thorn every day of my living memory. An independent mission would be a way to prove myself, both in his eyes and my own. How hard could a trip across the plains be, especially when I knew exactly where the tiara rested? And the second was that I wanted to impress Rayne, show her I could fend for myself, and maybe one day, when we were grown up, protect her, too.

"I'll go alone," I said. "Less suspicious that way. Who would think to attack or rob a poor orphan boy trekking through the back end of nowhere?"

The logic felt weak as it crossed my lips. An unaccompanied orphan would be a prime target for unsavory drifters as I crossed the high plains. I needed another justification. "And it seems bad timing to send Red Bean riders into Outer Pang after Vendark's threats, yes?"

There was a fair bit of argument back and forth about the merits and logistics of my trip, but eventually, we reached a compromise. I would take the strongest royal horse, tacked out without its usual finery. That way, I could return more quickly. A few days instead of a half month.

* * *

As the first rays of Cheeseday sunshine slanted across the stable yard, disappointment at my send-off crept across my chest like a constricting rope. Master Thorn's back had stiffened overnight, and he bade me a safe journey from his bed, pressing a pouch with several goat's teeth—including a molar—into my hand along with a carved wooden case containing a fine set of travel cutlery. "Today's puppet show is canceled, my boy. But never fear. I'll be working on the design for your runcible spork while you're away. We can start fabricating them as soon as you return. Maybe travel onward into Meer to try selling them?"

I'd pestered him about traveling to Meer or the Golden Shores for ages without success. Perhaps this concession was his way of expressing pride that I was undertaking this solo mission.

But other than the groom holding the horse's reins, only Princess Tasha awaited me in the yard. No Rayne. Not even Jing Jing had bothered to rouse himself from whatever cozy nook he'd claimed as a bivouac. He was probably roaming the royal guest house looking for filch-worthy wares.

Tasha pointed to my horse's swollen saddle bags. "I ordered a selection of salads and dried fruits for your pack, enough to see you there and back," she said. "And don this cloak before you go. It can get mighty windy up on the plateau."

A heavy cloak lay draped over the same rail where Vendark had assaulted Master Thorn the previous afternoon. It was of amazing quality, triple-layered, heavy, with pockets and a hood lined with a lattice of pillowflowers. I'd never seen the tiny blue and white blossoms before, but knew at once what they were—the legendary durable softness and inexplicable ability to flourish even after being uprooted resulted in their demand for bedding and lush furnishings.

With a final unfulfilled look back to see if Rayne would wave from a window, I mounted and ushered the horse through the stable yard toward Evermere's outer gates.

* * *

My first insight about the solo mission was the silence. I'd never really noticed that Master Thorn emitted a constant stream of observations, opinions, and edicts as I pulled the cart along dusty tracks, making it rare to travel without conversation. His banter made the plodding pass quickly and was the reason I knew more than children trained at the finest schools, but blind spots in my knowledge showed up occasionally. How could I not have heard of a tiara? After crossing the Moss Bridge, Port Evermere was barely out of sight beyond the first upstream bend in the river before I filled in the silence by talking to my horse.

"They forgot to tell me your name, but I think I'll call you Mister Apples, since that's what Princess Tasha said you liked to eat. Is that okay?"

The snort that rippled from snout to shoulders gave me a moment's doubt that horses couldn't understand our language. I leaned into the graceful, braided crest mane and patted his neck, a moment of shared understanding between two creatures destined to haul others on journeys not of our choosing. I gripped the horse's flanks with my inner thighs, feeling the muscles ripple as he trotted. My heavy cloak feathered the cooler river air past us, and the breeze shifted as we ascended into the low hills.

"Nobody's looking, Mister Apples. What say you to a sneaky snack, even though it's only early morning?"

Master Thorn had taught me to settle the well-being of all workers before your own. That's why he'd lean forward and hand me the first sandwich as I pulled the cart. It's why he sweetened every deal for raw materials by slipping the miners a trinket or delicacy to reward their underground toil. It was only right that Mister Apples got his apple before I investigated the saddle bags for my own snack.

As I returned to an upright riding position, my apple-finding task got much simpler. A rosy guild apple appeared, peeking from the saddle bag behind the crook of my left knee. Before I could grab it, the apple rose further from the pocket, supported by a pair of delicate hands, dwarfed by the apple's circumference. The pale, freckled skin continued along two elegant forearms as elbows crested above the saddle bag's flap. Confused, I hadn't yet grabbed the apple when a peal of muffled laughter erupted from deeper in the pocket.

Rayne's face peeked from the saddle bag with a scorching smile. She held the apple aloft, still waiting for me to grab it. "You should see your face, Minimus! You look like a baby who's tasted his first iceberry."

I plucked the apple with one hand and cupped the other so

she could step from the pocket into full view. My words tangled as I asked many questions at once. "How did you—? Does Tasha know—? Or the queen? No wonder the bags bulged so! I'm such a fool for not noticing."

"Don't be ridiculous, Minimus," she said, finding a position straddling my left thigh where she could steady herself with a hand on the saddle's gullet. "You're too polite to deny us our surprise reveal."

"Wait—you mean the Princess is here too? But I watched her wave as I rode off."

Something stirred in the corresponding saddle bag on Mister Apples's right side. The noises were decidedly unladylike, and I knew in an instant that recreational pick-pocketing was now on our trip's agenda. Jing Jing needed no help, and sprang from the pocket to cling to Mister Apples's mane, leaning out and making a noise that sounded very much like laughter. He snatched the apple from my hand in a motion too quick for my eyes to detect, and he coiled his tail around the bridle, delighting in the apple's disappearance behind gracious horse lips.

* * *

The farmers' fields and southern hills of the Red Bean Queendom had morphed into the featureless high plains of eastern Outer Pang. Dry and supporting only coarse grass too stubborn to wilt, the monotonous vistas made time grate against us. The elevation took away the desert air's hot sting, but the parched breeze attacked lips and hands in a ruthless quest for moisture. Mister Apples needed no guidance, following the worn traders' track across the barren land.

We noticed the blotch on the horizon before its familiar roaring sound reached our ears. At a distance, it looked like an impossibly tall palm tree, topped with a bulbous purple crest, but I knew that specific color. It was no tree, bound to the earth, but the contraption of science we'd gaped at overhead on the road to Mossmarch. At first, it proved difficult to tell which direction it traveled, but as it grew larger, I remembered it moved at the wind's mercy; the breeze in our faces brought the airborne vessel closer. Soon, I could see its dragging rope, and my pocketed hand glided over the now familiar form of the complex metal instrument Jing Jing had stolen during our previous encounter with the unusual airborne device.

The craft's pilot, his bush of wiry hair as disheveled as ever, regarded us through a long spyglass and fiddled with something unseen in the basket suspended below the purple bulb. The deep-throated rush of air stopped.

"You there! Boy!" the pilot called, gesturing wildly. "Grab the line and fasten it around that boulder. I'm coming down."

I couldn't imagine he recognized me—I'd been just another child of many speckling the approach to Mossmarch—but we were the only travelers today, so there was no doubt where he directed his words. But one look at Jing Jing, who had wisely pulled a lapel of my cloak around himself, and he'd surely erupt with anger. Still, what could he do to us? It was simple enough to ride off. Without further thought, I dismounted and grabbed the trailing rope with calloused hands.

There was enough slack in the dangling line that I could scoot to one of the many boulders that littered the landscape and slither its woven fibrous length in a loop. I circled the boulder twice to be sure of its grip. The basket nearly grounded when the rope pulled taut, and I worried momentarily that the remaining forward velocity would topple the old man from his contraption onto the packed earth. The basket listed, but he seemed familiar with the peril and clung to its rim until it righted itself and bumped onto the wiry grass. The purple sack filled with invisible magic wilted and wrinkled a fraction but remained fluttering in the light breeze above the basket. I motioned for Rayne and Jing Jing to remain atop the saddle as I approached the grounded airship.

As I ambled over, the wind-befuddled hairdo made a brief appearance over the basket's rim—just long enough to heave over an anchor tied to a short rope. The basket was even broader than I'd estimated, and the sac that hovered overtop was larger than any tree found in the forests of Outer Pang. The man's helmet bobbed above the wicker margin as he worked away at something hidden within. It popped up once I drew close enough to touch the odd conveyance.

Goggles that could be pulled down to protect the unusual man's eyes from the weather obscured the helmet's face, which appeared to be fashioned from a conch shell. I instinctively rubbed my forehead, imagining the harsh feeling of a shell pressing down on it, but realized the man's gray curls offered him a layer of protection I lacked.

"Thank you, dear boy, thank you. I'm a little off course and have seen no one else for two days, so figured I'd land for a chat. Tea and cake?"

I wasn't sure whether he was requesting or offering, but he ducked down again, and the rattle of china on saucers made it clear he would provide the tea, at least. But I needed to resolve something before fully engaging with this man.

"Uh, greetings, sir," I said, and pointed to Mister Apples, who stood bent over, nibbling at the sparse grass a short distance from the basket. "Do you see my horse over there?"

The man fumbled a set of oval-rimmed spectacles from a pocket high on his faded blue waistcoat and peered at Mister Apples and the two compact figures perched atop him.

As he focused, he spluttered. "By the great bushy brows of the tufted warthog! That's the little scamp that stole my compass! Where'd you capture him?"

"Well, I didn't exactly capture him. He's, I guess, my *brother*? My friend, anyway."

The man switched his gaze to me, brow furrowed. I felt obligated to break the awkward silence. Reaching into my pocket, I pulled out the device Jing Jing had stolen.

"Here's your thingy back. Your *crumpless*, or whatever you called it."

"Ooh, thank you, boy! No real harm done, although it set my mapmaking back a couple of weeks. I take it the little lady would enjoy a cuppa, but what about your simian brother?"

I didn't know whether *simian* was an insult, a compliment,

or more of the scattered balloonist's *science*, but the reference was plain enough. "Oh, Jing Jing could drink a gallon of tea if you let him. I'll lead the horse over," I said. "And did you mention *cake*?"

I introduced Rayne, not mentioning her connection to the royal household, and also presented Mister Apples. The horse took no notice and munched away at a patch of weeds.

"I am Ezra Longshanks," the man said, passing around tea, "official scientist of Queen Jada of Mossmarch's court, master balloonist, and mapmaker for the western queendoms. Someday, hopefully, the eastern queendoms, too."

We sipped from the fine china cups, Jing Jing without a saucer offered. "What's a balloonist do?" Rayne asked. Her smile had a radiance I wasn't sure Ezra fully appreciated, but it tugged his lips into their own responsive grin.

"Ah yes, it's the terminology that all too often scares people away from science, I'm afraid. A balloonist, m'lady, is one who operates a balloon. And a balloon is this big sack of air you see above us." Ezra Longshanks gazed and gestured upward while positioning his cup and saucer on the padded basket rim, which seemed too precarious to be a good idea.

"Well, I can see it's full of air, but what magic makes it float?" I asked. "I half expected to see a family of hovering goats in there, but it's empty."

"But *can* you see the air inside?" Ezra asked, his earnest gaze boring into me.

I pursed my lips and thought for a moment. "Well, no. But I *know* there's air in there. It's not water."

"Aha! You see? You are a junior scientist already," he replied, delight animating his face. "And what would you say if I told you the air within my balloon is not as heavy as the surrounding air? And that lighter air wants to float above heavier air the same way an air bubble wants to float to the top of pond water?"

I laughed. "Well, that's plain silly. Air doesn't weigh anything."

Ezra smiled and held up his index finger. Without replying,

he reached into an inner pocket of his waistcoat and extracted a folded paper fan. He handed it to me, jostling his teetering teacup with a sleeve but somehow without sending it tumbling to the grass. "Don't open the fan—swish it back and forth."

I obeyed, unsure where the demonstration was headed.

"Now open the fan," he said, coaxing me with a hand gesture. "What do you feel if you swish it now?"

As I fanned myself, I smiled. "I feel a breeze on my face." Then I fanned my companions. "Rayne? Feel something?"

"Ah, yes. But is it easier or harder to flap the fan when it is closed or open?" he asked. "Harder when open, right? It's moving more air."

Rayne was smiling, too. "And if air weighed nothing, you could swoosh as much around as you wanted, and it would be no harder than moving the closed fan. So it *does* weigh something, Minimus. Just very little, and easy for a sturdy boy like you to fan Jing Jing and me all day."

I nodded. Ezra Longshanks continued, pointing upward again. "And you know what makes the air in my balloon lighter than your air? It's *hot* air. I let air pass through my tiny furnace here, and it goes up inside the balloon. It's only a little lighter than normal air, so it takes a whole lot to raise the balloon and my basket from the ground. The difference in the weight of the hot and cool air must equal my own weight, including all my equipment and the balloon basket."

I nodded. This made sense. "Like how pieces of paperbark rise into the air above a campfire, right?"

"Precisely, lad. That's it. A balloonist is nothing but a crazy scientist floating like a piece of paperbark above a fire of his own making."

This was not the only bit of scientific magic that Ezra demonstrated. After correcting my pronunciation of the word *compass*, he showed me how it worked, how its dial spun round and pointed north, no matter how hard you tried to fool it. How you could peer through the matching notches to line it up level with the horizon. Of course, he could tell which direction was east or west when the sun was up, but Ezra described how he used the compass on cloudy days or moonlit nights as he drifted in his balloon at the breeze's mercy.

I savored the beetleseed cake as Ezra unrolled map after map from carved wooden sleeves, recounting trips criss-crossing the queendoms. Rayne pointed to Scalisport in Meer, where she and Tasha would set sail on their delegation to Oceanplat. I marveled at Ezra's ornate sketch of Yinti in the Queendom of Golden Shores on the Fading Sea coast and daydreamed that Master Thorn and I were already setting off to sell our runcible sporks, cart pulled by Mister Apples.

After I downed a second slice of cake, the scientist's eyebrows arched, and he looked up at the fluttering balloon membrane overhead. "Joy! Looks like the wind has shifted and is blowing from the south. I must cast off now and enhance my survey of the Red Bean Queendom and beyond to the Caves of the All-Seeing Eye in southern Meer. Queen Jada wants a better map of Red Bean, and I'd be a fool to disappoint her."

I collected the plates, cups, and saucers, and handed them across to Ezra. He filed them absentmindedly into a latched drawer as he fussed with the iron furnace. The hot—and lighter—air made the balloon's purple fabric squeak and creak against the englobing rope mesh as it strained to rise.

"Thank you again, boy, for being so honest as to return my compass. Now, if you'd be so kind as to unravel the tail line and hoist my anchor, in that order?"

I let Mister Apples continue grazing as the three of us sat astride, watching the magic of science transport Queen Jada's balloonist into the northeast sky.

Master Thorn and the Red Bean Princess

CHAPTER 12 - CENTRAL OUTER PANG

Appleday of Moon, Year 127

"I miss the puppet shows," Rayne said, watching me shake scant beads of dew from the tarpaulin under which we had slept. I nodded as I rolled it up and strapped it to Mister Apples's saddle. For all his harsh words, I missed Master Thorn, too.

He always said, *A good man makes the best of an unhappy situation, while an unhappy man makes everything a situation.* I took this to heart and pointed ahead, where the traders' trail bisected a patch of forest. "At least we'll be in the shade once this sun turns from warming to roasting. And our canteens will be full of cold water from the spring ahead."

Rayne laughed, also taking Master Thorn's advice. "Shade, water, good company... and a cheeky monkey. What more could a girl ask for? Do you think we'll reach the Gorge of Razors today, Minimus?"

"Princess Tasha said we should reach the gourd by Lemonday. That's tomorrow, but I think we've made good progress, so maybe we'll get there by the end of today instead," I replied.

* * *

The shade as the track passed through the forest fringe was welcome, especially to Mister Apples, who emitted a palpable aura of sweat vapor as he trotted. The dull thunk of a dagger embedding itself in a tree trunk to my left was less welcome.

"Not again," I muttered, slipping a frying pan from the saddle bag and swinging my head in frantic arcs, trying to locate the knife thrower.

Not seeing anyone, I called out, "We are but simple travelers! I hope we have not offended you, whoever you are."

A bush ahead on the left shook, accompanied by low chuckles.

"It offends me when you call yourself *simple*, boy. There's nothing simple about someone who carries the finest tableware in the western queendoms."

Rayne recognized the voice, too. "Sala Doon! Show your skinny self, you rascal."

Sala turned sideways and slipped from between a berry-laden bush and an ivy-clad tree trunk. A second person, who I was less heartened to see, followed. It was the thief, Mirko Leatherfoot, who had swindled us of knives and money at the Mossmarch market. I was never one to hide my emotions, which is why I could never be a swindler like Mirko. My disdain and surprise must have been obvious, and when I looked at Rayne, she bore a similarly unfiltered look of dismay. Jing Jing screeched and pointed at the cloaked thief. I wasn't sure why his irate gestures were so vehement; he seemed to take the swindle close to heart, as if Mirko had stolen something from him personally.

"Ah, yes, I heard you'd met my friend," Sala Doon said, ambling past to pry his dagger from the tree. Knowing his accuracy, he'd intentionally missed us with his throw, and I noticed he used a less precious dagger. He'd doubtless saved the ones Master Thorn had given him for special occasions, such as stabbing noblemen. I imagined Lord Vendark meeting the tip of a Master Thorn knife thrown with unfaltering aim by Sala Doon.

Mirko spoke up, approaching us with palms up and a roguish shrug. "I would apologize, but it's against code. What kind of thief would I be if I went around saying *sorry* to my *donors*?"

"Robbers gotta rob—it's our job!" Sala added.

Rayne spoke up, pointing an accusatory finger at Mirko. "Tell you what—we'll forgive you if you repay us. I don't really care whether you apologize. I have such a wave of not caring whether you say sorry that Master Thorn would probably call it an ambivalanche."

I couldn't restrain the corners of my lips from showing my amusement. I'd never heard Master Thorn say *ambivalanche,* but it sure sounded like a word he'd invent.

"*Repay?*" Mirko asked, raising an eyebrow, dark and shapely enough to look intentionally groomed. "I'm not sure I know what that word means."

"I don't even expect the knives or the goat's teeth back," Rayne said. "But if you tell us *how you did it*, and let Minimus know what to watch out for on future market days, we'll consider everything forgotten."

"Now that's a good deal," Mirko replied. "I'm all in favor of educating today's youth."

* * *

Thieves may have their code, but Master Thorn and I had our rules, too. One was *no lessons on an empty stomach. Empty stomach, empty head.* I moistened and fried dried strips of rainbow trout and diluted some lightningfruit paste as a sauce before I would allow Mirko to describe his techniques. Sala ushered us to a fallen tree, where we sat munching as Mirko held forth.

"The first rule of subterfuge is to never put yourself in an unplanned situation. I already knew the layout of your stall, the wares on offer, and had practiced the switch I intended to make. Did you see me at Seven Rocks?"

Rayne shook her head, but I realized why Mirko had seemed vaguely familiar when he appeared at the Mossmarch market. He'd been the customer poking around the stall in Seven Rocks, mostly hanging back. Maybe it was a gesture or something about his appearance that registered when I saw him again, but it was not a vivid memory. He'd made himself suitably, if not perfectly, inconspicuous on his first visit to the stall.

"The rest," Mirko said, "is practice, practice, spider thread, and more practice. Here—let me show you in slow motion."

Mirko beckoned us over as he lay a handkerchief across a flattish section of the log and fished a metal cup from his pack. "See this strand of spider thread?"

I nodded. "Barely."

101

"That's why I use it. Watch! I loop it around a goat molar … like so … and tie it tight. Then I tie the other end to my pinky finger. It must be exactly the right length."

Mirko lay the goat molar on the handkerchief, from where it levitated. "Whatever you do, don't look away from my pinky as I put the cup over the tooth. Even if I slap my other hand on the log."

When he slapped the log, I couldn't help but turn my attention there. Flicking my gaze back, I overturned the cup that he'd placed upside down over the goat's tooth, and, of course, there was nothing there. Mirko opened the palm of his hand to show he still possessed the molar. "Again," I said. "I promise to watch closer this time."

Rayne laughed, a glint in her eye as she turned to me. "I'm glad it wasn't only me that missed it. Fools love company."

After showing us a few more flourishes and finesses, Mirko gave Rayne and me a short length of spider thread each. "Now, it's a simple matter of practice."

As I packed away the plates and cups, I asked Sala Doon how he became such a knife-throwing legend. "I expect that's practice, too. Or competing in the inter-queendom trials. Something like that?"

His brow furrowed beneath the upper fold of his cloak's hood. The next words he spoke spilled out in a wistful, philosophical tone. "It's almost the reverse of competition. When I was about your age, my sister and I were messing around in a tree, building our own eagle-sized nest out of dry branches and twigs. The nest's middle gave way, and my sister plummeted through the resulting hole. The last part of her that remained in my vision was her waving ponytail."

"Oh my goodness," Rayne gasped. "Was she okay?"

"We were pretty high up," Sala said. "She broke both her legs and had to stay in bed for a month. They're still somewhat crooked to this day. But whenever I throw a trick shot, I first visualize the knife's trajectory in my mind, and then I imagine it's going to pierce the knot in my sister's ponytail, saving her from falling. So, it's love that guides the throws, not anger, revenge, or competitiveness."

It was only after the forest was a dim splotch on the horizon behind us and the Gorge of Razors was visible ahead that Jing Jing pulled a floating goat molar from the tiny pocket in his waistcoat. It still had a strand of spider thread attached to it, which the monkey used to swish the floating tooth around like a child's toy.

Manic monkey chatter accompanied my laughter. "Robbers gotta rob!" I said, tossing my little friend and his prize into the air and catching him as he returned.

Master Thorn and the Red Bean Princess

CHAPTER 13 - MOSSMARCH

Lemonday of Moon, Year 127

The witch Alianthe had been absent from the Western Continent for many years. She enjoyed neither Outer Pang nor the predators there, but it was time for another nudge. Just the slightest of touches would be sufficient, and only one person could possibly detect her guiding guile. Alianthe was not sure whether that person was yet aware of the critical role expected, indeed needed, of them. Time would tell.

A certain man slept beneath the baked tiles of a Pangan noble's roof. He slumbered fitfully, coursing with dreams that Alianthe had not poisoned, despite her talents extending into such areas. She couldn't help but dip herself into the jumbled images of the man's sleeping memories.

The man's dream was full of sensations. The cold, damp stones of a cellar floor as his father's lash descended time and again. The electric scourge of skin perforating down his back as the blows landed, and the lazy globs of blood that dripped onto his exposed calves as he cowered and covered his ears.

His boyish thoughts flooded the dreamscape—of how he would pity his father's weakness once he grew to manhood, sparing him any retribution. How he would never treat anyone under his power this way. How he would be a gracious and respected Outer Pangan lord, refuting his noble-born father's petty cruelties. But the acidic poison that coursed through his system as the lash wounds turned to scar tissue and were reopened, time after time, never allowed his self-promises to bloom. Each time an opportunity for generosity arose, the seething evil in the criss-crossed scars somehow made the man react exactly opposite to his aspirations, the poison burning him with the fire of self-destructive malice.

The dream shifted and the man watched in horror, unable to restrain his own hand from slashing a dagger across a donkey's throat. His hand, his arm, and his mind seethed with the desire to spite his father even as his heart felt the wrongness. The dagger strike would wound both man and donkey. He knew his guardsmen, his queen, and every ear that heard the story from whispering lips would think him twisted and petty. But as always, his animal need to lash out whenever he faced belittling words won out over his desire to be honorable. He felt such a coward.

After conjuring a darkened ganglion and recruiting a spider from the rafters to lower it to the sleeping man's chest, Alianthe altered the man's dreams, almost as an afterthought. She showed him the future, though he would dismiss it upon waking. A cough. The wrong footwear for slick cave rocks. A stumble at an inopportune moment. A failure. She knew it was petty, but relished the idea nonetheless. It seemed a fitting response to the man's repeated injustices.

The spider released her magical cargo, and it sank slowly among the sleeper's chest hairs, kissing the skin before diving beneath. A snatched breath interrupted the sleeper's rhythm, and Alianthe felt her conjured ganglion take hold. The sleeper was now fated to cough at the least convenient time.

The witch departed eastward to the mountain. There, she could intervene if this nudge proved too subtle.

CHAPTER 14 - INNER PANG

The Same Day

Night had fallen before we could reach the ruins of the rope bridge to the Island in the Sky. We had camped upstream beside the Gorge of Razors, reveling in the salty breeze that swept up the deep crevice from the sea. We reached our destination early in the morning.

It took some coaxing and several leaps across the crack, showing Mister Apples that he need not balk at the jump. The gorge's depth spooked him like it had originally frightened me, but if I could overcome my qualms and leap across without a worry, so could he. Eventually, the horse made the leap to the Island in the Sky, with me astride and Rayne cheering him on.

A pent-up breath left my lungs when I spotted the gourd exactly where we'd left it. Rayne leapt inside, searching for the forgotten tiara. "Minimus, it's not here!" she called. "The pulp's disappeared, and there's nothing left but the hard rind's moldy inside layer."

We'd come all this way to discover that someone else had taken the tiara. My hopes of returning a hero were dashed. I turned away from Rayne's forlorn face, so she wouldn't see the tears of frustration and self-pity roll down my cheeks. But I couldn't hide the sharp intakes of breath, and my tears made dusty pools on the trail's dry surface.

Rayne ran to me and urged me into a sitting position. "Oh, Minimus, don't worry. It's okay—Princess Tasha has other jewelry she can wear. I'm sure the royal silversmiths need a new project, anyway. And we had this brilliant trip together, so it's not all bad."

She lay her head on my calf and rubbed it. It was remarkable how much sensation her gentle caresses could express on my hairless lower leg. My tears soon retreated.

Jing Jing walked sideways to us, using a forepaw as a third contact point with the ground. Pausing before me, he held up his other forepaw and squeaked in a plaintive, rising tone. He waved a nugget of bird droppings between two fingers.

"Yes, Jing Jing, I agree," I said. "This *is* a big clod of poop we find ourselves in."

Jing Jing jumped up and down three times, dropped the poop, and gestured at several similar specimens littering the ground near the gourd.

"You little genius!" I shouted. "Treasure poop!"

Rayne looked up at me, her lips a near perfect *O*. "What? I hardly think some bird spoor is going to replace a jeweled tiara. Why are you so excited?"

"Treasure birds!" I said. "You know—the ones that collect shiny things for their nests. They've been here."

I expected Rayne to be equally excited, but her next words shot off on another tangent. "Wait. You can identify varieties of bird poop?"

"Uh ... yeah. Can't you?"

"It's not very ladylike," Rayne replied. "But never mind that. How will we find the treasure birds' nest?"

I knew that wouldn't be a problem. We had the most skilled treasure bird-rooter in both Pangs at our disposal. You wouldn't believe the trinkets Jing Jing had retrieved from such nests during our journeys. Picking up a pellet to judge its freshness and giving it a cursory sniff, I nodded to Jing Jing and waved him along. "Do your thing, lad."

The monkey sped into the bushes beside the track, following some scent or set of clues only he could decipher. I held my breath, lest the noise of breathing stole some subtle monkey sound from my ears. Rayne was silent, too, holding my pinky with both hands. The rustling receded into a silence so complete, the ever-present insects' background drone seemed like thunder.

"Sometimes he takes a while to—" I began. But Jing Jing's return interrupted me. He held aloft *two* tiaras. One, from its size, was clearly princess Rayne's, but the other would fit a full-sized woman's head. Adorned with a central aquamarine gemstone, it featured two lines of glittering diamonds set in gold, with a central spire and peaks above the wearer's temples.

Rayne squealed with joy. "Robbers really do gotta rob! But who could lose a tiara that big?"

* * *

We couldn't risk another encounter with Mirko Leatherfoot now that we had both his secrets and the filched molar, so we took the well-traveled road on the border's Inner Pangan side. It would take a day longer to return to Evermere, passing through the town of Mista and skirting Inner Pang's capital, the City of Jade, but I didn't trust our luck to avoid a snarling third encounter with Lord Vendark, either. Outer Pang held many threats, so our tiaras would travel through Inner Pang instead. I would enjoy pointing out familiar places to Rayne, having criss-crossed the region for as long as I could remember.

Despite the rope bridge's rickety planks that spanned the gorge's wider span from the Island in the Sky to Inner Pang, Mister Apples crossed without protest.

We arrived in the rambling but not unpleasant town of Mista at noon, ready for delicacies from their market and mugs of their legendary tea. Fields of red-leafed tea surrounded the town, stoking anticipation of a warm brew for visitors from every direction.

Jing Jing offered me his purloined molar, and I exchanged it, spider thread still attached, for a jangling pouch of minor teeth, bowls of lentil and cheese stew, and three steaming teas in various-sized mugs. Jing Jing sipped at the rich drink from an earthenware cup like the other marketgoers, while they gave Rayne a child's cup. I guzzled from a soup bowl that I'd pointed out behind the tea stand's counter. At first, the wrinkled proprietor thought I was jesting, but she filled it after my promise to pay extra and drink the entire bowlful. She was not disappointed, and nor was I.

As the market stalls thinned at the southern end of town, I saw a familiar tent accompanied by an equally familiar booming voice. I was about to turn Mister Apples toward the eastern edge of town when that voice turned its attention to me, calling from the tent flaps.

"Boy! You there on the horse. Come here. I owe you an apology."

If anything, Vik Gaard's hair was even more untamed than the last time we saw him, the scar crossing his right eye socket even more pronounced against his tanned skin. I tugged the reins and urged Mister Apples in his direction, coming to a stop near the beastmaster's tent but not bothering to dismount. This hinted at disrespect, but my pride still smarted from our last encounter.

Vik seemed to take no offense, approaching Mister Apples and stroking his neck as he looked up at Rayne and me. "What are your names? Master Thorn never told me—he simply called you *my boy*."

I hadn't known that Master Thorn had spoken to Vik Gaard at all while we visited Seven Rocks. "I am Minimus Mu, and this is Rayne of Evermere."

Rayne elbowed me. "And we have Jing Jing here, and the majestic Mister Apples," she said, patting the horse.

He smiled broadly, and I felt my tense shoulders lower a little. "As you might have guessed, I am Vik Gaard, traveling companion to many stray animals. And speaking of animals, I'm surprised that Master Thorn splurged on a horse, and a good one by the looks of his condition. That man's always been a bit of a skinflint."

"Uh, yeah. Tell me about it. He wouldn't even give me money to see your show in Seven Rocks," I said. "But it's not our horse. It's on loan." Rayne elbowed me again, more subtly. "Yeah—on loan from a... merchant in Evermere. We're here to arrange... a shipment of tea."

"Are you even old enough for a mission like that? I mean, you're clearly *big* enough," he said.

"It's been said that a year at the school of Master Thorn is like two years doing anything else," Rayne replied.

Vik's spluttering laugh showed he understood Rayne's mix of compliment and fun-poking. "Ha! It's been said only by a certain Master Thorn, I imagine. Let's tie up Mister Apples here for a drink at the trough, and I'll show you around inside the tent. The first show doesn't start until mid-afternoon."

Jing Jing remained outside to monitor Mister Apples' saddlebags and eyeball any marketgoers with unsecured valuables. Vik held back the flaps with a well-muscled forearm, and I ducked inside, Rayne striding to my right.

"In a way, Master Thorn paid for this visit," Vik said. "When I approached him in Seven Rocks to use you as the *face in the flap*, he said it'd provide a good life lesson for you. And you must admit, everyone laughed really hard."

"Not *everyone*," I grumbled, realizing I had yet again been a pawn in Master Thorn's enterprise.

Tessa the two-headed wolf lay curled up on the ground a step inside the tent's entrance. For all her ferocious barking the last time we'd met, she barely raised a disinterested ear as we passed. Vik bent and gave a firm scratch to each head. "Found her with a broken leg in a ditch near Og, the poor thing."

"And here's the tartan chameleon. I've trained this guy with twenty-seven patterned swatches of cloth. His skin can now match any of them. Here, pick a cloth and try it."

I let Rayne choose a square of fabric, then held it beside the knobbly lizard. Both eyes rotated independently to observe the cloth. It seemed impossible, but the vague green skin tone gave way to a wave of purple-tinged paisley curlicues that swept from the lizard's crested head to its whip of a tail in a matter of seconds. Rayne giggled with delight.

"And look at my latest addition. I'm not sure what act of my show I'll include them in, but they're ever so cute," Vik said as he pulled back a sheet covering a bamboo cage.

Inside were four tiny sabreclaw kits. Their fur rippled, downy-soft and tufted. Juvenile scythe-shaped claws scratched the cage floor, looking like they could do serious damage despite the kits' small size.

"Their mother was in a bad way following a vondabeast tussle gone wrong. She didn't even have the strength to swat at me as I pulled the mewling kits away from her. Maybe she knew in her heart that I was their only hope of survival."

They were beautiful, but I knew they would grow to become among the most savage creatures to roam the plains of Inner Pang, their magic-infused claws deadly to both man and beast. I wondered how Vik could even consider including them in his show.

As if he read my mind, he described a few things he'd learned. "I was younger and more foolish when I got this," he said, pointing to his scar, "but to communicate with a sabreclaw, it's all about protocol. Watch this!"

Vik turned sideways and unlatched the cage door. He kept his gaze fixed on Rayne and me as he reached into the cage for the nearest kit. "First, never look at them directly. That's a challenge, and it means you want to fight. Edge your way toward them. I learned this by watching a pride of sabreclaws interact over the course of a week. And this next bit I learned almost by accident. Watch my hand movements."

Vik moved his hand in a short set of syncopated rhythms. He patted the floor twice, turned his wrist three times to point his thumb to the tent roof, then gave the floor two further pats. After observing those motions, all four sabreclaws bounded over and snuggled up against his forearm. Their rasping purrs and fully retracted claws drew a striking contrast to the snarling, slashing powerhouses I'd seen take down heavyweight prey five times their size on the plains. "I mimicked their mother's tail movements. I think it might work to calm adult sabreclaws, too, but I haven't had an opportunity to try yet."

After a full tour of Vik's menagerie, he set us on our way with a clap on my back, a low bow for Rayne, and some faintly steaming buns from the neighboring market stall. Rayne stood on Mr. Apples' saddle, ripped off clods of warm bread and threw them through the air while I attempted to catch them in my mouth. Several bounced off my nose and cheeks, and the more I laughed, the worse her aim and my success became.

CHAPTER 15 - EVERMERE

Spiceday of Moon, Year 127

Our return was meant to be triumphant, but the Red Bean Queendom had other fears and conundrums on its collective mind. With twice as many tiaras as we'd set out to retrieve, saddlebags full of Mista tea leaves, and all of Master Thorn's goat teeth still jangling in my purse, I had imagined nothing but beaming smiles upon our return. Instead, I saw scowls and clusters of Outer Pangan soldiers. Their presence indicated a threat, their faces peering and sneering around the docks at Port Evermere.

Whispers abounded as Mister Apples nosed a path through the port and onto the main road to Evermere. Stevedores continued their usual business, lugging cargo to and from river barges, with choruses of curses warning idlers to clear out of their way. But new flags fluttered at the port. The Banner of the Golden Shores adorned a troop of horses, their tan skin and froth-white braids complementing the azure waves of their queendom's emblem. Armored in gold breastplates, their riders eyed the Outer Pang foot soldiers with open suspicion.

A carriage bustled past us toward the port. I'd never seen the flag of Meer before, but quickly identified its green field and circle of golden leaves. As with most things I'd learned, the flag's description sprang from the narrator's lips in Master Thorn's recurring puppet show about heraldry. It was unusual to see the local queendom's flags, and other queendoms' banners normally flew only on rare official visits. But within a matter of minutes, Rayne had pointed out troops from Inner and Outer Pang, Golden Shores, and Meer. Nothing about this spectacle signaled good news.

The central square in the outer part of Evermere was impassible, which forced me to usher Mister Apples through side streets teeming with people large and small. After an agonizing few minutes traveling against the flow, we reached the royal stable's gates. A stable boy took the reins and led our horse to some well-deserved hay. Master Thorn stood beside Tasha's father, Lord Alfred, on an open gallery which backed onto the stables and had windows open to the central square. He motioned us up with urgent gestures, but his broad smile as he watched me scoop up Rayne and bound up the stairs two at a time put me at ease; it had been the longest separation of our lives. Jing Jing sped ahead and leapt to the rail, giving a passionate but unintelligible speech to Master Thorn.

He winced as he enveloped me in a deep hug. His back seemed much improved but still troublesome. I was gentle as I returned the embrace, soaking it in while surreptitiously lowering Rayne to the floor. "You're back just in time, my boy," he said after releasing me with a series of claps to my shoulders and biceps. "There's a major announcement brewing. There are *five* other queens here, not counting Queen Violet."

"Aren't you going to ask about the tiara?" I said.

"Tiara, shmiara," he replied. "Hang on—did you get it? Let me inspect it before you give it back."

"Actually, we found two—" I began, but Lord Alfred signaled me to silence.

"Wait. They're about to start."

The open window from the gable gave a good view of the square. Alfred and Jing Jing peered over the bottom sill, while Master Thorn and I leaned against the rail that divided the opening halfway up. As usual, Rayne was at my level, legs crossed and tapping my chest from her shoulder perch. We were at eye level with Queen Violet, who sat upon an elevated throne atop a plinth. The throne put her at the same elevation as six other figures—five full-height women dressed in diverse finery and a man wearing scholarly robes and a felt hat. Princess Tasha sat in a similar but lower throne, perched with her dainty feet slightly in-turned.

Five of the seven women wore tiaras, although each was as different from the others as I could imagine. I whispered to Rayne, lifting Tasha's tiara from its refuge in an inner cloak pocket. "Does she need this, like, right now?" I asked. "Seems like everyone else is wearing one."

Rayne whispered back, leaning in to speak right into my ear. "I'll see if I can slip it to her at some point during whatever ceremony this is, but there's no way I'm sneaking up on stage right now. Do you know who everyone is?"

I shook my head.

"The one next to Queen Violet, with the white-blonde hair and the dark, high-collared dress? That's Queen Jada of Outer Pang."

I squinted to protect my eyes from the glare. An open-topped, black metal crown, devoid of jewels, restrained her hair. "Why isn't she wearing a tiara?"

"Good question. Formal royal appearances normally demand proper headwear. But wait—maybe the other tiara…?"

I fingered my other inner pocket, making sure our mission's second treasure was still safe. "You think?"

"But how'd it get …? Anyway, forget that for now. The one on Queen Jada's left? That's Queen Liu of Inner Pang."

Her red gown, embroidered in golden thread with a tapestry of fabulous animals and architectural works, matched the vivid color defining her lips' perfect cupid's bow. Her tiara was an exquisite textured work of gold, rising in the center to clasp a dark and sparkling ruby.

"Oh yeah. I've seen her before, but only from a distance. Master Thorn took me to her coronation in the City of Jade when I was little. Well, littler."

"Not sure who that guy on the far left is. He looks a shade embarrassed to be sharing the stage with six queens. The one to the right of Tasha, with the hair teased straight up? That's Queen Seela of Meer. She visits us often."

The woman in question had a bemused look on her ebony-skinned face, and wore a series of necklaces, each dangling in an arc perfectly nestling its neighbor above. Her tiara looked like an arch of conjoined, diagonally pointing hat pins, each capped with a diamond. Her tight curls rose from her scalp like a basalt column, the tiara affixed halfway to the top. The height of her hairdo made her tower over the other queens.

But height was not the key marker of a powerful presence. The queen to her right looked even more imposing. The sides of her head were shaved to a fine stubble, and the tufts of wiry hair that poked here and there above her aquamarine-studded tiara served only to accent the tattoos above and below her right eye. Cresting waves darkened her cheekbone, while a trio of black-limned sails rippled above her eyebrow.

"As you might have guessed, that next one is Queen Angstaad of Golden Shores. And at the far end, I believe, is Queen Valance of Oceanplat. She must have really hustled to sail here in the week we've been away! I wonder if this will cancel our diplomatic sea voyage to visit her?"

The Queen of Oceanplat had loose red hair that rippled to her pale, bare shoulders. A gown of shimmering blue that matched the cobalt workings of her tiara rippled with her every movement.

The assembled royalty represented the four Queendoms surrounding the Red Bean Queendom, plus their closest offshore neighbor. A hush swept over the crowd below as Queen Violet stood on the throne's platform, raising a forearm horizontally before her and clasping a silver bracer to it. I hadn't noticed it amongst the glittering finery, but a tiny green bird fluttered from a high perch above the stage to settle on the bracer. It must have been the size of a hummingbird.

"That's a thunderbird. Have you heard one before?" Rayne whispered.

I thought it odd that she asked if I'd *heard* one before instead of whether I'd seen one. A moment later, I discovered why.

I was too far away to hear Queen Violet speak, and it didn't seem like she was trying to project her voice, but I recognized her intonations as they rang across the courtyard. It was her voice, but it burst from the thunderbird's glowing beak. No one would have trouble hearing her words. Even the stableboys busying themselves attending to Mister Apples jerked their heads in the direction of the impossibly loud bird.

"Ladies and gentlemen of Red Bean, you may wonder why

we have assembled all these queens. It seems there's a gripe from our neighbor to the west, and this meeting was called at Queen Jada's behest."

As Violet sat, Jada stood tall, her lips forming a tight and slight smile. A ribbon of hair crept over the margin of her dark crown. She placed a similar bracer on her forearm, and the thunderbird swooped over. When its beak opened again, a fresh voice sprang forth—deeper, less elegant, and more direct than Queen Violet's.

"Thank you, my rhyming neighbor, for arranging this meeting at short notice. I bring unfortunate news for you—but good news for the citizens of Outer Pang." She spread wide her arms, as if to include the crowd of Red Beaners, nearly dislodging the thunderbird from her arm. I looked down to see if any of her troops were in attendance, but I saw none. A few murmurs rose from the throng.

"I'll have my scholar explain the situation. Lord Rose, if you would?"

The foppishly-dressed gentleman at the stage's far end raised his face as if startled from a snooze, and fumbled to affix his own bracer. The thunderbird fluttered over, glancing back at Queen Jada as if fearing she might pursue it.

"Uh, h-h-hello, everyone." The scholar paused while he fumbled open a heavy, leather-bound book to a page marked with a black ribbon.

Master Thorn took the pause in proceedings to mutter an aside my way. "My uncle, the Master Thorn I may have mentioned, was involved in a scheme to farm gorge cod. Came a cropper because of a thunderbird. He was hiding in some thick bushes out near the Watchtower of the Pang Wastes, hiding from an irritated sabreclaw, when a thunderbird repeated him saying, *I'll be safe in here.* His manservant reported that Master Thorn lost two limbs and a panoply of organs before expiring and becoming sabreclaw dinner."

Alfred shushed him as the scholar found his place and spoke once again. "You see, in our research, we discovered it says right here, in article six hundred and forty five of *The*

Binding of the Queendoms, that *the humans of each queendom, up to and including the Queen, handle the protection and safekeeping of all animals within their demesnes."*

There was much nodding in the crowd—caretaking of animals was a well-respected tenet of every queendom. Master Thorn managed a further side-remark before Alfred elbowed his shin. "Minimus—*demesnes* means all land associated with a queendom. I should have included that in one of the puppet shows."

The felt-hatted man continued. "And it's very clear how the borders of each queendom are drawn. *The Binding* describes the process in great detail in article fifty-one. The boundaries are undebatable."

Queen Jada of Outer Pang's gaze bore into Queen Violet, and a hint of a smile fluttered at one corner of her lips. It was a spiteful smile that suggested a thunderstorm of malice to come. The queens of Meer, Golden Shores, and Oceanplat shuffled a little closer to Violet offering implied support, and Tasha sent a smoldering glare in Queen Jada's direction.

The tome thunked shut as the scholar lifted an even larger volume from the platform. He unlocked the book's folding metal clasp with a thick iron key that shook as he withdrew it from his pocket. With a few muttered page turns, he located the section of interest.

"You will all be familiar with *The Catalog of Lands, Waters, and Beasts.*"

Most heads nodded. Even those among the crowd who couldn't read would have heard the descriptions and stories from its revered pages. It was the most complete index of the known world's wildlife, plants, and geographical aspects, cataloging from the Abject Turtle through to Zzangle Lake. Master Thorn had a copy in the cart's tiny library, and had recited its entries to me since I was a toddler.

With a pause to accommodate the acknowledging sounds from the throng, the scholar continued. "I'd like to read you the entry for *Little ones of the East Pang Forest.* It says, *These small human-like creatures inhabit the area from the East Pang Forest to the*

River Moss. They rise knee-high, have adopted the common language, built settlements, and formed a single society."

An assortment of gasps, rising voices, and discussions flowed across the square after a momentary silence. A fraction of those present seemed to understand the implication I'd missed, including the Queens of Meer, Golden Shores, and Oceanplat, who clustered beside Queen Violet, speaking among themselves without resorting to the thunderbird.

Queen Jada raised her forearm again, and the reluctant thunderbird flitted over. "Quiet, everyone!" she said in a commanding voice that quelled all but an undertone of hushed conversation. "Just so it's perfectly clear, what the founding books say is that each queendom handles caretaking of its local beasts, and that creating a Red Bean Queendom was a mistake. Its residents are not humans, but beasts. This courtyard, the city and port of Evermere, and all surrounding lands are chartered parts of Outer Pang, according to the boundary rules set forth in *The Binding*. There were never really nineteen queendoms, only eighteen.

"I offer you all my royal protection, and anyone that threatens you or the Outer Pangans shall face swift and violent response from my soldiers. I will allow the forces of all other queendoms one day to vacate my queendom."

Now I understood. This had nothing to do with reality. It was a passive war based on a loophole in the rules as defined in two ancient books. There was no denying the rules, but anyone with sense understood that Red Bean citizens were people, not beasts. Yes, they were small, but they did not categorize bigger humans as beasts. At least, I hoped not, or I'd be an outcast from the human race, too.

The thunderbird alighted on Queen Violet's bracer. Her glare belied a passionate fury that her measured words concealed. "Jada, I see how you twist the texts against my lands, but the power is not all in your hands. You summoned the other queens as witnesses, but I'll not remain mute. I call for the trials of the All-Seeing Eye to resolve this dispute."

Queen Jada smirked again, as if she'd anticipated this. Her

voice rang across the silent courtyard without using the thunderbird. "You have no standing here and cannot call for anything."

An even louder voice cut her off. Queen Angstaad's look suggested that if her wiry arms clutched a sword, she'd have leaped across Tasha and Queen Violet and made appropriate use of it on Queen Jada's less athletic form. "You're more of a beast than anyone here, Jada. Even if Violet cannot call for the trials, I certainly can. Justice will yet prevail. Let's have at it, you witch."

Jada's smile beamed wider and more lopsided. "Very well. The laws are the laws, Angstaad. I accept the dispute call, but you know how it will end. Same way the other eight have. The caves are so close, let's begin the trials tomorrow."

I'd heard the tales of the previous eight inter-queendom disputes, and Jada was right. There was no way this would end well. All eight attempts by the disputing queendom's chosen champions had ended in failure, many after only the first of five trials. The trials were a civilized way of resolving disputes and had prevented inter-queendom wars for many generations, but this method seemed unfair to the Red Bean Queendom. Queen Violet's lords and ladies were at a distinct size disadvantage when it came to feats of strength.

The Caves of the All-Seeing Eye were a few hours' ride north from Evermere, so at least failing in the trials wouldn't require a long trip. I was sure that Master Thorn would let us travel to witness the pomp and spectacle. It was exciting even though it seemed the ending would spell disaster for Tasha, Rayne, and their whole queendom.

"Well, Violet, let's get this over with," Queen Jada said, her voice feigning boredom. "Choose your champion."

The first trial was one of strength, and four of the previous attempts had failed; even Colwyn the Colossus of Wraithwatch left the first cave dejected. I struggled to see how any Red Bean citizen, given their tiny stature, had any chance of success. There was not even a whisper audible while the crowd waited for Queen Violet's response. The thunderbird did not betray the whispered consultation between her, Tasha, and the three aligned Queens. After a minute that seemed like an hour, the huddle broke apart, and Violet named her champion. "My *people*, I have chosen a champion for you."

As she paused before announcing the Red Bean hero, I had time for a hushed question to Rayne. "Hey—what lord will she select? Whose name rhymes with *you*?"

I thought about princess Tasha's animated gestures in the huddle. A bad feeling crept into the depths of my stomach. Rayne looked up at me, wide-eyed. She, too, could think of someone whose name rhymed with *you*…

Master Thorn and the Red Bean Princess

CHAPTER 16 - EVERMERE

The same day

Queen Violet pointed to the window where Master Thorn, Alfred, Rayne, and I watched. "I choose as our hero, Minimus Mu!"

I felt the blood drain from my face and a knot constrict my stomach. This couldn't be right. I wasn't even a Red Bean citizen. She must have said someone else's name that sounded like mine. Maybe a lord was named Finneus Moon, and he'd slunk behind me, unnoticed. But then I saw Princess Tasha waving at our window, beckoning me to the stage.

Master Thorn nudged me and used a harsh stage whisper without turning his face away from the royal stage. "Boy! When royalty summons, you *move!*"

I bent to allow Rayne to take up a spot beside Jing Jing. She locked eyes with me the whole time. When she said, "Minimus, this is an honor. You don't need to worry," her voice wavered. I looked away and trudged down the stairs to the stable floor.

My feet shuffled in cautious steps across the city square's cobblestone floor. I was broader than the full-height people clustered against the stable walls, and I surprised a trio of leaners as I unlatched and opened the door from the stables into the square. I squeezed through the rear of the crowd with ease. But at the throng's center were native Red Beaners, and accidentally kicking one aside would emphasize my foreignness. But they matched my caution with a willingness to form an open path. I felt like a magnet repelling people away from my strides as I stepped to the stage front.

My waist was at stage level, so I angled my head upward to speak as I arrived. There was no way I would address any queen, so I kept my gaze focused on Princess Tasha. But not *too* intently, because that would be both weird and disrespectful, as a commoner. I tried to focus on an unlit oil lantern behind the stage when averting my gaze from her.

"Uh, hello, P-Princess," I stammered. "I, um, got your tiara back."

She smiled, and I felt my hands shake a little less in my pockets. Pulling out the miniature tiara, I held my arm out toward her. "D-do you want to wear it? Seems only polite."

The Queen had just nominated me as the Red Bean assignee to perform the never-completed trials of the All-Seeing Eye, and that was the best I could muster? I felt like I was shrinking, but a furtive scan of the crowd showed I towered over the locals, as gargantuan as ever.

Princess Tasha clapped and clasped her hands, then pranced down the steps built into her chair and plucked the tiara from my outstretched palm. With a practiced motion, she slipped it onto her head, slotting it below the ornamental gold leaves that pinned up her hair. It fit so perfectly and complemented her skin tones so well, I knew the smiths had fashioned it just for her.

"Minimus Mu, you are a gentleman and source of a thousand smiles. Might we call on you to defend our queendom in the trials?"

I didn't think everyone in the square could hear her words, as she did not use the thunderbird, but they certainly heard Queen Jada's scathing tones, echoed through the bird's magical amplification.

"*This* is your champion? This *boy*? He's not even one of you. Choose again, Violet. Properly this time."

There was a pause while the thunderbird fluttered back to Queen Violet. Her voice spoke with sweetness on the surface but ice and daggers underneath.

"If it's rules that concern you, Jada, let's not fight. Give me a minute; I'll make sure this is right."

I expected her to select her actual choice of champion now. Mentioning me had been only a ruse, the meaning of which I couldn't fathom. But then Queen Violet spoke to me directly.

"I have a question for you. Exactly where were you born, Minimus Mu?"

Born? Nobody remembers where they were born. Or recalls anything until the age of three, really.

"Uh, I don't know. My mother abandoned me, and I … Master Thorn adopted me. I can't even remember her—and she's the only person who'd know. Maybe it was in—"

I was unable to suggest that I was probably born in Inner Pang before Queen Violet cut me off and asked a further question.

"I'm so sorry, Minimus. That's a terrible situation, but a tribute to Master Thorn that he took you under his wing. But I'd like to ask you one more thing. Did you recently return from a mission whereby you single-handedly retrieved Princess Tasha's royal tiara from the Island in the Sky?"

It was hardly boldness that made me respond in full voice— more like I subconsciously matched the thunderbird's volume as best I could without shouting. "Well, your highness, I used both hands, but yes, I did retrieve Lady Tasha's tiara."

Queen Violet turned once again to Queen Jada, a faint smile decorating the corners of her mouth. "There you have it! In section eighty-seven of *The Binding*, it's all written down. *Persons of unknown birth origin will be deemed citizens of a queendom if they provide invaluable service to the crown.*"

The thunderbird paused, fluttering in midair as Jada dismissed it with a languid backhanded wave. "Fine, fine. If you want to send a boy to do a woman's job, go right ahead. He'll not make it past the second challenge."

In a backhanded way, this gave me some confidence. Queen Jada seemed to think I would pass the first trial, at least. And I knew the first one—a feat of strength—was beyond even the most powerful Red Bean citizen. There was no substitute for bulk, and I'd doubtless eaten five times as much as even the adult locals.

Then I had a brilliant idea. The second tiara retrieved from the treasure bird cache was of such exquisite workmanship and adorned with such fine jewels that it must be Queen Jada's notably absent headpiece. Or if not, it wouldn't look out of place among the other queens' tiaras. I could offer it in return for her dropping this obscene attempt to hijack the Red Bean queendom. I'd be a hero without having to lift anything heavier than a piece of fancy jewelry. Well, a hero to everyone except a certain trader in fine tableware who would never let me forget the priceless artifact I was about to forfeit.

There was an audible gasp as I held the glittering arc of gold at full stretch overhead. It could have been awe at the tiara's beauty or perhaps outrage at such grubby fingers handling a work of art this grand. Sunlight refracted through the aquamarine and glinted off the diamonds.

Somehow, Tasha's commanding voice had infiltrated my veins and burst out with a proclamation that felt foreign to my lips. I'd never called out like this before, except for the time a rapscallion in the City of Jade tried to hightail it with a handful of Master Thorn's forks. "Wait, everyone! This is all so stupid. Queen Jada—I don't know if this is your tiara, but even if it's not, why don't you take it as a gift? Leave the Red Bean Queendom as peaceful as you found it, and have your wise man add a note to the back of his big book?"

Eyes widened along the stage, except for a single pair that narrowed with suspicion: Queen Jada's. The hand holding the tiara aloft shook—hopefully noticeable only to me. I glanced over my shoulder, searching for Master Thorn's reaction. Everyone else in the square looked shocked, but he looked calm and a beaming smile twitched the corners of his well-twirled mustache. The slightest of nods let me know I had his endorsement. Rayne covered her mouth, but her eyebrows danced. These were the only approvals that really mattered. My hand steadied.

I snapped my attention back to the stage and straightened my spine to stand as tall as possible. But all was not well in the land of royal negotiations. Queen Jada motioned an accusatory finger at the thunderbird, the black-varnished fingernail an order the bird could not refuse. She tapped a toe while awaiting its reticent arrival. A loose feather dropped from the thunderbird and dipped in a series of arced swoops toward the crowd's first row, highlighting the silence.

"Boy!" she spat, nostrils flaring and her venomous gaze skewering my optimism. "That tiara is *mine*, not yours to offer.

It was snatched from my palace window not three weeks ago by a devious, thieving monkey. You will hand it over *now*, or my guardsmen will retrieve both it and the grimy peasant hand clutching it. And there will still be no Red Bean Queendom, only Outer Pang. The law is the law."

I tried to slide the image of my severed hand to one side and wondered about the tiara's theft. A monkey? From the palace in Mossmarch? In the last few weeks? I slowly rotated back to the window above and behind me. Jing Jing turned sideways to better hide himself behind Rayne's wispy frame, but I could still make out a single eye peeking over her shoulder, its blossom of an eyebrow raised almost to the peak of the monkey's silver-crested scalp. Had he stolen it when he'd pranced off in a huff from our stall, then lost it somehow, and recovered it from the treasure bird nest?

By the time I returned my gaze to the pale and seething face of Queen Jada, the thunderbird had fluttered to perch on the Red Bean Queen's forearm.

I realized I'd committed a strategic error. How could I be such a fool? If I'd returned Jada's tiara, she would surely have claimed me as an Outer Pangan citizen, using Queen Violet's logic. It would be but minutes before my severed head rolled to the gutter, her mocking laughter the last thing my ears would hear.

"You can stop pointing your bony little finger at my champion, Jada," she said. "The law is the law, and we'll solve this now, not later. I see how you behave, and we'll not have this brave boy called a common knave before his victory at the caves. Let's have a look. I'm sure we can settle this according to your book."

Queen Violet turned my way once again. A wave of supreme self-consciousness cascaded over me, and I lowered the raised tiara and engaged in an internal debate about whether to pocket it again or, if not, how to best hold it to appear nonchalant as I reflected on my life's failings. In the end, I did neither and gripped it in awkward tension at my side. But she gave me a subtle glance of amusement that I was familiar with from observing Tasha's facial expressions—maybe she had something else up her sleeve?

"Minimus Mu, is it true? That the tiara lay unfound on the ground—not anywhere nearby, but on the Island in the Sky?"

My voice was still unwavering despite my heart thumping loud enough that I could hear its throb in my eardrums. "Yes, your highness. In a treasure bird's nest."

Queen Violet turned to face her adversary with a further expression of legal disappointment at her lips. "I'm afraid it's not *your* tiara, you see. The boundaries defined in the Book exclude the Island in the Sky from every country. We must treat it like the sea, where treasure goes to the finder, as per section two seventy three."

The scholar cleared his throat. "Um, section two seventy two, actually." He looked like he wanted to swallow his own tongue, followed by the rest of himself, such was the glare from his Queen. Queen Violet, too, raised an accusatory eyebrow in his direction for nullifying her rhyme.

Invoking the trials, affirming my citizenship, and now denying the return of her tiara—Queen Jada's weaponized books had been turned against her three times. The thunderbird was unneeded for the snarl of rage that tore from her lips. It echoed from the surrounding stone walls.

"Keep that trinket," she said in words directed at me alone, returning to an icy calmness. "The trials will soon be over, you'll be *my* citizen, and I'll have your head hung from the walls of Mossmarch while I smile upon your misfortune from under my rightful tiara."

CHAPTER 17 - SOUTHERN MEER

Gingerday of Moon, Year 127

I'd heard of the Truthsayers' Guild, but there was no puppet show to enlighten me about its origins. Well, not before the day the caravan left Evermere for the Mountain of the All-Seeing Eye. A royal horse pulled our cart. I'd hoped for Mister Apples, but the grooms had released him to a distant pasture, and he was not available for our unexpected morning departure. Master Thorn made Rayne and me huddle near the bank of drawers that dominated the cart's back end while he set up the stage, prepared the puppets, and kept a loose hand on the reins as the wheels rumbled across the cobblestones toward the North Gate and the road to Meer, following a snaking line of vehicles and marchers.

"Come here, Apostle. I, Sifu Pan, have a special mission for you," the lone puppet called to someone offstage. This was a typical Master Thorn tactic—use a standard puppet that would introduce itself by name as it began talking. I swear this one had been a pirate, town crier, swordsman, and mermaid in past plays, but I settled right into his role as leader of some organization. Rayne giggled beside me, less jaded about puppetry than I, still enjoying the idiosyncrasies of a Master Thorn production.

A second puppet peeked around the miniature stage's curtain. This one's face was hidden deep beneath a hood, its body surrounded by a swirling cape. I hoped the horse knew where it was going because Master Thorn must have relinquished the reins. Maybe Jing Jing was driving, which sounded like a worse idea than simply letting the reins dangle.

The apostle spoke in a high-pitched voice. "Yes, Sifu? What mission must I conduct for the Truthsayers' Guild? I am ever your servant."

The first puppet's head bobbed as it spoke. "Remember, Apostle, how I pricked you with the land urchin quill, and you now cannot but tell the truth? There is an extra-special need for your divine constraint. The trials of the All-Seeing Eye are being contested in Southern Meer. You must accompany the champion on his mission to the trial caves and report on his activities—if there are any challenges or accusations of cheating."

"What an honor, Sifu! I will ready my travel pack. What is involved in the five trials?"

"Good point, Apostle. Although the founder of our order discovered the Meeran gem hens that roost in the five caves and devised the trials around recovering their gems, nobody knows *exactly* what the tasks are, and nor should you reveal any specific details you observe. Only answer in general terms when questioned. The trials rely on secrecy to ensure any queendom invoking them does not have unfair advance knowledge. All we know is they are trials of strength, accuracy, bravery, wisdom, and endurance. They must otherwise remain shrouded in mystery."

"Understood, Sifu. Will it be only the champion and me allowed in the caves?"

"Often, they send along a composer of songs, to record the tale of the trials for retelling across the queendoms. They do not allow any beasts of burden; the champion must carry any supplies desired. And no helping! You are there in an official role, so do not submit to any temptation to assist the champion, no matter what difficulty he or she may face."

Rayne called out to the stage. "Sifu Pan! I have a question. Are animals allowed in the cave with the champion?"

"Well, my beautiful young lady, as I said, no beasts of burden. The rules go no further than that."

Rayne continued. "What if there are people accused of being animals? Could they go in?"

The two puppets bounced over to stage left, and Master Thorn's face peeked out beyond the curtains. He used his normal voice while neglecting his puppetry. "Huh, good question. I guess if you went in with Minimus, you'd either be cheating, and we'd forfeit the trial, or you'd be admitting you were an animal, allowing Queen Jada to justify annexing Red

Bean. Sounds like a bad idea."

His head popped behind the stage again, and the puppets resumed their original positions.

"Prepare yourself, Apostle. There is no time limit on each trial, so you may need to remain at the mountain for several days. I've heard this champion is likely to succeed where all others have failed. Oh—and take an urchin quill along, lest you need to indoctrinate an alternate truthsayer."

The second puppet bowed low and exited the stage.

* * *

The train of vehicles, draught animals, and people snaked along the packed earth roadway, heading north from Evermere toward the Meer border. Beyond lay the Caves of the All-Seeing Eye. I was in the pleasant limbo where I guess every trial champion dwelled while journeying to the caves. The queen had selected me as the prestigious Red Bean champion, but like all who had attempted the trials before me, I would likely soon be a failed champion. Doubtless, disgrace and lingering feelings of inadequacy would chase me like Del Cartan harrier hounds for my remaining days.

Rayne and I chatted quietly as the cart bounced along. She brought up a good point. "Master?" I asked. "If Sifu Pan forbids any discussion of the details of the trials, how come *everyone* talks about them? I heard the stable hands debating how heavy the lift will be in the trial of strength. One claimed it was an iron sphere and the other had heard it was a stone cube."

"Ahh yes, young lady. A wise man once said *laws may make heads roll, but they never stop tongues waggling.*"

"I haven't heard that quoted before," Rayne replied. "Is that a Pangan philosopher's line?"

A twinkle in his eye, Master Thorn stroked his beard while replying. "Sort of. I just made it up."

"The girl that tidied our room told me she'd heard I would need to lift a hippopotamus from a pit of snakes," I said.

Master Thorn laughed. "You see, my boy, there's a lesson here. You know what's worse than a complete lack of information? *Wrong* information. Those waggling tongues often produce sounds when disconnected from their owners' minds."

I shook my head. "So none of this helps? What do you think, Master?"

"It's a trial of strength, Minimus. You can be sure you'll need to lift or move something heavy. That's why I'm not worried about the first trial, boy."

After meandering through the forested hills and crossing the Meeran border cairn, the roadway zig-zagged across a stretch of stinking marshland. Crushed-rock causeways bridged spans of the waterlogged pond, making the path to the mountain a hopscotch of muddy islands and bumpy interludes.

I was glad a horse pulled the cart. It meant Master Thorn, Rayne, and I could press mint stalks to our nostrils to ameliorate the gaseous stench of the most odorous sections.

"Master Thorn?" I asked. "Why do you pronounce *swamp* as if it rhymes with *camp* while most people rhyme it with *pomp*?"

"I'm sure I have mentioned several times already, my boy, that you shouldn't listen to *most people*. As we know, and as they prove time and again, most people are morons. And besides, the word swamp is a combination of the words *sweaty* and *damp*. Hence, *swaaamp*. So clearly, the way I pronounce swamp is both correct and superior."

Rayne giggled beside me. I wasn't sure whether she was laughing at Master Thorn's logic or at the silly conversations we enjoyed while traveling.

* * *

There was space for a significant encampment at the foot of the Mountain of the All-Seeing Eye. The steep-sided peak rose from the foothills to four snow-capped points. Master Thorn had told me it was more of a high hill compared to the tall mountain ranges in the Far East, but the way it dwarfed the surrounding hills made it majestic and mountainous in its own context. A flat, grassy expanse, open to the mountain face but ringed by trees behind, was already bustling with activity when our cart pulled up. Burly, bare-chested men were using pile drivers to whack in pegs for elaborate tents. A crew of kitchen workers busied themselves like ants, building a huge brick oven, gathering firewood, and porting barrels of cold mountain stream water into position. The delegation from Outer Pang set up their tents in a far corner of the field. Everyone else steered clear of that area, leaving a gulf between the main encampment and its offshoot. The banners of Outer Pang flew from tall, bending poles, showing a lime-green field with a red sun, rays radiating to the edges.

A detachment of the Red Bean Queen's guards, mounted on ponykins, tiny golden horses suitable for their statures, directed our cart toward the side of camp furthest from the Outer Pang tents. A felt-lined yurt was already in position, and liveried runners flitted in and out, carrying plush blankets and cushions. This was the utmost luxury compared to where we normally slept, secreted beneath the cart with our thin drop-cloths the only protection from sandstorms and predators.

A trio of cooks poked at a steaming pan near where we parked the cart. A quick chat with them revealed Queen Violet had assigned them to cater only for us. At least they wouldn't have their champion fail the trials because of a growling stomach!

* * *

After the well-wishers had retreated, including a heartfelt visit of thanks from Queen Violet and Lord Alfred, our original traveling group mused on tomorrow's challenge as embers lifted on the campfire's thermals to wink out overhead. While the rest of us chatted, Jing Jing sprawled asleep in a human-like pose, his calloused feet warming at the fire's edge with his arms linked beneath his half-turned head.

Master Thorn, of course, had some advice. "If it was me in the trials, I'd do what I always do: examine the scene, think for a moment, then devise a perfect plan. That's the way to do it. When you get to the cave, imagine what I'd do and then follow the plan."

I'd seen many Master Thorn plans. Most seemed to skip the actual planning phase and jumped right into chaotic action, but I felt it unfair to bring up past examples at this point. I nodded, hoping my practiced facial expressions hid my skeptical mirth.

Rayne prodded my side. "You should listen to him, Minimus. There's no time limit, so don't rush into anything without thinking it through first. The important part is that you come back to me. To *us*, I mean. Even if you fail a trial, nothing will change between us. You know that, right?"

Doubt still gnawed away. How could they even choose me as a champion? I was just a boy. "I don't know. You've seen Queen Jada's scholars. They'll probably find a way to say I'm cheating or something. And those tasks! I heard everyone else who's tried has failed. I'm a gnat where they were workhorses. How can I ever succeed?"

Princess Tasha looked me in the eye and somehow refused to let me look away. "Minimus Mu, look at you! You are the most educated cart puller in all the lands, the rescuer of princesses with the strongest of hands. And lest all that go unheeded, the finder of twice as many tiaras as needed. Or you can channel your monkey, who thinks he'd steal the five gems while the All-Seeing Eye blinks!"

We all looked at the sprawled Jing Jing, who idly scratched his bulging belly, still asleep.

"About that extra Tiara, Master Thorn," I said. "Remember in Mossmarch market when Jing Jing ran off? After hearing what Jada said, I'm guessing that Jing Jing climbed into the keep and stole it from her windowsill or something. But then Mirko Leatherfoot somehow snatched it from Jing Jing, who'd hidden it under our stall."

"And then the treasure bird stole it from Mirko before we

found it on the Island in the Sky?" Rayne asked.

Master Thorn stroked his beard and nodded. "Could be. All three characters in that story are predisposed to thievery."

Princess Tasha hissed a breath between her teeth. "Four, if you count Jada."

* * *

After the fires dotted around the camp had reduced to embers and Tasha had returned to her parents' section of the encampment, I pulled a blanket over the cushioned mattress in the yurt and raised an arm to form a tent within a tent for Rayne and me.

"I wish there was some other mission for me. Like fetching another lost thing. You and I could ride off for another few weeks and look for it. Now everyone's depending on me, and they're going to be angry when I fail."

"Don't think like that," she said. "The first test is strength. Remember when you jumped the cart over the missing bridge? That was so easy for you. The first trial is yours. And that's more than almost every other champion could manage. Even if Jada gets her wish, I think our allies will stop her. You saw Queen Angstaad, right? When everything is over, you can ask to stay in Evermere. Master Thorn can run his cart himself, and you can stay close to the palace. We'll be able to see each other every day, like during our trips."

I hoped so. It seemed unlikely, but I dreamed it was true as I slept, with Rayne snuggled in beside me.

CHAPTER 18 - SOUTHERN MEER

The Same Night

The witch Alianthe had never appeared in Rayne's dreams before. The girl recalled half-formed memories of when coal rayvns visited her at the orphanage, but this time a voice pierced the veil of sleep and spoke to her directly.

It was a voice both familiar and strange, compassionate yet inhuman. Rayne dreamed she trod shoeless across a featureless plain. Lazy white snowflakes limited her vision and chilled her toes. Against the pale flakes underfoot, an occasional black rose petal broke the monotony. Here and there among the gliding snowflakes, glossy feathers drifted, their dark radiance seeming to keep them aloft rather than allowing them to settle amongst the snow and dust.

"Child," the voice of Alianthe said, coming from neither within nor without; not ahead, behind, or aside; not above or below. It drifted from a distance and direction Rayne's mind could not define. The black petals stirred, slowly spinning around her. "You may find that humans fail you," Alianthe said. "Not all humans—your genuine friends will remain clear to you. But I can see things that will come to pass, and we animals *need* you. The future of our magic depends on you and your allies."

Rayne spun in circles, searching for the source of Alianthe's voice. Unsuccessful, she called out to the snow-filled sky. "I cannot save anything! I'm just a girl. And a tiny one, at that. I don't have control of a queendom, like Tasha, or the wisdom of the elders, or even much freedom. I think you came into the wrong person's dream."

"Wisdom does not spring from age, girl, just like power does not require a muscular body," Alianthe said. "Look within yourself, and you will find that your words can be as powerful as magic when spoken with passion to the right people at the right times. It's what I practice. This is your wisdom, and you must follow it."

Rayne's lips parted, but she could think of nothing else to ask. Black rose petals and glossy feathers spun in a tornado around her as the voice spoke its last dream words.

"Your advice and love will make your friend succeed in the trials ahead. They must. If he fails, there will be no way you can stop magic from fading. This I see, child."

Master Thorn and the Red Bean Princess

CHAPTER 19 - MOUNT MEER

Garlicday of Moon, Year 127

Sleep eluded me throughout the night, and I abandoned any pretense, slipping from under the blankets as dawn's light glowed through the yurt. It seemed I was not the only person restless at this early hour; Master Thorn peeked his head through the entrance slit.

"Tea?" he asked. "And I prepared a bowl of hot oats with your name on it."

I took this literally—when I'd graduated from child-sized portions, Master Thorn crafted a large soup basin with my name engraved in capital letters around its inner lip.

"Scoot out here, too, Rayne. I'm ready for the puppet show," he said, beckoning.

The yurt held folding chairs of different sizes, so Rayne and I sat in unexpected comfort, sipping Mista tea while Master Thorn assumed his position in the cart at the end of marionette strings.

After some unnatural Master Thorn lip music that served as an introductory theme song, the frightening figure of the Giant jiggled into the frame. It quivered while a deep voice introduced the scene.

"Long ago, in year two of the new calendar, the trials of the All-Seeing Eye were convened for the first time. Wraithwatch cheered on their champion, the infamous Colwyn the Colossus, as he headed to the first cave for the trial of *strength*."

Colwyn had an even deeper voice than the narrator, and more exuberant. The marionette raised its arms wide. "Excellent people of Wraithwatch! Thank you for accompanying me across the Fading Sea to witness success in the dispute with Astella. The mountains belong fully to us, and we'll soon redraw the borders."

A noise that I took to represent a wild, cheering crowd polluted the air from offstage. The Giant's hands moved in clumsy harmony and lifted one of Master Thorn's fanciful animal creations overhead. The animal looked something like a lion with sheep elements and was predominantly red. Colwyn's voice continued.

"You have seen me lift the great Ox of Hornport! I rolled the grindstone of Merwyn Millhouse across the Plain of Plenty! This feat should be child's play—I'll be out in five minutes with the first trial gem."

More simulated crowd noises accompanied the Giant's move offstage. A brief silence preceded a series of grunts and straining noises, the stage remaining empty. When Colwyn the Colossus reappeared, his massive marionette head hung listless, and his oversized marionette feet dragged as he moved to center stage.

"I'm sorry, Wraithwatch. That thing is *really* heavy. The mountain border will stay as-is. Let's head for the boat home."

The puppet stage curtains slapped shut in the usual urgent manner. I didn't like this puppet show one little bit. It was hardly the encouragement I'd expected from Master Thorn. "Don't worry, Minimus," Rayne said, stroking my right calf. "Colwyn probably strained a muscle or something. You'll be able to pass the trial of strength. You were born for this."

As abruptly as the curtains snapped shut, they reopened. The show was not over. A smaller marionette bounced to the fore. It was the puppet Master Thorn often used to represent an exotic foreigner, with its multicolored jacket and puzzling green flesh.

His narrator's voice called out, "The next trials occurred in the year fifty-seven, when Far Inchaway argued that the bridges of Lakkenfall should be ignored when drawing borders, and that all land east of the lakes belonged to them."

The marionette took some jiggling steps around the stage, beckoning with its comical hands. This champion used a squeaky voice that seemed unlikely to reflect historical accuracy. Rayne giggled at my side. "I am Pierro, champion of Far Inchaway, as clever as a timbercat, as quick as a wakefish, and as determined as an Inchaway mule!"

Simulated Lakkenfell heckling interrupted from offstage, in

Master Thorn's normal voice: "Yeah! A *dead* Inchaway mule!"

Master Thorn's attempt to emulate half the crowd laughing at the retort was a work of comedy genius, and I laughed along with Rayne despite my glumness.

But moments later, the curtains snapped shut after Pierro's failure to complete the trial of strength. The puppet show plumbed new depths of discouragement.

Yet the show continued, Pierro again taking center stage.

"Far Inchaway, I'm back! It's year fifty-nine, and I'm here again for the trials to prove that Del Carta cannot simply fish wherever they like in the Bronze Sea! I have waited for two years to overcome my last failure. Are you with me, people?"

The invisible crowd cheered him on as he wobbled his way into the offstage cave. After a couple of grunts, the green-skinned marionette returned. In its upraised arms, it held a prop I'd never seen before. Master Thorn had added a red gemstone to his puppetry armory.

"The first trial is over! Easy peasy!" Pierro shouted. "I had a plan, and that made all the difference."

Rayne smiled up at me. Her eyes seemed to shimmer as she paused for the right words to bloom on her pursed lips. "Your plans always work, Minimus. Nothing can stop you in a trial of strength. And even though we're young, we've both faced a lot more than normal kids. You can use your experiences to help you make the plan."

I liked the eventual moral of this historical puppet play and felt much cheerier. A plan would form once I entered the cave and discovered the trial's true nature. It would be shrimple.

* * *

I found myself on the ledge that clung to the mountain face, with five exits to the Caves of the All-Seeing Eye. The cheering crowd assembled in the clearing far below jolted me from whatever reverie had consumed my thoughts. I had left the encampment and followed the trail the short distance to the guardhouse that straddled the narrow causeway, choking access to the caves with only the sheer-sided path providing access. Chasms dropped on either side to boulder-strewn crevasses. Only skilled climbers with plentiful equipment could circumvent the guardhouse, and they would be easy to spot by even casual observers.

The inter-queendom guards had allowed me to pass through the guardhouse passage's narrow confines as the Red Bean Queendom's legitimate champion, and the two companions I found myself with had joined me there.

I raised a hand almost to my right cheek before checking its progress. Was there a residual tingle where Rayne had kissed me? She'd held Jing Jing's paw, restraining the monkey from following me to the caves. I dared not wipe it away. That feeling and the crinkle-eyed smile that Master Thorn beamed at me as I turned to leave were the only two good things in my life. I sucked in a breath, drew what energy I could from the encouragements shouted from below, and tried to look confident as I hefted my small pack and strode to the leftmost cave and the first trial.

Master Thorn had stuffed the pack with items he figured might help me in the trials. A lantern, spyglass, and magnifier might help me explore the caves. A length of fine Red Bean rope may prove useful, too. But he considered the most important items the snacks and cutlery I'd use. He knew me too well.

"Have ye ever sailed to Oceanplat?" one of my companions asked, breaking the solemnity of my march as I looked back over my shoulder. "It's a fine voyage on a summer day. Spray on your cheeks, sun on your brow, and wind in your hair. Not that ye have much in the way of hair, but ye take my point, aye, Champion Mu?"

Nobody had called me *Champion* before, and this stopped me in my tracks. That, and my rudeness. Master Thorn would have threatened grave consequences for my failure to introduce myself to the two men that edged along the ledge behind me.

"I've always had a dream of sailing the seas," I said. "But so far, I've only waded into the Sea of Sorrows. My last dip didn't turn out too well either, and I can't even swim. I really must apologize for not introducing myself earlier. I was distracted, but still, it's inexcusable. I'm Minimus Mu, associate of Master Thorn, the cutlery trader. Apparently, I'm a citizen of the Red Bean Queendom."

"No apology needed. Everyone knows who ye are after the last two days, so no need for an introduction on your part. It's us that should feel ashamed, Champion. I'm your assigned historian minstrel, Virgil Longspeaker of Oceanplat. Ye can probably tell by my accent."

I'd had a historian minstrel *assigned* to me? "Wait—you're coming into the cave, too?"

The tassel on Virgil's knitted cap bounced with comical animation as he nodded. "Aye, lad. Me and Dan, here—"

An exasperated voice drifted from my second companion, edging behind Virgil. "I *told* you not to call me that. It's Dando. Or better yet, *Apostle* Dando."

I leaned out as far as I dared from the narrow ledge and glimpsed gray robes with gold trim beneath a shaven-headed and expressionless visage. This was quite a contrast to Virgil Longspeaker's patterned kilt, red jerkin, and slung lute.

The minstrel continued. "Right, right, sorry there, lad. Apostle *Dando* of the Truthsayers' Guild and I will both go into the cave with you. Sorry—caves, plural, I meant to say. He's here in case any disputes arise. As you know, the truthsayers cannot lie. Makes them perfect witnesses. And judging by the way those queens argue, it'll be good to have him along to confirm events. That Queen Jada seems like the type to accuse ye of cheating, eh?"

Virgil left no space for a reply, continuing without taking a breath. "Aye, but he's not as important as me, obviously. I'll be composing a suite of songs, poems, and stories about your epic failure. Or success! Joke! Feel free to laugh at my supreme wit! Whatever happens, ye'll have tales told about ye for centuries to come, lad."

I didn't smile at his joke, but cheered myself up by asking,

"Do you ever put on puppet shows?"

* * *

The three of us edged to the maw of the first cave to the west, with me leading the way. Before sticking my head around the corner, I ventured a last look at the throng fringing the camp below. I fancied I could pick out Master Thorn and Rayne waving and willing me good fortune from a hillock bearing the Red Bean royal pennant.

Although I desperately wanted to know the details of the trial, it proved hard to take the last few steps to the cave entrance. My two companions halted behind me, awaiting my next move. As I'd discover, Virgil liked to fill silences with chatter.

"Apparently, I'm forbidden from revealing any details of the trial mechanics when I compose my songs," he said. "So I found it odd that Hommold of Ven, assigned to the previous trials, twenty years back, gets pretty specific. He mentions in no uncertain terms that the champion of Ven, Elle Asquith, failed to lift a massive stone globe."

"I'm not supposed to speculate, but I heard it was made of crystal, not stone," Dando added.

There was little point in delaying proceedings any further. The truth lay a few paces away. With a deep breath for courage, I entered the cave.

It was dim but lit by reflected light entering from the entranceway and by striations of sun fungi, shedding their characteristic green glow. The fungi punctuated the cave walls on all sides, illuminating even the deepest recesses. The cave opened before and above the three of us. It was high enough that a hundred bats could have flapped in their chaotic patterns without prompting involuntary duck and cover reactions in us. The floor was sandy, ghoulish in the fungal light, and a subterranean stream babbled its way along the cave's right-hand margin, disappearing into a crevice in the rock.

Two features stood out immediately. The first was an enormous stone sphere, with its bottom quarter settled into a depression in the floor near the back wall. It looked hand-carved and smoothed by some long-dead artisan. The eerie light picked out glints of embedded.

The second noteworthy item squawked at us. The Meeran hen's eyes were unexpected: two multifaceted shapes glowing with an inner golden glimmer, almost as if the eyes were emulating the gemstones the hen could produce. Other than that, it looked like any other chicken. It sported white feathers, mottled here and there with patches of brown plumage. The beak was a proud yellow, and the squawk communicated typical poultry outrage at being disturbed. It paced the sandy floor, nudging idly at the boulderish sphere.

The scene was oddly relaxing, but I jumped a little as a minor chord snuck from Virgil Longspeaker's lute. He sang a few bars, *sotto voce*, but his voice was so quiet I couldn't make out any lyrics. This irritated me only a smidgeon.

I approached the obvious obstacle that stood between me and success: the massive ball of rock.

"It's nearly as big as you!" Apostle Dando said. True to his guild, this was a self-evident statement. The stone came up to my chest. I laid a hand on its cool surface.

Virgil laughed, a hearty, bellyful of sound. "Dan! Did ye say ye were from the Truthsayers' Guild, or the Stating-the-Bloody-Obvious Interrupters' Society? Let the lad get to work."

"It's *Dando*!" the apostle grumbled.

The colossal stone globe's mass would be a challenge, but nothing short of a trial lift could verify the degree of effort needed. But there was another problem. Grip. The stone was big enough around that I couldn't lock my fingers on its opposite side. I would need to grip its sides and exert enough power in my fingers to stop it from slipping from my grasp. If only it had handles!

I circled the sphere, hunched with my nose almost skimming its surface, hunting for any imperfections that would afford extra purchase. Nothing.

I straightened back up. Master Thorn suggested I needed a

plan to succeed. But what was there to plan, other than to lift the rock, grab the gem, and descend into the crowd for a light lunch? I ran my fingers through the crop of short hairs at my crown. The babbling stream's percolations provided a calm space for me to consider the predicament. I faced the rock, looking across it to the cave's back wall, allowing my eyes to attune further to the modest light.

A simple plan. Or a shrimple plan. Any kind of plan would have been good at that point. Then I spotted them. Four depressions in the stone's surface pointing up to the cave's ceiling. A carved handhold!

I stretched a hand across the rock's upper contour, fingers nestling into the recesses. One handhold at the stone's apex wouldn't help much, but maybe there was a second set of finger holes I couldn't see. Perhaps that clever dog, Pierro, the only successful champion to emerge from the first cave, had positioned the stone to make the feat harder for those who followed him.

Part of being strong is knowing that gravity is normally your enemy. But you also learn when it can come to your aid. If you want to knock down a house with a boulder, you don't throw a boulder at the house; you roll it down a hill toward the house. This was one of those situations.

I hooked my fingers into the holes atop the stone globe and pulled myself from the sand, so my full weight dangled. I hoped that the pull toward my side of the rock would cause it to rotate, even though it nestled in the depression below the sand.

Virgil strummed a few chords before settling on the right key for the start of his epic ballad.

"Minimus Mu, with heart so true,
Fingers stuck to the weight, like glue;
I'm not sure what he tried to do,
But it didnae work, he'll try something new."

Apostle Dando commented on the improvised song, his

voice a dry monotone. "That's the worst song I've ever heard."

"Shut it, Truthsayer! It's a work in progress." cried Virgil, his lute-strumming halting in a jumble of discordant notes.

I wasn't sure if Dando intended humor, but I giggled, then laughed outright. My arm shook as I tried to keep my grip on the stone. "Stop making me laugh, you two. There's nothing that will ruin a feat of strength more than laughing."

The jiggling expanded to my torso and legs as I laughed even harder. It must have been the extra movement that broke the stasis; there was a grinding noise beneath my chuckles as sand grains objected to a slight shift in the globe, shuddering at the margin where the sphere met its rocky cup. Gravity did its job as I hung from one hand, and I pumped my dangling legs as they shifted closer to the sandy floor. The boulder was rolling in its depression!

The lute strumming resumed.

"If it weren't for Dan's inquisition,
The weight would've maintained its position.
But you can't go wrong with a humorous song.
All along, Mu followed his vision!"

I clung on as the rock inched its way through a quarter spin, then released my grip. The holes were now halfway up the boulder's nearest side. Apostle Dan looked at me, then at Virgil, saying, "The song is still rubbish."

I leaned so that I could see the globe's opposite side. There was a second set of finger holds, exactly opposite the ones I'd used! That sneak, Pierro. Sixty-five years ago, he'd rotated the stone after retrieving the gem that I presumed lay beneath. That was some cheek—seeking to thwart future attempts. I doubted any of the four champions that had attempted the trial since would have left the finger holds in such an awkward position, given they failed in their attempts.

I reached around the globe. My wingspan was wide enough that I could lock my fingers into both sets of holes with ease. That was step one of my plan—figure out how to grip the giant mass so that I could attempt a lift. Master Thorn's cart had an axle and a nice flat bottom; heaving an object around had as much to do with its shape as with its weight. I now felt confident I could attempt to move the globe, but there were two steps to complete before that. Stretching and snacking.

I didn't mind sharing the spoils from the Red Bean Queendom's royal larders with Virgil and Dando, but there was no way I was leaving the cave—success or failure—with an empty stomach. I showed them my fine set of traveling cutlery as we unwrapped the delicacies from their gold and red ribbons, tiny wooden boxes, and intricate folds of greaseproof paper.

We left nothing but crumbs. I suspect my two companions could have eaten more, such were the flavors and textures of the breads, pastes, fruits, and nuts in the meal, but it made sense for them to leave the larger portion to the one doing the most physically demanding work. Their unspoken charity heartened me.

I found the snaking stream's current surprisingly warm as it washed away the clinging remains of our snack. After stretching every muscle I knew—a routine perfected in previous lifts—I approached the stone sphere and locked my fingers into the holds on either side, positioning my callouses at the right points to give me the best purchase. The Meeran gem hen squawked thrice. I took this as encouragement, rather than a warning I'd momentarily strain a hamstring.

I stretched every muscle taut before I exerted full force; it was always best to prime each sinew before committing everything. Poised, I poured everything into the lift. The sand beneath it ground, just as it had when I rotated the sphere. I felt the stone rise a fraction, my forearms and biceps bulging against its grainy surface.

Then it sank again, which was unexpected. My arms and back still forced the great globe higher up my chest, so it puzzled me that the thing was settling back into its depression. My toes felt chilly, and I realized the predicament. As I lifted the sphere, my feet sank into the sandy floor. I'd lifted the rock a couple of hand spans, but I'd sunk a corresponding depth into the sand. I released my grip.

"Don't put that part in the song," I told Virgil.

"Aye. To be fair, I was struggling to find a word that rhymed with *failure*," he said. "Plus, I need to protect the trial's secret nature, so I need to be intentionally vague. Or not, if I follow Honnold of Ven's illustrious example. I figured I could focus on your youthful innocence and surprising musculature instead of what ye're lifting or the techniques ye use."

Finding firm footing had not been part of the plan. I'd envisioned the cave as having a flat stone floor that would give me an excellent base against which to perform my feat of strength. I made a note to enter future trials without assumptions, realizing as I did so that this meant I was subconsciously optimistic about succeeding in this cave, despite the setback.

As I dug into the sand, fine grit lined my fingernails. The dark but dry volcanic sand flew away in clouds as the hole grew. It was painstaking work, the hole much wider than ideal as half the powdery sand I cast out shimmied down the hole's slope to its bottom. I'd hoped it was a thin layer of sand atop a hard floor, but those hopes receded with each handful excavated.

Despair flooded in, and I gave up when the hole was waist-deep. Even if my fingers struck a hard floor now, the rock would be too high above me to lift. The look on my face convinced Virgil and Dando to help me fill in the hole. Eventually, the scene returned to its pre-lift state, with level sand and little hope of success.

I scanned the cave for signs of anything I hadn't noticed previously that might help. This was how Pierro failed on his first attempt but succeeded on the second and third. He'd probably brought something to lie atop the sand and provide good footing, like wooden planks or a lattice of ironwork. And a lever. All I'd brought were snacks and cutlery. I wasn't complaining about the snacks, but my spoon didn't offer much leverage against the giant boulder.

I realized I was going to disappoint not only Rayne but a

whole queendom. She'd reassured me that my worldly experiences would help me make a good plan. Yes, I had shown my strength in many places I'd visited with Master Thorn, but pulling a cutlery merchant's cart hadn't really prepared me for this. I wished I was back on the trail, sharing snacks and laughter with Rayne and her princess, or carrying them into the surf, happily unaware of the lurking fanglimb.

The scarlet beach had almost prevented that moment of happiness, too, as the cart's wheels sank into the squeaky sand.

Sank...? Sand...? But the wheels were fine as I'd pulled the cart along the wet margins formed by lapping ocean waves.

"Guys, give me a hand! We're going to divert the stream in this direction. Dig a shallow trench toward the rock."

It took much longer than expected to get a tributary of the cave's stream to dampen the sand before the stone globe. Water being water, it cared little for being told where to go. At one point, I lay down and let the stream divert along the length of my body as Virgil and Dando made a dam of sand to coax its flow along a new course.

Virgil panted by the time the flow dampened the sand where I would stand to perform the lift. "Strictly speaking, we aren't supposed to help ye with the feat of strength," he said, clapping wet sand from his burly hands.

"Just don't mention it in the song," I said.

Dando nodded, shaking sand from his robe. "And if we are talking about strict speaking, we didn't help him lift anything. Strictly speaking, we only built an elaborate sand castle while we waited."

I looked him in the face. Was that a hint of a smile toying with the corners of his lips? I couldn't tell.

After a short warm-up and re-stretch, I tested the wet sand's firmness, stomping the area where I would brace for the lift. Footprints appeared, shallow and hard-edged. This was good. The sand, when dry, was so powdery and wispy that little sign remained of any pacing across the cave. It was time to give it a try.

I assumed the same position as before, fingers locked in the holes. I glanced quickly at Virgil Longspeaker. "Better have a rhyme for *back sprain* ready, just in case," I said.

He sang a capella as I tensed.

"No need to explain
The risk of back sprain.
Minimus Mu has a plan;
He's so supple, quintuple
The strength of any other man."

He'd called me a *man*. That was the first time I'd heard that word used to describe me. My abdominals flattened and arms bulged. Most of the strength for the lift coursed through my legs as I imagined pushing the hard sand on the floor away from me. There was a moment of apprehension before the sphere inched upward. My toes pressed divots into the sand, and my heels sunk—but only a fraction. I had a stable base and far more leverage than my previous attempt.

With a teeth-clenching cry of strained anguish, I felt the boulder clear its dish-like depression. My core burned as I twisted the mass away from its home and dropped it to my left. It thudded to the sand, so narrowly avoiding my toes that I had to yank my leg to pull it free of the sand at the boulder's base. The Meeran gem hen danced in animated delight, hopping from foot to foot and squawking in what sounded like a full one-sided conversation.

Virgil and I were more animated. "Boy! Ye did it! Look at the size of that gem!"

"You almost crushed your toes," Dando said, voice still affectless.

I punched the air, tilted back my head, and roared a wordless cheer of victory that I was sure reverberated down to the crowd far below. I danced myself in a high-stepping circle and then leant over the gem that had lain in the stone bowl beneath the carved boulder. It was half the size of my fist, a multifaceted ruby with a dark pyramidal shadow at its core. It had a greenish tinge in the fungal light of the cave, but I knew it would sparkle with divine radiance in pure sunlight.

The Meeran gem hen wasted no time, brushing my gem-clutching hand away from its nest area as it settled down. It was only moments before it produced another gem with the same internal figure. The hen hopped to the front of the bowl, positioning itself between me and the gem, its golden eyes glowing in warning. It crooked a wing at an inscription that had been hidden behind the globe, and I'd overlooked in my excitement.

CONGRATULATIONS, CHAMPION! ALLOW THE HEN TO REPLACE THE ROCK.

I was unsure whether the hen read my mind and directed me to the inscription, or if I'd imagined the gesture. Either way, my unasked question resolved itself; there was no need for me to repeat the feat of strength now that the hen had laid a new gemstone. I wanted to see what the hen would do to move the rock back into place, but I was far more interested to show the gem to the waiting throng, waltz down the causeway, and rest before what I hoped would be a celebratory feast.

As the lute sprang to life and the gem gleamed in the sunlight where I held it high, I spared a glance over my shoulder into the cave. A mad flapping from beneath the hovering stone sphere preceded a thud I felt rather than heard as it fell to cover the new gem. The finger holes looked like they were atop the rock once again, and I saw the dimly lit bird scratching at the sand around the diverted waterway.

Maybe it wasn't Pierro who'd hidden the fingerholds. I made a mental note to avoid trusting all chickens.

CHAPTER 20 - MOUNT MEER

Nutday of Moon, Year 127

I slept better on the night after my hero's welcome in the clearing beneath the Caves of the All-Seeing Eye. Perhaps it was the dinner in the royal tent—who'd have thought they could prepare such exquisite courses without the castle kitchens? Or maybe it was relief that I had succeeded in my primary area of expertise: lifting heavy objects. I felt less stressed about the upcoming trial of *accuracy*, where self-expectations were low, failure would not bruise the same way.

In my heart, it felt like I'd already met Master Thorn's hopes and dreams. He'd saved, taught, and raised a misfit orphan to an accomplishment only bested by Pierro, the champion of Far Inchaway, seventy years ago. That added a lightness to my step, unexpected for a boy of my bulk.

It also heartened me to see that Princess Tasha offered Rayne full leeway to spend time with me. It seemed like a good plan from the queendom's perspective—memories of the evening chats with her before we sprawled on the camp mattress's wide and glorious quiltedness were exactly what a champion needed to propel him to success. When I woke to the first rays of sunlight seeping through the thick woolen tent, my first glance was to the artlessly arranged tresses of Rayne's flowing hair laid across every margin of her miniature pillow.

Once again, Master Thorn was awake and hustling. A cup of root tea warmed my hands before I'd even put on my sandals, and once Rayne had brushed the grogginess from her eyes, he beckoned us both to the puppet theater.

Master Thorn used the same puppet to represent Pierro, this time embarking upon his third trial. He'd succeeded three years earlier in the test that would face me only a few hours hence. There was considerable court drama preceding Pierro's appearance at the caves. It seemed the man's ego was bigger than any friendship could bear.

As his puppet jiggled on near-invisible threads, the crowned puppet representing the Queen of Far Inchaway sent him on his way to the caves with a less than encouraging message.

"You should do this for your queen and queendom, Pierro, not to further yourself. All these demands! Land, titles, chestfuls of goat's teeth—no trove of physical wealth can make up for the basic warmth and decency you lack. I wish you good luck, sir, but only for the good of the queendom. I fear you have outlasted even my deep reserves of patience."

Pierro's voice parried in tones as low as Master Thorn could muster. That was odd because yesterday, the puppet had used a squeaky voice, but as a regular attendee at Master Thorn productions, it was best to ignore such inconsistencies. "I will overlook your insolence, *Queen*. We have a deal, and I expect you to fulfill your part when I return with this week's third jewel in my mercenary hand. I'll be back shortly, with or without any luck you may wish upon me."

A cave mouth slid in from stage right, and the puppet disappeared into it. Master Thorn's traditional narrator's voice followed. "And so, Pierro entered the third cave, seeking to further his successes in the feats of strength and accuracy with a feat of bravery."

There were some scuffling sounds offstage, with grunts from Pierro, some impacts that sounded suspiciously like a sack of dried beans whacking against the base of a frying pan, and a final strangled cry. The narrator's voice returned.

"That was the last anyone saw of Pierro, except, of course, for..."

A puppet's dismembered arm shot across the front lip of the stage, landing in Rayne's lap. She squealed with laughter. The felt arm was nearly as long as her own but far less delicate.

"... except for his arm! Which spun from the cave and into the ravine, spurting blood. They would have preferred a victory in the trials, but no one in Far Inchaway missed him."

Oddly, the threat of losing an arm and never being seen again did not bother me. The challenge of bravery was a matter for tomorrow, and I paid more attention to what Rayne's earnest face was expressing.

"See, Minimus? You already have the advantage over Pierro. He had no friends, nobody to give him good advice. You've got Master Thorn and pretty much everyone in five queendoms backing you up. And everyone we met on our ride—don't forget they all liked you, too."

"Well, maybe not Mirko Leatherfoot," I said. "At least, not after we revenge-swindled him."

"Ha! True! But you've also got *me* on your side. My advice is ten times better than any callous thief."

"A hundred times," I said. "Maybe a thousand, or whatever comes after a thousand."

* * *

Virgil and Apostle Dando fell into stride with me as I approached the gatehouse clamped to the midpoint of the caves' causeway. I was better prepared this time and rummaged in my sack for ribbon-festooned snack bundles I'd had the royal chefs prepare for each guard. I think they were required to remain neutral, judging by the way they wished me luck only in hushed voices, eyeing Dando as if he might tattle on them.

I'd added a few exquisite snacks to my pack—this time, I had requested additional treats for Virgil and Apostle Dando. Rayne had sent me off with a reminder that my friends were at my side even as I left them behind, and another kiss on the cheek. I was as prepared for the unknown as a cutlerer and a princess's handmaiden could make me.

As my trio edged along the ledge fronting the caves, I wished for a second trial of strength. I grasped at only the barest reassurance that the second trial was achievable. Pierro had succeeded, but only on his second attempt. Like the first trial, he must have learned something in his failed attempt that guided his packing for the second visit.

"Virgil, what did Honnold of Ven sing about the second trial?" I asked. "I heard something abut throwing a javelin through a Spiran nose-ring from twenty paces."

"I hate to disappoint ye, lad, but Honnold only witnessed

155

the first trial. Elle failed to lift the rock, remember? But I seem to recall reading some records from Far Inchaway versus Del Carta. Something about Pierro throwing ball bearings?"

I kept silent, not wanting to berate Virgil for not telling me this earlier so I could stuff some metal balls into my pack.

The second cave was high-ceilinged and doubly lit. The fungal glow that illuminated reaches of the cave sunlight couldn't touch was blue-tinged this time, giving an impression of nighttime. Underfoot, sand ran from wall to wall, and this time there was no running stream to compete with the ruffle of gem hen feathers and the clucking noises that drifted to us from a recess high on the cave's back arc.

We ducked out of the sun's glare and waited a few moments for our eyes to adjust to the dimness. The dampened sounds of the Meeran gem hen tickled our straining ears with faint teasings. It was almost as if the hen muttered to herself, complaining about our intrusion.

Once accustomed to the blue glow, I could discern shadowy movement in a gap high on the rear wall. I had to shift my feet a little to get a clear line of sight between spindly stalactites chaotically yearning for the floor. Once positioned, I saw more detail, the hen strutting the margin of a cave within a cave, a flat-bottomed recess that slunk away from the cave wall, high above the sandy floor. The lip she patrolled was as high as Mossmarch's city walls, with no sign of a way to ascend to its level.

Instead of squinting to discern more, I pulled Master Thorn's spyglass from the sack and twisted it to focus on the gem hen's position. The miniature cave was only twice the hen's height with its full depth unseen in shadow. Its ceiling formed a gradual arch that pinched to the floor at each side. Centered, a nest of twigs sat in the forks of a stony Y shape that protruded from the ceiling. The multifaceted red point of a large gemstone rose above the twigs. I let Virgil and Dando scan the inaccessible lair.

"There's no way up there," Dando said.

Virgil stifled a laugh and shook his head. "I can't wait to

hear your final report," he said to the truthsayer. "Minimus, what are ye planning?"

"There's a scattering of objects on the floor of the hen's niche. Looks like I'll need to throw something up there big enough to knock the gem from the nest. Or the nest from its supports. Even then, I have to hope the gem bounces from the ledge to the cave floor instead of rolling deeper in. It would take an even better shot—a ricochet off the ceiling—to nudge the gem toward us."

I could see why they named this the trial of accuracy. It was going to take a divine shot to thread a projectile between the cantankerous stalactites, reach the correct height, and have enough force to extricate the gem. Rayne's recommendation to harness the combined power of friendly faces rang in my ears, so I did what Master Thorn would do in my situation.

First, I scoured the cave for anything remotely useful. Unless you consider powdery sand useful, there was nothing interesting. Whatever Pierro had thrown to dislodge the gem either lay scattered on the ledge or had been removed from the cave. Maybe he'd thrown apples, long since rotted to nothing. In keeping with Master Thorn's puppet portrayal of the Far Inchaway hero, I pictured him removing the rocks or whatever he'd thrown that bounced ineffectually to the cave floor before leaving in victory. No point in leaving anything useful for the next unfortunate hero.

Could I use the magnifying glass to channel the sunlight and set the nest alight? I toyed with combinations of spyglass and magnifier before realizing this would only work if the nest was both in sunlight and at my feet.

I arranged a few potential hurl-worthy items from my sack. The caterers had packed the more delicate snack items into small wooden boxes, so I removed the foodstuffs and laid them on a silk square on the sandy floor. I had eight such boxes, weighted inside with the compressed ribbons and wrappers from the other food. I would hurl the magnifying glass if all else failed, and maybe the spyglass.

The next step on Master Thorn's plan would be practice.

He was forever pestering me, telling me that if I wanted to approach excellence, the only route was practice. "Want the perfectly balanced spoon? You need to make hundreds of imperfect ones. Bend that iron bar into a smooth S curve? You'll be making a lot of V's and L's along the way." I needed to practice my throws before risking a miss and littering the floor near the gem hen nest with failed throws.

Virgil Longspeaker strummed, hummed, and sang along as I calibrated my throws.

"Minimus Mu had but ten tries,
To strike the gem and claim the prize.
With little margin to spare,
He took time to prepare.
His success was not a surprise."

In the time it took for Virgil to settle on these lyrics, I felt my right arm had learned the amount of power needed to fling the lunch boxes to the correct height. I practiced by throwing them to one side of the hen's lair, where they could bounce off the cave wall and return to the sand below. But I could tell my throws were mostly off to either the left or right. The shot would need to fly dead straight if it had any hope of avoiding the stalactites and striking the nest.

I was used to using the terrain to my advantage. Threading the cart along the path with the fewest lung-busting rises or positioning our wares at the spot in a market where the most customers would pass were second nature to me. I knew I could use the stalactites to my advantage, blocking an errant throw and returning the projectile to the floor without losing it to the distant ledge would give me extra attempts. The spyglass, used from several angles, allowed me to plot a clear but narrow path to the nest.

I explained my thinking aloud, gesturing along the ideal angle. Apostle Dando could report that I'd made the best attempt at the nearly impossible task if they questioned him after my failure.

Heartened by the positive lyrics Virgil had devised and my channeling of Master Thorn to give me the best possible chance to make the throw, I shifted my weight from foot to foot until I had the most stable base possible. I squared my shoulders to the distant nest, noticed my hand shaking as it held the first of the eight wooden cubes, and expanded my chest into a lung-busting breath to calm myself.

Just like the practice attempts, I cocked my arm and willed the correct amount of power into the throw. It cleared the first stalactite but clattered against the second, dropping to the sandy floor. I left it where it lay, keeping my perfect position as I readied the second box. This one cleared all six stalactites lining its flight path but was a little short on power. The box hit the front lip of the recess, bounced upward, then slid into the darkness beyond the nest. The gem hen squawked in protest and slunk into the shadows.

After the first round of throws, I'd lost two boxes to the ledge, but my aim seemed to improve. The last two throws skimmed the stalactites before falling short, their momentum slowed by the glancing impacts.

I threw the six recovered projectiles from the same spot, my confidence renewed. Four of them navigated the hanging obstacles, and one struck the outthrust stone arm supporting the nest. It teetered but did not dislodge the gem. That left me with only two shots for my third round of attempts before I'd need to resort to chucking the spyglass and magnifier.

"You can do it," Dando whispered, as if the volume of his message might evade his truth-telling if he was later questioned about his neutrality. I wasn't even sure if anyone outside doubted that Dando and Virgil would help me if they could. It seemed an accepted but unspoken aspect of the trials, that there were rules but that common decency outweighed them.

"Maybe a snack first?" Virgil ventured. "It worked last time."

A snack was always a good idea. We squatted by the fine cheeses, dried fish, and juicy fruits I'd arrayed earlier, taking turns selecting and commenting on their deliciousness. I'd brought three long-handled forks this time, so we each had an elegant way to sample the treats. I hefted a fork in my hand, but it seemed too light and awkward to throw with enough power to reach the ledge with any hope of freeing the gemstone. We shared the water flask, and I realized it had potential. I plonked it beside the spyglass as a throwable item of last resort.

Despite having only two boxes and the three irregular objects remaining, the invigoration of the snacks renewed my concentration. The first box flew true through the tunnel of stalactites but skidded along the floor of the hen's hideout. The final one sailed over the nest, rebounding from the ceiling beyond to an undiscoverable resting place in the darkness.

I exhaled, fully emptying my lungs. I had only three remaining items to throw, and they would fly differently than the identical boxes. The magnifying glass would go first. I raised it several times in my right palm, letting my muscles feel the difference in weight.

I clasped it with my pointer finger curling around the bronze band encircling the lens. It felt comfortable, and although it would spin as it flew, it seemed like a good choice. My release felt clean, and the magnifying glass rotated, handle over lens, as it sped between the ceiling spikes. Watching, I knew it flew true. It spun through the twigs on the nest's left side, breaking several off. The gem lolled in that direction but then stopped, resting against the stony arm supporting the nest. I'd made an impact, but not quite enough and not quite centered. An unspoken curse raged through the nether regions of my mind.

Two shots left. I hefted the flask three times to get the grip right. It had a lot of power behind it, and had it struck the nest, the gem would have surely flown free. That was not to be—it caromed, spinning to the right side of the gem hen's recess, causing further squawks.

I toyed with throwing the spyglass like a stunted spear, but decided releasing it like a thrown axe would produce the most accuracy. Its dull metal casing gave it a ghostly appearance in the blue glow of the cave fungus as it twirled its way toward the ledge. It, too, skittered away harmlessly, making the gem hen flap and leap to avoid it.

Thus ended my heroics. The second trial had stymied me. I cursed my simple clothes and the underwhelming contents of my sack. My two belts would never reach the nest, even if coiled, and I lacked Sala Doon's fancy boots that would be heavy enough to dislodge the gem if thrown properly.

Properly. I'd thrown with a practiced hand through a narrow path that afforded me some error, but Sala Doon wouldn't have said these were proper throws. He'd told me you needed to throw with love, that he always envisioned throwing as if it would save his sister's life. Rayne had been right, but I'd been too confident to realize Sala had provided the guidance I needed.

Were my sandals weighty enough to throw that far? Maybe. It was worth a try—there was little difference between a failed champion and a failed, shoeless champion.

I slipped my right sandal from a calloused foot and gripped its heel between thumb and forefinger. It felt just heavy enough to make the distance, but I was unsure whether it would wobble in flight. I raised the sandal into position, resetting my feet as its leather grazed my shoulder and my elbow pointed straight up. Eyes closed for a moment, I paused like this, imagining that Rayne perched in the nest, imprisoned on high, and that I had only one chance to throw her an escape rope to clamber down.

I pictured this until it was burned into my mind, then opened my eyes and zeroed in on the nest. The sandal straps thrummed as the imbalanced shoe spun. The throw had enough power, but did it have the accuracy?

I must have closed my eyes during my shoe's flight. I opened them only when I heard one stifled and one exuberant cheer from my companions, followed by an outraged series of crows and scratching far above. The blue light caught the falling ruby as it vanished in a cloud of scattering sand at the cave's back wall. My numb legs shuffled to the divot in the powdery sand at the base of the wall, and I barely felt my hand close around the precise edges of the hen's gem.

CHAPTER 21 - EVERMERE

Sproutday of Mountain, Year 114 (Thirteen Years Earlier)

The witch Alianthe had surrendered to the urge. It had pulled at her, driving her ancient, hollow bones, her arcane, black-pupiled eyes, her blood running hotter than usual. She had made the arduous trip across the Fading Sea, had crossed the ancient forests of Inchin and the high steppes of Inner Pang, to reach the city of Evermere. The work she'd started two years before required a nudge; the humans were blind and helpless in this task.

She conferred with her kin. Alianthe had assigned three to watch over the child after they had flown her safely to the orphanage door two years earlier. They entered daily through the curtainless window, visiting, nagging the dour-faced sisters if they felt the child's blankets too thin or the gruel portions too miserly.

Alianthe slid a black-petaled rose from the lone vase the orphanage sisters maintained in their spartan entry hall. It was their symbol, a reminder to jostle the sympathies of donors and patrons. She sped to the Palace of Evermere, the premonition dancing in her peripheral vision, guiding her to the correct window, the proper person, at the right time.

The woman was too busy to understand Alianthe's message, flitting between palace staff members and visiting humans. But the man would understand. He was more attuned, more grounded. He'd have made a good witch, given magic.

Alianthe lowered the black rose to the thick windowsill of the white-haired man's chambers, high in the palace tower. She opened her beak and purred. When the man looked up from his breakfast, she lifted the rose, shaking a petal to the sill.

An eyebrow raised, the man spoke—to himself, maybe, or to Alianthe. "Ah, the Orphanage of the Sisters of Ambition. What would the queendom be without them? A token that it's time to find a playmate for the princess. The best handmaidens are friends since the time of first memories."

Her kin would make sure the visitor would choose the correct child. Alianthe left a flutter of darkness on the sill as a reminder to the man, although a flame flickered deep within her, a sign that her message blazed in him, too.

There were two further tasks that needed her nudges. In the market square, Alianthe nosed through three bins of ripple-gourd seeds until she found the right one. Her paws dug a hole of the perfect depth in just the right location outside the city walls. In the next twelve years, the gourd would grow large enough to accommodate two small people.

Her last visit was to the nest of a mother drift goose. The still-flightless hatchlings peeped at her approach, but they were old enough to commune with the witch. She chose the right one, nuzzled the scent of the ripple-gourd seed into its memory, and started a countdown in its mind. The spell would spur it to act on the correct day, years hence, when its wings would be broader than any other bird's.

The witch Alianthe departed, satisfied, turning her attention to other tasks.

CHAPTER 22 - MOUNT MEER

Hexrootday of Moon, Year 127

I discovered a new pair of sandals on a silk square outside my tent flaps when I eased them open and stretched into the warm, early morning breeze. The square fluttered away as I lifted the sandals, catching on the weathered wooden stake that secured the guy rope to the clearing's patchy grass. I slipped them on and sighed. It was as if someone with exactly the same foot shape as mine had broken in the sandals but without visible signs of wear. The cobbler that made them was as skilled at her trade as Master Thorn was at making cutlery.

"Look at those!" Rayne called. "Are those *gold* buckles? Looks like Queen Violet couldn't bear the thought of a one-shoed champion."

I had invited Virgil Longspeaker and Apostle Dando to have breakfast with Master Thorn, Rayne, and me. Dando wove between neighboring tents, dragging a stumbling and bleary-eyed Virgil by the cuff of his sleeve. The lute bobbed where it was slung over Virgil's right shoulder, and lazy blinks led to spells where he kept his eyes closed and let the truthsayer lead him.

"He's still drunk," Dando announced.

Virgil opened one eye and surveyed the scene. "But not as drunk as I was last night, aye? Nothing a splendid breakfast won't cure."

He motioned a flapping hand at the table between Master Thorn's tent and mine. A starched white tablecloth shone with the unadulterated smoothness of a fresh snowfall, punctuated with bread, jams, and gleaming cutlery. Orange clay plates invited us to sit on the folding chairs. Master Thorn sat already, and a short attendant in the Red Bean Queendom's livery stood astride a table-side platform, steaming cups of tea at the ready.

Accompanied by the clink of butter knives and Virgil's conspicuous tea slurping, Master Thorn recited the story of his grandfather facing the great Lion of Og. I'd heard him recount the story countless times, so focused on the proportion of plum jam to butter on my toast.

"My grandfather held the belt that Minimus wears even now," he said, following up after the gory details of how the other three pit fighters had been bitten, pounced upon, and slashed to bits by the rampaging lion, twice the height of a grown man. "He coiled the buckle end around one fist and held the other end in a puny show of defiance."

This part I'd heard before. But the next was a stark revision.

"He flushed with boldness but knew his doom approached with each slap of the lion's massive feet on the arena floor. No matter how strong the belt, he knew his strength was no match for the lion. One paw swipe and he'd be flung over the pit wall, likely headless. 'Come at me!' he roared at a face as tall as his whole body. 'I'll take an eye if you get closer.'

"Do you know what *really* happened next? The lion took a half-hearted swipe, one claw skewering a new hole in the belt and ripping it from my grandfather's hand. But the lion was tired from mauling the other three men, who whimpered and cowered even as they perished. Although my grandfather was no match for the lion's great strength, tussling with him seemed more trouble than it was worth. The lion snorted, shook the belt from his claw to the hot sand, and turned to gnaw on a dismembered leg.

"The original Master Thorn stood a moment in disbelief. He snatched up the belt and faced the crowd. They cheered. A trickle of courage flowed through him, and he flicked the lion's haunch with the belt's tail. And the legendary Lion of Og did nothing more than direct an annoyed growl in his direction before returning to his meal. For his bravery, my grandfather— and his toughened belt—walked free that day."

I strained to look at my own left haunch, a finger finding the oversized belt hole that must have been where the lion claw pierced it. "So he didn't strangle the lion with the belt? That's how the story usually goes."

Master Thorn shook his head. "I took a bit of artistic license with that part," he said.

Apostle Dando shook his head and averted his eyes, but Virgil perked up. "A man after mine own heart! Ye'd make an excellent balladeer, Master Thorn."

Virgil took a moment to tune two lute strings before giving an experimental strum. "But here's an auld verse about today's matter.

"Pierro, from Far Inchaway,
Faced his trial upon the third day.
With a distinct lack of charm,
But no sense of alarm,
He went up, expecting some pay.

"The crowd, in their silence,
Heard cave roars of violence!
He came to some harm,
'Twas ejected, his arm.

"It rolled down the slope
With no gem from the hen,
Despite Pierro's queen's hope
He was ne'er seen again."

Rayne shot Virgil a dark look that seemed to physically jar him. "Well, I mean, ye know," he started. "That was Pierro. Face like a slapped arse and temperament of a barrens badger. Nothing like ye, Minimus. I'm sure whatever's in that cave will love ye as much as the crowd hereabouts. Well, excepting those lot from Outer Pang, mind."

Rayne clutched my pinky finger. "And you're braver than him by far. Remember how you saved me from the fanglimb? And saved the princess, Master Thorn, and Sang of Seven Rocks!"

"What? Really? A fanglimb? Blimey, there's no end of epic ballads to compose around here. Job for life," Virgil said.

"Ah, yes," Master Thorn replied. "All true. All true. And

that reminds me, Minimus, Sang stuck his nose under the back edge of my tent this morning before it was light. Remember his girl Elsa's mother? He brought you a pie from her."

Master Thorn handed me a bundle wrapped in layers of rough red cloth. I sniffed it without unwrapping. Maybe lemon? I vowed to keep it under wraps until the cave. "Rub my earlobes for luck," he said in a low voice as he hugged me. "It may help."

* * *

It was as if a weight pressed on our trio from above. There was no conversation to lighten the load as we departed the guardhouse. The warm and lazy day inspired our strides as slats of sunlight angled through the dappled clouds, lighting the pollen that drifted in the still air. The guards once again seemed delighted by my proffered treats, and their eyes wished me well, despite protocol. But the knowledge that this task was the only one known to end not only in failure but in death colored our mood. Even Virgil Longspeaker had not spoken for several minutes as we ascended the sloping ridge.

It was Dando that broke the silence. "This is the dangerous trial. Pierro spent his last day here. But you know what the old songs don't mention? The fate of his truthsayer."

I hadn't even considered the safety of my two companions. Powerful forces had ushered them into this awkward arrangement in much the same way as I. Some royal, doubtless reclining on a padded divan below us even now, had ordered their assignment to the task. I felt a flush of embarrassment rise within me; I hadn't considered they were risking their lives just as much as I was. We were all victims of circumstance, but it seemed only my story, cheerful or cautionary, would survive into future generations.

"Well, ye can make a sound assumption," Virgil muttered. "Have ye noticed that the ballad of Pierro's third trial is from the perspective of someone *outside* the cave? Why do you think I refused none of the ales offered yestereve?"

Virgil stopped for a moment, and pointed a finger at Dando's chest. "But hang on! If Pierro was the only champion before Mu to make it to the third trial, how come there are so many whispered stories about what lies within the cave? I heard an abomination bird creeps to its nest in the cave through some secret entrance on the mountain's backside. Riddle me this, truthsayer!"

"You think the guards from the causeway never have a peek into the caves in the long months they're stationed here?" Dando asked. "Or mountaineers that sneak around from the mountain's other side? Lots of possibilities, my off-key friend. The only thing I don't understand is what kind of fool would venture inside the cave of bravery for a root around."

The apostle darted a look my way and covered his mouth. "Oh, sorry, Minimus."

We turned right, where the ridge met the mountain face, away from the first two caves on the left. After edging along the ledge in silence, I peered around the ragged opening into the third cave and allowed my vision to accommodate the darkness within. The cave materialized as if from a damp fog as my eyes adjusted.

The third cave's composition was like the previous two. Sandy floor, high roof with an occasional stalactite, and lit by the dim glow of fungus. Orange this time. A clucking and ruffle of feathers told my ears that a Meeran gem hen nested in some unseen crevice in the cave's depths.

This cave had one stark difference from the other two: it was untidy. Low piles of jumbled material dotted the sand, pointed shapes jutting randomly. It was the acrid waft and buzzing flies that nudged my brain enough to identify the piles. The upthrust, jagged masts were bone. Broken bones rose from picked-clean animal carcasses. A fence of ribs curved from a heap of disintegrating wool. The curled horns of a golden mountain ram topped the empty eye sockets of a staring skull. The fear was palpable; Master Thorn would doubtless have attempted to palp it if he was there.

There was only one explanation for the grisly tableau before me. I knew the peril we faced. I closed my eyes for a moment and tried to visualize Rayne's face as she told me how brave I was. Was that this very morning? And what had her face looked like? I found it hard to remember anything, my breaths rasping, sharp and rapid in my ears. Forcing myself to pause, I sucked two breaths as deep into my lungs as I could manage.

"I faced a fanglimb. This is only a sabreclaw," I told myself as I took three steps into the cave, not knowing I spoke these words aloud.

"*Only* a sabreclaw?" Virgil said from behind me, his voice incredulous. "Only the fiercest land predator! They're the sole beasties capable of this slaughter. The same claws that can neutralize the mountain ram's magic can cut a man in half."

"Three men, probably," Apostle Dando added.

Virgil was right. The golden mountain ram would erupt into a fiery explosion if threatened, but sabreclaw talons quelled their natural prey's magic, protecting the cats in a way inaccessible to humans. This scene was undoubtedly a sabreclaw den.

I could have turned back when I understood the implications of the heaped carrion within the cave. I could have accepted failure and returned to the camp below, another squandered attempt at the challenge of bravery to be sung about across the continents. But I knew the consequences. The disappearance of a whole queendom. The subjugation of not only Rayne and Tasha, but an entire populus. Queen Jada derided them as animals, but who was she to cast aside a thriving, vibrant society as if it was dung for the midden? Being small was no reason to be looked down upon, just as being big and strong was a vile reason to be excluded by other children.

I hadn't known I was brave before the fanglimb attack. Even after, I wouldn't have believed I was brave if Rayne hadn't told me. I'd rather a sabreclaw sliced me to ribbons than slink back to camp to face a lifetime of recriminations.

"Don't worry, guys. I know something I can try," I called back to Virgil and Dando. I spared a quick glance over my shoulder and saw only their heads, one atop the other, as they leaned to peer around the cave's mouth. All four eyes were as close to circular as possible, and four eyebrows fled up creased foreheads.

I stepped further into the cave, my eyes now adjusted. The gem hen fussed near a twig and feather nest in a recess to the far left. A passage sloping deeper into the mountain opened to my right, and the glow of the fungus ridges picked out eight eyeballs reflecting the orange light. An unmistakable rumbling warning growl tumbled across the cavernous space, echoing from the walls and stone ceiling far overhead. Judging by the distance between the glowing eyes, it was a mother sabreclaw and three kits that advanced with the slaps of oversized paws on damp sand.

"Oh great," Dando drawled, trying to hide the tremors of fear behind feigned nonchalance. "Mama sabreclaw can train her children using each of us as helpless practice prey."

Vik Gaard had primed me with the steps to avoid suffering the same fate as the mountain rams in the next few seconds. I looked away from the eyes, keeping them only in my peripheral vision, whispering for Virgil and Dando to imitate my movements. The sleek bodies paced from the passage into the cave's open expanse, majestic stripes mimicking dappled sunlight on their thick fur. Eight ears rose to full alert, pointing in my direction as I made sure I presented a side-on profile and crouched. Vik had mentioned that eye contact, facing the sabreclaws head-on, and standing tall were all signs of aggression that the beasts would not tolerate.

All I needed to do now was remember the secret hand movements that would show my peaceful submission and signal that I was neither a threat nor prey. But now that I knew what had sliced Pierro's arm from his body, the only movement that would enter my mind was an arm rolling down the mountain face.

Was it three slaps on the floor, then a fist? I tried that.

The three kits circled me, and it was all I could do to avoid eye contact as my escape route vanished. The growls escalated.

Maybe it was only two slaps? Yes, that seemed right. I tried to visualize Vik performing the action, but my memory was a blur.

A wave of fetid breath accompanied the next growl, and I got my first and likely last close-up glimpse of needle-sharp teeth lining the gaping maw of an adult sabreclaw. It was only inches from my face, offering advance notice of my doom. Drool splashed the back of my hand, and a glowing golden claw, longer than a dagger, drew blood from my right pointer finger as it sliced through the tip of its fingernail. It took all my concentration to keep my eyes averted. The kits growled an octave above their mother from my flanks and rear.

The thought that I'd never see Rayne again gave me enough space from the paralyzing terror to remember the time we'd spent together fetching Tasha's tiara. Riding on Mister Apples. Touring Vik Gaard's tent. I replayed his movements when he calmed the caged sabreclaw kits. I closed my eyes and watched him pat the floor twice, saw him rotate his wrist three times with an upturned thumb, finishing with two further floor pats.

Screwing my eyes shut so I could die without witnessing the vicious swipe of a razor-sharp claw, I repeated those actions. Slap. Slap. Thumb, thumb, thumb. Slap. Slap.

I heard breathing, the expansion of terrifyingly massive lungs right in my ear. The growling had subsided. I waited for a strike that never came. Repeating the rhythmic hand movement, I dared to open one eye.

The mother sabreclaw retreated a step, the magic in her claws dimming. The kits reappeared at her side. My lungs burned; I realized I'd held a breath for somewhere between a few seconds and an hour. I exhaled heavily and gasped in another lungful of air, delicious despite the hint of rotting carcass. Once again, I repeated Vik's gestures.

Food. Food would seal the deal. I rummaged in my pocket, keeping my eyes averted and my other hand ready to tap out the submission signal. Out came the pie delivered under cover of night by Sang of Seven Rocks. I unwrapped it with a few deft flicks. Lemon—it was a lemon pie, the citrus wafting from the slits in the thick golden-brown pastry.

Breaking off a chunk, I offered it at full stretch to the adult sabreclaw. She sniffed it, then pushed my hand gently away with the pads of her gargantuan paw.

"Stupid me," I muttered. "Cats don't like lemon."

I held the chunk between quivering lips as I fished out another snack. Hexroot cakes spiced with desert rose powder. Would they like them? If only there was fish in my pack; I knew Sabreclaws would relish tidbits like that.

I raised my chin, letting gravity roll the lemon pie into my mouth as I stretched again, offering six of the cakes to the sabreclaws. At least if they raged away now, I'd die with the sharp contrast of sour lemon and sweet pastry on my tongue.

Feline nostrils flared, and the gray hairs that tipped the sabreclaw's ears rose like antennae at the scent of hexroot. Mother sabreclaw teased the cakes from my palm with unexpected gentleness and, with barely audible encouragement, urged the kits forward. The ends of her stiff whiskers poked my wrist as she gestured to the kits with head shakes. All four sabreclaws took tentative nibbles, then bigger bites.

I straightened up slowly, careful to remain respectfully stooped and avoid eye contact. "I'm going to say hello to this nice hen over here at the back of the cave. Is that okay?"

The sabreclaws regarded me as they continued to pick at the hexroot cakes, but didn't seem alarmed or aggressive at my movements. Keeping half an eye on them, I sidled to the gem hen's nest. It clucked at me, imparting some wisdom I'd never comprehend, and stepped aside to let me pluck the gem from its nest.

* * *

Virgil and Dando followed me into the yurt. My hands were shaking still, and I'd given only the merest attention to the cheering well-wishers and pinched faces of the Outer Pangan troops, needing to unwind before I could face anyone other than my friends. Master Thorn ushered me through the flaps.

"Boy! Your finger is caked in blood. Put that gem away; let me tend it."

Our crew of three hadn't said a word on the way down, but Virgil began babbling as Rayne and then Princess Tasha slid in beneath the tent flap.

The minstrel raised his thick kilt, revealing rough leggings. "Gods, Minimus. I literally pissed me breeches, and I was barely inside the cave. Look! I'm soaking. What…? How…? I don't believe ye did it. Tamed them. No wonder they chose ye as champion."

I snorted at his stream of excited words, which broke the barrier, letting the pent-up tension fizz from me like a fountain. I laughed a little, then a lot, relief coursing through me. Rayne, Master Thorn, and Tasha joined in, making me realize they'd been as tense as I. "I wouldn't mention your wet pants in the ballad, but I'm pretty sure it'll be in the truthsayer's report, no matter what you compose."

Dando laughed, a high-pitched giggle I hadn't heard before. "It's my duty! And I recommend wearing robes for future trials, Longspeaker. My right leg is damp, but you'd never notice, looking at me now, would you?"

Virgil punched Apostle Dando on the arm, an affectionate and glancing blow. "Ye'd better repeat that part in the report, too, my tactless pal."

Master Thorn made us all sit and wouldn't allow a recap of events. It wasn't that he was a stickler for the rule banning speculation about the trial mechanics. This was a matter of manners. He wouldn't tolerate any serious discussion until he'd served everyone with steaming cups of tea. The royal caterers would lay out a banquet, but for now, we were content to sprawl on the thick rugs, insulated from the hubbub beyond the yurt walls.

Although it was against the covenant of the trials, I let Virgil and Dando give a breathless recounting of the confrontation with the sabreclaws, interrupting only to describe how the beastmaster Vik Gaard had shown Rayne and me the secrets of communicating with the giant cats.

Their questions answered, Tasha and Rayne launched into a story of their own. We'd missed some tense action in the camp while we'd been in the cave.

"… and Queen Jada threatened to ignore the trial results," Rayne said, indignation dripping from every word like golden drops from a honey dripper. "She told Queen Violet that even if the trials proved she couldn't be treated as an animal, the Red Bean is culturally barren, and no one could blame her troops for accidentally trampling our people and towns."

"And this time, there was no doubt," Tasha continued. "Queen Angstaad's sword rasped fully out. She said Jada couldn't smell culture if someone rammed it up her snout. I thought she'd violate the pact, leap the table, and attack, but her swordmaidens gripped her sword arm and held her back."

Rayne looked up at me, locking eyes. "You should have seen it, Minimus. It was like a schoolyard altercation. Everyone was shouting at the same time. Pushing but not daring to throw a punch or raise a sword. Well, aside from Queen Angstaad, but she's always whipping out her steel. I saw Sang of Seven Rocks at Queen Jada's side, but he wouldn't meet my gaze. At least he knows this is all wrongheaded. In the end, Tasha's father had to step in and calm things down."

A slight smile teased the corners of Tasha's lips, and a faraway look softened her eyes. "Yes, father's voice seems both quiet and loud; you'd be rapt in an empty room but catch his voice above a crowd. Whatever he said, I can't remember, but the queens all regained their tempers."

Rayne finished the thought, gripping my elbow. "Promise me, Mu. You must be careful even *after* you succeed in the fifth trial."

I wished her confidence was contagious. A coldness surged up my spine at the thought of the upcoming trial of wisdom. It was hardly one of my talents.

Master Thorn and the Red Bean Princess

CHAPTER 23 - MOUNT MEER

Oatday of Moon, Year 127

As Master Thorn draped the underside of our merchant's cart with its muddy cotton curtains the previous night, I'd wondered why we needed to establish our traditional sleeping arrangement. We had luxurious tents a few steps away.

He'd stroked his slender, snowy beard, nodding. "You seem tired and nervous, boy. Let's get back to our usual beds and shelter. Nothing soothes more than familiarity. I even recreated Rayne's cozy nesting spot beside yours, like on our journey across Outer Pang."

Rayne nodded. "Sounds relaxing, Master Thorn. Come on, Minimus, it'll be fun."

And so I awoke in the usual way, with wan light scintillating through the thin drapes, the shadows of the cart wheels' spokes slanting across our blankets, and the sound of light rain pattering on the cart above us. Master Thorn snored in tones more soothing than rasping, and Rayne stirred sleepily beside me. I slid from beneath the blanket, raised the flap that concealed us beneath the cart, and trotted the few steps to our tent to retrieve my new sandals and make a start on breakfast. The clouds were more dull than threatening, but drizzle dampened my hair nevertheless.

I snatched a sandal and was hopping while fastening its heel strap when I realized something was wrong with the scene inside the pointed tent. I froze, still perched on one foot, and bent to attend to the sandal. Dim rays of light shone through a score or more holes in the tent's side that pointed away from the encampment, lighting lazy dust motes. The bedroll where Rayne and I had slept the previous three nights bristled with feather-crested arrows. At least a dozen were angled down into its quilted surface. More stood embedded in the surrounding rug, and a slender javelin pierced the only remaining pillow.

I scanned the tent for intruders but saw nothing else amiss. I relaxed when I noted the streamers of rain descending beneath each hole in the tent wall. The puddles below and the interweaving paths the raindrops had taken along the tent's inside face told me the attack had happened deep in the night. Slapping the other sandal to my foot, I scarpered back to the cart and slid myself beneath.

My voice came out as a hiss, sharp enough to awaken both sleepers. "Master Thorn! Someone shot our tent through with arrows in the night. And a javelin! Right where Rayne would have slept."

Master Thorn eased into a cross-legged sitting position, rubbing his back with both hands. "Huh," he said.

I expected more of a reaction. A raised eyebrow of puzzlement, perhaps, or at the very least, a hint of alarm.

"I guess it was a good idea of mine to sleep under here, eh?" he continued. Rayne was awake now, crouching. At least *someone* shared my anxiety.

"Well, not entirely my idea," Master Thorn said, vainly attempting to tame wisps of hair enough to tie them into his usual topknot. "It was Sang of Seven Rocks that suggested it when he brought that lemon pie. It seemed an odd thing for him to recommend, although it's sensible advice to soothe frayed nerves."

"By the sun's light!" Rayne said, her voice trembling. "Maybe the pie was only a pretext. We owe that boy gratitude beyond reckoning. Although after saving him from the fanglimb, maybe we're even. Just you wait until I tell Tasha!"

* * *

Our party of three wore wide-brimmed farmers' hats, woven to keep off the worst of the sun's sizzle or the clouds' drizzle. The men at the small guardhouse made little attempt to conceal their partisanship, urging us upward to shelter for a few minutes in the hut. We shook ourselves free of drips as we paused and drank some warming cups of hexroot tea they'd prepared for us. Virgil composed an extemporaneous ditty about their generosity as we prepared to trek upward for the right turn to the fourth cave.

"I keep expecting to encounter a disembodied eye drifting around the cave, checking up on us," I said. "I guess the All-Seeing Eye is just a name, not something we'll actually see."

Dando answered, cocking his head and furrowing his brow, which contrasted with the slight smile that crossed his pursed lips. "It's weird that you haven't noticed the All-Seeing Eye in the previous trials. It's been watching you the whole time."

A shiver of ice crossed my chest. I imagined one of the fanglimb's pickled eyeballs escaping from the jar in Master Thorn's cart and hovering in the shadows, stalking me. "You can see it now?"

"Well, sort of," Dando replied. He pointed at his own face. "When Sifu Pan sent me on this mission, he said, *Apostle, you will be the All-Seeing Eye for the trials. The caves are named after our order's oversight, and you must maintain our traditions.* It seems like this is the only principle of the trials that is never broken. Having a truthsayer as witness isn't meant to prevent gossipers revealing elements of the trials. It's only to discourage the most vile attempts to cheat."

Relief replaced the creepy feeling that had coursed through me. "You had me inventing my own ghost stories there, Dando. I feel both calmer and better informed now. I'll pay more attention to the task at hand, I think, knowing that the All-Seeing Eye is a friendly one."

"It sounds less hazardous, the trial of wisdom, doesn't it?" Apostle Dando asked as we edged along the narrow path. "At least compared to the trials of strength and bravery."

"Aye," Virgil agreed. "Provided yesterday's sabreclaws don't have extended family that have expanded into this cave. Ye saw they had some sneaky back entrance into cave three, right? Maybe those tunnels also lead here. But hush. We've arrived."

I reached the third cave's margin and peeked around its lichen-adorned entrance. A pair of glowing eyes turned in my direction, visible in the dim rear area of the third cave. No growling, though. Maybe yesterday's demonstration was enough to bond me to the sabreclaws for more than an hour or a day. I looked away, as Vik Gaard had taught me, and the mother sabreclaw lowered her beautiful striped face to her waiting paws, silvery whiskers flexing as they rested atop claws like threshing scythes. I wondered where the kits were, but they soon came into view, curled sleeping in the lee of their mother's furry bulk as I padded across the cave mouth and continued to the fourth cave.

The cave for the trial of wisdom was much smaller than the previous three. It was more like a wide passage than those amphitheaters. The glowing fungus here was violet, giving the sandy floor a hue like spilled crimsonberry wine as the passage wormed away from the radiant light of the overcast day.

Perhaps to demonstrate a modicum of courage, Dando followed in my hesitant footsteps, acclimatizing to the low lighting, with Virgil bringing up the rear. After bending to the right and leaving the outside world behind, the passage opened into a chamber the size of a bustling tavern kitchen. Not like the bustling kitchen I'd glimpsed in Evermere, but like the heaven-scented kitchen in Seven Rocks that produced the best pies I'd ever tasted.

This space did not smell like pastry or sweet fruity fillings; it was goaty with a hint of feathers—unsurprising since a goat hovered with its hooves at my eye level. Atop the goat, a Meeran gem hen puffed its chest, ruffled its wing feathers, and clucked to its companion, as if gossiping about the disparity between my soiled tunic and finely crafted sandals.

The drifting goat was both typical of its kind and unusual. Although the coarse, shaggy coat looked violet in the light, I knew it would be off-white if it floated into direct sunlight. It had a scraggle of beard no longer and no less tangled than normal, and its eyes bulged ever so slightly, as was common among its kind. Unusual, though, were its horns, each ringed and ridged arc as long as my handspan. They curved upward to almost touch at their points, in decidedly un-goatish colors. One was blue, taking on an indigo hue in the weird light, and one was a rich red.

The goat changed direction and drifted in our direction. That was the only sign of its magical navigation. A goat's legs dangled, relaxed, during flight, flexing them only to push themselves around. The eyes bulged a little more as it examined each of us in turn. Naturally, I looked away under its regard— Master Thorn had drilled into me that goat ogling was a sure signal of greed and best avoided.

Finishing its inspection of its visitors, the goat let out a muted but plaintive bleat, accompanied by clucking from its passenger. Master Thorn would undoubtedly have a term for the combined sound. Probably a *cleat* or a *bluck*.

"I don't see any gems in here," Dando said. His hushed voice didn't echo as it had in the other three caves.

He was right. Unless they'd buried one in the sand, there was no way to conceal a gem hereabouts. Sandy floor, the ceiling only half my height again, rough walls—the only feature of note was a stone slab the size of a dining table for four, that rose to knee-height from the sand. I paced around it. No sign of a nest or a gem, but the slab's uneven surface bore an inscription, its words tainted with traces of violet fungus. The three of us read it in unison, the words tumbling audibly from Virgil's mouth. I guess as a songsmith he was naturally unable to read silently.

CHOOSE WISELY. ONE HORN IS HARMLESS, THE OTHER BRINGS DEATH.

The goat had followed us to the slab, and we all backed away from it as we read. At least our wisdom extended that far—none of us wanted to die from an incidental graze of a horn.

"By the All-Seeing Eye!" muttered Dando. "Here's me thinking this the safest trial, and now there's a one-in-two chance of death."

"Only for Minimus, though," Virgil said, adding, "Oh— sorry, mate."

I took no notice of the implied doom. "There must be some

clue here to guide a wise person. And as Master Thorn told me this morning, if I just do what he would do, things will work out because of how wise he is."

Virgil chortled. "Brother, we were there at breakfast, too. After saying that, Thorn described all the foolish things he'd done. I even wrote several in me notebook as future ballad material. Laid goliath leeches on his earlobes to see if they would help him relax. Tried to peek into Lady Pun's second-story window while on stilts and fell into rhinothorn bushes. Adopted an orphan who eats his own weight in food every week. Designed fork with tines on both ends. All failures."

I raised an eyebrow and ventured a reply. "Maybe he was giving me examples of things *not* to do. But let's see what clues lay hereabouts."

We talked through the meager points of interest in our surroundings. Violet fungus. Goat-hen friendship. Low ceiling. Only one exit. Cave number four. Not much else to go on.

There was one obvious next step, though: tea and snacks. I opened my pack and surveyed the day's delicacies. Soon we sprawled on three sides of the stone slab, butter-laden knives flashing across slices of still-warm bread. The aroma of pickled cucumbers took the edge off the hircine odors, and tin cups brimmed, in danger of sloshing tea onto the sand.

"Maybe the fungus color is a clue," Virgil said, wiping his lips with the back of a hand. "Wait, sorry. I'm not supposed to help ye. Forget I said anything. Unless it helps, of course."

"But he's got one blue and one red horn," I said. "How does the fungus play into that?"

Virgil cocked his head. "Good point. Maybe the clue is in the words here. Or maybe Apostle Dando could grab both horns, and the two of us could return to camp, victorious!"

He slapped Dando on the back, laughing, causing the truthsayer to sputter tea down his gray robes. The hen bristled at the commotion, but the goat was unfazed and drifted to the stone slab's side, feet hanging limp almost to the sand. It looked uncomfortable, the way the hen's claws gripped scrunched-up bundles of wiry goat hair on either side of its pronounced spinal ridge, but the hovering creature seemed nonchalant about his passenger.

I nudged a pair of melon rinds, the crumpled and stained paper that had surrounded the lump of cheese, and a glutinous mess of pomegranate seeds to the goat's side of the table, careful to avoid any contact with his horns. As required by the goat code of honor, it devoured the lot, seeming to enjoy the greasy paper most of all. A modest belch shivered its beard before it settled to the cave floor, curling its legs beneath itself. The hen hopped free and scratched idly at the sand, uncovering nothing of interest. Still no gem in sight or plan blossoming in my mind.

"I don't know what nugget of supposed wisdom Master Thorn would roll out in this situation, so I have little to navigate by. But I got some advice from a rapscallion by the name of Mirko Leatherfoot. I can't say he's a friend, especially after I stole from him what he'd already taken from Master Thorn—and more—but he taught Rayne and me an excellent lesson. Before robbing anyone, he told us, scope the place out, then give yourself space to think. You'll avoid any rash mistakes that way."

"You're taking guidance from thieves now?" Virgil asked.

I shrugged, then nodded. "What do you think these tasks are about? We've invaded the nesting spot of a gem hen and want to steal its treasure."

"That's true," Dando replied. Virgil gave him a raised eyebrow for a moment before we all laughed. The goat bleated, as if joining in.

"Sifu Pan, my master in the guild, always tells us to sleep on a big decision. Like I did before I volunteered to travel from Golden Shores to become the resident truthsayer of the All-Seeing Eye. It helps."

I smiled. "So, you're saying it's nap time?"

Virgil plucked a simple melody, its slow strains reminding me of the minstrels that would entertain me behind the cart when I was too young to rove away. After the previous night's stealthy attack, I figured a little rest would help me stay alert this evening. And a full belly lent itself to a spell of shuteye meditation, even if sleep never came.

"I can keep a lookout. Prod ye if the goat moves its horns near anyone," Virgil said. The goat looked dozy enough that it wouldn't hassle us anytime soon.

I turned onto my back on the slab, resting my shoulders against it, with legs extended on the cool sand. With my eyes closed, I visualized the inscription, seeking clues in the words. I listened to the lute's tune, the confined space's harmonics, the slow-breathing goat's exhalations, and the scratching of the hen. With the expectations of the Red Bean Queendom weighing on my mind, I doubted I could sleep, but removing distractions surely couldn't hurt.

Now, even the less obvious sounds invaded my consciousness. Virgil's finger pads stretched the strings over the frets. The friction of hen feathers as wings shifted. A gurgle in the goat's stomach.

I don't think I fell asleep, but relaxation flowed through me as my eyelids fluttered open. Virgil's tune had reduced to nothing more than intermittent strumming. I shrugged my shoulders and rolled my head before crouching and examining the sleepy-eyed goat.

"Okay, my cloven-footed friend," I said. "I've contemplated the cave. Nothing. I've read the inscription, and can't find a clue there. The hen's not talking, and my friends are out of ideas. And although the snacks and rest were surely wise, Mirko Leatherfoot's advice to think it over has suggested no obvious path to success. But still, I like my chances of saving the queendom. Let's get this over with."

Dando's eyes widened. "Are you sure, Minimus? There's an even chance of you dying. You can still leave the cave."

I forced a smile and gave him a slight nod, acknowledging his good-hearted advice, but I knew the many fates in the palm of my hand tipped the scales toward action, not self-preservation.

If I chose wrongly, the remaining food in my pack would do me no good, and if I touched the correct horn, a full banquet would await us below. It was hardly the goat's fault I needed to make this fateful choice, so I slapped the last swirl of butter and the discarded beetleberry husks into the palm of my right hand and offered it to the rising goat as I raised my left hand to make the final decision.

Two sniffs were all it took for the goat to make its own decision. Butter first, then husks. A coarse and disconcertingly black tongue removed every trace of butter from my palm.

Blue is the color of the sky, I thought. *And of the sea, where I've always dreamed of voyaging. But red is the color of Rayne's hair. And the color of my new queendom.*

Okay, red it would be. I let the goat finish grinding the husks and swallow them. My hand shook as I reached for the red horn.

"Are ye *sure?*" asked Virgil.

My hand steadied. Of course, I was sure. This was the wise thing to do. Or at least the only honorable path. To guess. To risk death to save a queendom. At least I'd learned something from Lord Vendark's crazed confrontation with the donkeys. I'd been kind to the goat, despite the fact it could momentarily kill me.

"Okay, little goat. It's now or never. I'm just going to grab your red horn and hope for the best. You're the only one that knows what will happen. What do you think?"

The goat bleated. My hands shook as I reached one to either side of its narrow face. Squinting against the consequences, my palm closed in on the red horn.

Just as my hand was about to close around the red horn, the goat jerked away and slapped its blue horn against my other palm. Its juddering bleat sounded like a crazed laugh.

"No!" I shouted. "I meant to touch the red horn. Give me a second chance!"

The echo of my own panicked voice told me I was still alive. Had the laughing, hovering creature done me a favor? The goat swallowed hard, then belched, a full throat-rumbler. A gemstone nearly the size of my fist flew from the goat's throat. Reflexes on high alert, I caught it as it dropped, whipping forward the had I'd jerked away from the blue horn's contact. The gem hen squawked and fluttered, jumping in place, before arching through the short flight to the goat's back.

Three forceful exhalations marked the end of our tension once the gem appeared.

"Phew!" Dando said. "That was close."

"Ain't that the truth?" Virgil replied.

I nodded, pocketing the gemstone. "It's always wise to treat our animals with kindness, I guess. Maybe this should be called the trial of charity, not wisdom. In the end, the goat governed the trial, not really me. That's where Lord Vendark went wrong. Like with those donkeys."

Vendark was wrong in other ways too, but we would find that out during the fifth trial.

CHAPTER 24 - MOUNTAINTOP

Sugarday of River, Year 127

The witch Alianthe conferred with her kinfolk. They had been above and among the human throng, watching, spying. They murmured, brooding that success in the trial of endurance would not be enough. The humans needed more evidence than a gemstone to undo the direction poisonous tongues pointed.

She found a branch with the requisite eleven leaves and clung there, rear claws encircling the branch and front paws crossed. Her eyes slipped shut like hoods to deflect the outside world's rain. She heard the footsteps of beetles on the tree trunk, the scrunch of worms skirting the roots below. Her heart beat three times, shivering her hollow bones; then two more, slower; then stopped.

The way became apparent to Alianthe. One nudge, one cheat would suffice. She re-started her heart, paused until she reattached to the physical world, and flapped away to the mountaintop.

Wind lemurs were fickle but also creatures of habit. A mob's prime lemur would perch in the place with the most commanding views of the surrounding area. Her range encompassed all the territory her precision eyesight could see, so the wind lemur atop Mount Meer ruled the largest territory in the western continent. She favored the rising sun. The winds most often flowed from west to east, following her gaze as she curled in repose, facing the Fading Sea. Occasionally, she would regard another compass point, the winds changing direction as her gaze alighted on the forests of Northern Meer, the Sea of Sorrows to the west, or the distant dunes of Inner Pang, southward. The wind would bend to follow her gaze.

Desiring a perch on the highest point also meant Alianthe knew where to find the prime wind lemur. She counted seventeen stripes ringing the dozing lemur's tail, curled in the bed of pebbles, twigs, leaves, and shed fur her disciples maintained to protect her from the bitter wind and snow. This was more rings than Alianthe had ever seen on a wind lemur, making it very unlikely she would face any challenges from within her mob. Tradition required a challenger to have no fewer rings than the prime. In a way, she was glad the lemur dozed. Implanting a dream was simpler than the protracted negotiation needed if she had been awake. After scouring the skies to the south to ensure her divination was correct, Alianthe once again stopped her own heart and descended into the wind lemur's dreams.

The lemur dreamed that a purple splotch appeared, airborne, visible from her south-facing nest over the steppes of Inner Pang to the south. This was true in both reality and the dream. Alianthe could barely make out the floating object in the distance; it would pique the lemur's curiosity upon awakening.

The lemur dreamed she wanted a closer look at the purple splotch, and in the dream, she crept to her north-facing nest, urging the wind to blow north and bring the unexpected item closer.

Resuscitating herself, Alianthe pinched a pebble in her beak and dropped it on the sleeping wind lemur from on high. With a languid stretch, the lemur stirred. Once her eyes fully opened, she popped onto her hind legs, peering southward. It was obvious to Alianthe that the lemur spotted the distant floating object. The creature stood on tippy-toes, stock still, before leaving a graffiti of claw prints in the snow between her east-facing and north-facing nests.

The wind shifted. Alianthe felt it in the ruffle of her feathers. Although she could not tell if the object drifted closer, she could feel it, her witchsenses alive.

That was the nudge. Now, she would cheat a little.

* * *

The witch Alianthe and the monkey Jing Jing shared a common language. As they clung to branches near each other in the tree with the best view of the caves, it was far from obvious to any human who might bother to look that they were aware of one another, much less communicating. The patter of beak and hand on the tree, a specific angling of the head, an occasional squawk or subvocalized chatter—none of this seemed like speech. But it was. Rich communication flowed.

The cheat was easier than Alianthe dared hope. The monkey had already encountered the floating contraption. Twice! It had seemed odd that her vision showed her a monkey performing the task she required—the mission felt better suited to a bird.

Alianthe discovered that Jing Jing knew nothing about science. He cared little about *how* the coal rayvn knew the balloonist would arrive or what he carried. But he sure loved climbing ropes, even when there was nothing to steal at the top. Every rope had a story at its knotted end.

As the balloon approached, blaring its intermittent roars of hot air, the trailing rope came into focus. It dragged past the foot of Alianthe's tree as it traveled overhead, and slinky monkey arms whirred into action along its snaking length. *Oohs* and *aahs* from the tense crowd below spun like confetti into the air as the balloon passed overhead and the monkey scrambled.

Jing Jing ascended the rope until the still-perched Alianthe saw his tail flick over the basket's edge and disappear. She imagined but could not see a curious lemur at full stretch atop the mountain, peering down the slope as the wind died to nothing.

The balloon drifted to a stop, descending ever so slowly. The rope slithered, lethargic, outside the fifth cave as Minimus Mu entered. There was an exchange of greetings between the boy and the strange-looking man in the balloon who hid behind oversized goggles, but the words faded to nothing over the intervening distance.

The earlier nudge in the Mossmarch noble's house, the wind lemur's nudge, and the instructions to Jing Jing brought a harmonious feeling to Alianthe's heart. Everything was in place as Minimus Mu entered the cave.

Master Thorn and the Red Bean Princess

CHAPTER 25 - MOUNT MEER

The Same Day

"Minimus Mu, ye're both a surprise and a peril," Virgil told me as I waved up the dangling rope to the balloonist, Ezra Longshanks, and turned to the mouth of the fifth and final cave. "Ye have a surprising array of friendly acquaintances."

I'd never considered it unusual, but on reflection, it seemed the life of a queendom-spanning trader's apprentice exposed one to a gamut of faces and personalities. I'd even made friends with the queen's guardsmen, both little, from Red Bean, and tall, from Golden Shores, that had stood alert overnight at the corners of Master Thorn's cart, deterring another roguish attack. But one blossoming relationship had turned sour, dragging at my confidence. When we'd passed through the mountain's guard station this morning, the guardsmen accepted the delights from the queen's kitchens that I'd selected for them, but could barely make eye contact. Could I have offended them somehow? It seemed unlikely—something external must have influenced them.

"And it's a good thing I have friends. Without them, I'd have failed every trial beyond the first," I said. "Whether I succeed or fail today, I hope that you mention them all in one of your brilliant songs, Virgil."

"Aye, lad, ye friends will feature large, chorus and refrain. Let's make today's song one of joy. Do ye fancy yourself for the task of endurance?"

I was glad that Dando answered that question. His reply shook off any forebodings that itched my underbrain. "This trial is even more in Mu's favor than the trial of strength. You've heard all he has endured during his travels, Virgil. This task is custom-built for him."

"The alemaster in the drinks tent last night said he'd heard Minimus will have to hang from one hand for an hour," Virgil said.

That would be a modest challenge, but it was less

demanding than the single-finger chin ups I was famed for across Inner Pang.

Dando raised an eyebrow at the songster. "Yeah, but we also heard that he'd have to walk on his hands all the way from the fifth cave to the camp. And also that there was a giant crocodile in the cave and Minimus would need to hold its jaws open and wait for the gem to roll out. That idea is just stupid. Wouldn't that be more bravery or strength than endurance? Who makes this stuff up?"

It was the waggling tongues at work. As Mater Thorn described, wrong information was worse than none. I waved my companions along, and we entered the dim passage that wound to the fifth cave. This one differed from the others. The cave did not open until we'd taken a good hundred paces from the sunlit ledge. Its twisting entrance passage blocked all external light. The deep cave left us to navigate by only the dull silver glow of its natural fungal illumination. The floor was dark, slick rock, covered with a smattering of sand and a trio of erosion-smoothed boulders. Several crevices and dim passages punctuated the cave's undulating back wall, and moisture suffused the air. Five of the openings were broad enough to squeeze through, giving me an image of the cave as a giant's glove, its fingers plunged into the rock seeking the mountain's concealed secrets.

Rivulets of water snaked down the walls, appearing black in the odd light, and a crescent of running water coursed from an opening in the wall on my right to disappear into a slot in the floor of the rightmost darkened finger, reaching for the mountain's heart. This stream ran faster and deeper than the one in the first cave, as if racing toward salvation.

There was no sign of a nest, a gem hen, or any indication of how to proceed. And something else seemed wrong. A smell, maybe, or a sound too quiet to hear. Perhaps it was the unknown spaces of each cave offshoot niggling and goading my senses. It seemed I would need to explore them to decipher the trial's nature, so I beckoned for Virgil and Dando to follow me to the leftmost passable offshoot. I paused to retrieve and ignite Master Thorn's lantern from the fancy pack that Lord Alfred of Evermere had gifted me. The silvery fungus glow was both dim and prone to making every shadow into a fortress for unseen horrors.

I was about to slide into the shadow-filled slot when the hairs on the back of my neck rose at the hint of an unexpected sound ahead. A snick of metal on metal? I strained to hear it repeat, turning an ear toward the depths, but instead heard something in my other ear: the sound of muffled monkey chatter.

Master Thorn and the Red Bean Princess

CHAPTER 26 - OVERHEAD

The Same Day

The throng in the camp below surged as close to the mountainside as practical while Minimus Mu undertook each trial. Some would gather early, keen to wish the boy champion well. There were many hands reaching to lend a reassuring pat, many voices desperate to pass along a mumbled or shouted phrase of good fortune. There were no ill-wishers; the Outer Pangan delegation kept its own counsel, afraid of backlash.

Some preferred to arrive later or stake positions on the hillocks rising behind the scrubby plain. Atop the hills were a few prime spots with sightlines where the nobles encamped to fix nervous eyes on the caves above. Wherever onlookers assembled, there was an unwritten and unbroken law: the much shorter Red Bean citizens were allowed to move to the front. For now, at least, the varied crowd behaved equitably. Who could say what might happen if Minimus failed the final task?

Master Thorn paced circles around the cutlery cart from the time Minimus left for each trial until he returned. Rayne and often Princess Tasha would sit on the cart, trying in vain to persuade Master Thorn to rest. But if he raised the spyglass to his eye once, he raised it a thousand times, checking on any signs from the cave mouth.

Both young women dangled their legs over the cart's side while they waited for the final trial's results. Guards from the Golden Shores and the Red Bean Queendom stood watch over the cart, pretending to neither gawp at the princess nor show intense interest in the activity by the fifth cave mouth. Furtive glances were in good supply.

Master Thorn stopped pacing to steady the spyglass. "There's the boy," he said to himself. "That was quick. Not holding up a gem, though. He's eating his pie—he must be confident! He never eats when he's nervous. Well, he does eat when he's nervous, but not as much as when he's at ease. I wonder how much pie he's eaten. Wait, is that Jing Jing? I thought he was with Rayne."

* * *

After the witch Alianthe had seen Jing Jing scarper up the balloonist's rope and disappear into the basket, there was a reunion of sorts. Jing Jing had paused, clinging to the basket's inner rim, wary that the animated pilot might harbor some malice after the monkey's earlier theft and slap him overboard. The old man's smile and gestures informed Jing Jing's next move; it was clear he was not only safe but welcome aboard the hovering contraption.

Everything was just as the coal rayvn had said. The wind had faded to a dead calm. A compact wicker cage held two thunderbirds. Their small, green forms hopped from perch to perch. The trailing rope dangled to the ledge outside the cave where Jing Jing had watched Minimus disappear a few moments earlier.

The monkey pointed at the cage, then sprang to the basket's rim. He motioned to the crowd before using his hands to mime a giant mouth opening and closing, then pointed to the cave mouth. Would the man understand his mimes?

Ezra Longshanks's eyebrows rose, and he tugged at the windswept tangle of curls engaged in a lawless wrestling match behind his head. "Clever boy! Was that your idea? I'm sure the crowd would *love* to hear what's going on in the cave. It's the perfect time to try out my thunderbird link. But you know I can't go down there. Nobody but the champion, his minstrel, and the truthsayer may approach the cave."

Jing Jing shook his head in response to the question about whether it was his own idea, but did not know how to mime his conversation with the coal rayvn, so shrugged.

"But nobody said anything about *animals* approaching the caves, did they?" Ezra said. He switched to a high-pitched voice which he found somehow more suitable for addressing a small monkey, as if the little ears might reject any deeper-pitched voices. "You could carry the thunderbird to the cave, couldn't you?"

It was only a matter of moments before Ezra had a spool of spidersilk affixed to the cage and tied at each end to the thunderbirds' claws. He ushered one of the slight birds to a perch facing away from the mountain and closed the cage door so Jing Jing could carry the other linked thunderbird to the cave below.

The monkey clutched the loop atop the cage's wicker roof, and his free hand and feet flashed with flecks of gold-limned magical energy as he sped down the rope, the nearly invisible spidersilk spooling out behind his descent.

Leaping from the rope's frayed, trailing end, the monkey paused, unsure of whether or not to enter the cave. A distinct smell of sabreclaw pervaded the area, and it was always best to stay in the open with a threat like that wafting on the air. He called to Minimus, hoping the boy was not so deep in the caves that the shrillest monkey calls could not reach his ears.

Within moments, Jing Jing heard the shuffle of sandals echoing along a narrow passage. Judging by the cadence and pressure of the footfalls, he knew it was Minimus.

"What are you doing up here, you furry-footed barbarian?" Minimus asked Jing Jing, holding a cupped hand up to shield his eyes from the sunlight. His eyes adjusting, he spotted the cage and the thunderbird. Tracing the toughened gossamer strand trailing from the spool, the boy looked upward, along the rope.

"Oh. Ezra wants to try his connected birds? From the cave to the balloon?"

The monkey nodded and held out a still-glowing palm. This was a sign that some form of payment was in order.

"I've got no goat's teeth on me. How about some pie? There's still a slice of the one from Seven Rocks. I could split it with you."

Jing Jing sprang and used Minimus's belt for leverage to attain a seat on the boy's shoulder as he waited for him to rummage in the pack. Dividing the slice of pie into four similar-sized chunks, the three humans and the monkey savored the flavors of sugar-laden pastry and fruity filling while taking in the sun's warmth.

"Stay out here, Jing Jing, I'll take the bird in with me. You won't like it in the cave. Once I figure out my plan, I'll get that gem and meet you here. Just wait. Hopefully, it won't take long."

Dando gave Minimus a sideways glance. "I'm pretty sure a trial of endurance might take a while."

High overhead, Ezra Longshanks fussed with the strand tied to his thunderbird's leg until it thrust out its chest, stretched its wings twice, and urged its powerful voice to life. Unbeknownst to the trio re-entering the depths of the fifth cave, science and magic would combine to thrill the crowd below. No longer would they have to wait in tense anticipation, murmuring quietly about imagined doings inside caves they could not see. Whatever was said within the cave would thrill them, live. The first words sizzled through the spidersilk from the listening thunderbird dangling cage-bound in Minimus Mu's muscular grip. The paired thunderbird in the balloon opened its beak and boomed out an amplified imitation of Mu's voice. Was this violation of the secrecy of the events inside the cave greeted with gasps of outrage? Hardly. The crowd below cheered as they heard Minimus Mu's puzzled question.

"What? Gem hens can swim underwater?"

CHAPTER 27 - MOUNT MEER

The Same Day

Water beaded and fell from the copper plumes atop the Meeran gem hen's ridged head as it surfaced from the swift-flowing stream. A few powerful strokes from its wings, and the hen was ashore, shaking itself free of the remaining water droplets. It regarded me with a disdainful air and clucked in what sounded to my ears like criticism.

I put the caged thunderbird on the cave floor's smooth black rock. It cocked its head to the side, listening intently.

"It swam upstream, from beneath the finger of the cave on the right," I said. "No point in checking out that cave on the left now—I'm guessing its nest is downstream. Maybe there's a ledge or something."

"Ye're going in to look?" Virgil asked. "When ye told me about your dream of a sea voyage, it surprised me when ye mentioned ye cannot swim."

"Well, I don't have to swim. I'll *wade* a little, feel around just there, where the stream dips below ground. But yeah, good point. I think I'll tie myself off first."

The Red Bean Queendom's rope weavers were true artisans. The coil of rope in my pack was slender but strong; I'd given it some test pulls while organizing the pack's contents, and even my most violent attempts couldn't fray it. I rolled a boulder to the stream's edge and fastened a loop of rope around it. The other end, I tied to my belt. If the belt could hold my weight as I dangled over the Gorge of Razors, it would surely save me if the current upended me.

I removed my sandals, lest they get washed away. It would be a shame to lose footwear of such fine workmanship. Dipping a toe in the cool rush of water, I said, "Here goes! Wish me luck."

Apostle Dando and Virgil both knew how the thunderbird pair were supposed to work—I'd told them about my encounter with the balloonist at dinner two nights previous.

Dando winked as he spoke. Anyone hearing his voice roll down the mountain could do nothing but nod at his dedication to neutrality. "I can't wish you luck, Minimus. I'm here only to observe and report."

Virgil smiled at the truthsayer. "And I'm too busy working on lyrics at the moment to sing any hearty sea shanties for ye little marine voyage, Mu. Although I know a good one about a whale-sized mermaid. I'll give you a rendition back at camp."

I stepped into the stream, gasping at the cold. The water was waist-deep where it swirled through the cave opening. The timeless passing of water had worn the stream's channel smooth, but enough texture remained for my calloused feet to maintain a degree of grip. The current's speed had kept the channel free of slimy plant life, and I waded with confidence into the finger of cave. After a few paces, the stream's bottom dipped, and the cave roof sloped until nothing remained but water rushing through a hole in the rock.

I braced a hand against the back wall of the passage, above the waterline, leaned my shoulder beneath the frothing exodus, and felt around with my free hand for signs of a nesting spot.

"I can't feel anything yet. I'm dipping under to reach a little further," I called.

The first few chords of a ballad about a boy who couldn't swim bounced off my concentration as I inhaled deeply and ducked my head. I took a step forward, feeling above myself for a crevice that could serve as a gem hen nest, but my hands detected nothing but smooth rock.

Then my right foot lost its toehold.

My heel slid from under me, and my right leg skidded downstream. The chute's floor fell away at an angle and stole what remained of my balance. My shoulders spun a quarter turn before my left foot lost purchase as well and left me at the mercy of the current.

It's poor form to blow out the air remaining in your lungs when dealing with an underwater surprise, but if you are a non-swimmer like me, it seems that's the first thing you do. The bubbles of my exhalation flew past both cheeks and tussled my ears, telling me I was face-down in the underground stream. I'd been jolted but did not panic. This was the reason for tying the sturdy rope to my belt, and I looped it around a wrist without a moment's hesitation. Less than half the rope's length had played out.

The current was strong but no match for my muscles, and my lungs had barely begun to burn before I was hauling myself back, following the taut rope. Seeing the fungal light overhead, I burst through the surface and sucked a breath into my grateful lungs. Virgil's song would likely call it a splutter or a heaving gasp, but I envisioned myself more like a runner catching his breath after a race than a bedraggled rat.

"I'm okay!" I called. A faint but distinct cheer echoed from the cave entrance. Warming energy flowed through my limbs.

"There's nothing there. At least nothing I could feel before I was dragged down the underground part of the stream," I said after hauling myself ashore and shaking water from my soaking tunic.

Ever the stater of the obvious, Dando replied. "It wouldn't be much of an endurance trial if you only had to reach into the chute's mouth and pull out a gem, would it?"

I considered this. It was a good clue about how to approach the fifth cave's mysterious task. "Maybe the nest is in another part of the cave," I said, slicking a cascade of water down my back as I ran thick fingers through my tufted hair.

"Nah. That makes little sense, either. The hen came from the stream, so she must have some business down the chute. I think I need to go *deeper* to find the nest and get the gem."

Then it hit me: this was a test of endurance for a swimmer. For me, it was impossible. I'd nearly run out of air after the merest skirmish with the chute's mouth. As a wader, even with my ability to haul myself along the rope, I panicked when made to spend more than a moment underwater, airless. Claustrophobia and a desire to breathe would beat out determination every time.

"How long do ye think ye can hold ye breath for?" Virgil asked. "A thirty count? More? Ye'll need to turn around when ye get to half ye limit."

"I can let the current drag me downstream pretty quickly," I said. "But then I need to leave myself enough time to find the nest, grab the gem, and haul myself back. Assuming the rope holds. It's hard to guess how far I can get."

And any estimate of breath-holding would only apply on land. Underwater, predictions were worthless. The fifth task felt more like a test of stupidity than endurance. Any misestimation and I'd drown, hauled out dead from the end of the rope by a performance artist and a truthsayer, with the hopes of a whole queendom lifeless alongside.

"I'll need to grow fish gills to complete this challenge."

I slapped my wet backside onto the rocky floor and leaned forward, elbows to knees, cupping my forehead. Of course, I'd attempt the feat. Courage always seemed to come at the wrong time, blurring the line between bravery and lunacy. But letting down Rayne, Tasha, Master Thorn, and the whole queendom was worse than perishing in a noble attempt. At least I'd escape the disappointment and tears as Queen Jada snatched control of the Red Bean Queendom. Maybe I imagined it, but it sounded like faint shouts of encouragement crept in from outside.

I clutched the sides of my throat, checking to see if I'd grown magical gills, but my hands came away disappointed. The knot around my belt stayed secure as I tugged it, and I checked the end tied around the boulder, too. There was enough rope to let me explore the tunnel well beyond the limits of my lungs. If only I could take the cave's air with me as I explored the Meer hen's watery passage.

I hugged Virgil in a tight embrace, and he responded with as much heartiness as his well-fed frame allowed. Dando was less enthusiastic but clapped me on the back as I lingered. "You're a brave man, Minimus Mu. Or boy, I guess. Scratch that—no boy would be brave enough to tackle this challenge. I can see it's not stupidity; it's honor, love, and courage. You're a man despite your age."

I enjoyed being called a man, even if it was unmerited. "I

feel like I've known you two for years. It's been a long five days."

I knelt by the thunderbird's cage, making sure my words were heard. "I'll go in now and wade downstream as far as I can. If I fail, I hope the songs you write, Virgil, and the truths you tell, Dando, will include that I'm doing this for people. Not for myself or my own fame and fortune. For Rayne. For Princess Tasha and the Red Bean Queendom that put so much faith in me. To show Master Thorn that I've learned from everything he taught me, even when he thought I wasn't listening. For Jing Jing and everyone that's helped me along my dusty path."

I hoped that the link between the thunderbird listening here and the other floating above was working fine. Despite the twisty cave entrance, I thought I could hear my own amplified voice reverberate. Although talking about my plan within earshot of hundreds seemed a violation of trial protocol, I'd happily claim innocence if, by some miracle, I returned with the fifth gem. How could I have known a mute thunderbird within the cave was transmitting to its linked partner in the balloon overhead?

The outside sounds faded, but I imagined a hint of my voice and the concerned tones of a crowd snaking their way into the cave. I imagined Jing Jing waiting for me at the cave mouth and Ezra Longshanks high above, tending to the spidersilk beneath the bagful of hot air in his airborne home.

His bag of air. Floating.

Instead of taking a final deep breath and throwing myself upon the stream's mercy, I emptied my finely stitched pack. The remaining snacks fanned across the floor. Cutlery, a spare set of sandals, and the other artifacts that Master Thorn reasoned might help me scattered as I flicked them away.

Virgil looked at me, narrowing his eyes. "Don't worry about that, Minimus. We can take the pack down if ye don't… um… ye know."

"Thanks to Ezra, I'm not going to *you know*. Let me grab that chunky rock over there," I said.

I checked the pack straps. They could fit under my armpits with my head inside the bag, just as I'd imagined. Virgil shuffled over, carrying a rock two-handed. He plopped it in my outstretched right palm. It seemed heavy enough for my purposes. I needed a brief experiment to reassure myself this plan would work.

Dropping the rock stream-side, I waded in once again, this time carrying the empty pack. I turned it upside down and pulled at its corners to expand it to its maximum volume, pointing its circular opening directly at the water's surface. Using the straps, I submerged the bag.

Yes, this would work. The quality of the seams and stitching on the bag was as fine as expected—only a tiny trail of air bubbles surfaced from one corner. It was as airtight as I'd hoped.

I sat near the thunderbird again and told my companions my strategy. "Just like Master Thorn taught me, I need a plan that will give me the endurance I need. See this pack? I'm going to use it like Ezra's balloon. In his case, the balloon is full of invisible hot air. It tries to rise above the cooler air outside but gets trapped in the giant bag. I'll do the same thing underwater. The bag's air will want to rise to the surface, but the waterproof fabric should hold it in. I'll put my head inside the pack, put the straps under my arms to hold it in place, and I'll be in my own little pocket of air. Then it won't matter that I can't swim. I'll wade my way along the stream until I feel the nest. That's science, apparently."

I hoped Ezra was nodding in agreement with my proposed use of his science somewhere above the cave entrance. If he was cursing my lazy brain and wondering whether I'd had silencer snails plugging my earholes when he described the balloon's operation, I was in for an unpleasant surprise.

"You'll find it by feel?" Dando asked.

"Yeah, should be shrimple." I smiled. "If I fumble the gem, I'll have time to catch it as it sinks.

"And what's the rock for?" Virgil asked.

"The pack full of air is going to pull me to the surface—and the rock should help me sink."

I had a plan, and this seemed like a suitable solution to the task of endurance. Sloshing into the stream, I shook the pack to make as much room as possible for my head, and pulled the straps down my arms so they could loop under my armpits. The straps were snug, and they chafed, but I had a nice gap around my face and ears. I felt around on the bank for the rock.

"Left a little," Virgil said. "A bit more. There, ye've got it. And step over the rope with ye left leg—it's trailing under ye there. Don't want to get caught."

I held the rock at my left side and extended my right palm ahead. It wouldn't do to rip the pack open on the rockface once I got to the chute. The noise of rushing water amplified with my head inside the pack. Maybe it was echoes or perhaps the fact that I'd removed some of my other senses, making me focus more on the stream's sounds and contours. I squatted, then sat on the stream bed, reassuring myself about the plan and the pack. A little water splashed up inside as I submerged, but I laughed aloud at how well it worked. Although the pack strained at my underarms, buoyant, the rock and my own body weight held me down. I had a personal pocket of air, even though I was fully underwater. To myself, I said, "Ezra Longshanks, you are a genius," mostly to prove I could still talk, although I expected no one to hear.

I stood up again and began my slow wade into the offshoot cave, hand waving in front of me until I felt the cave roof dip toward the stream. The water was deeper here, chest-high. I crouched and allowed water to flow over the pack as I took the first step down the sloping underground chute.

I kept my footing this time. With my left hand clutching the rock and my right hand swiping across the chute's contours overhead, I took a tentative step. Then another. After ten steps, the chute's floor leveled out, and the channel widened. I now needed to sweep to full arm extension to feel for any nesting ledges on either side or above. The air inside the bag was getting warm, and water danced onto my chin and nose from below.

A strange sensation crept through me as I took step after step in complete darkness. My feet seemed steady enough, toes gripping the textured rock without slipping, but I felt dizzy, as if I was about to lose my balance. I ignored it, took another big breath of warm, damp air, and waved my arm overhead.

There! An imperfection invited my hand to explore further. A ledge. A smattering of small stones scattered as my palm swept forward, exploring. Something pointy jabbed the flesh on the outer edge of my palm, hard enough to send a twinge of pain through my hand but not enough to break the skin.

Feeling around, I discovered a nest-like formation. Twigs, probably, intertwined. Quick and shallow breaths now, and I blinked away another spell of dizziness. The air in the pack was so hot. I was glad to have a personal air supply, but I'd failed to anticipate the rising temperature. I tried to slow my breathing and let the air sink deep into my lungs, but it seemed like this hot air wasn't refreshing me.

Victory! My hand roved over a hard, multifaceted object at the nest's center. I pulled the object below my chin, angling my eyes down, as if I'd be able to see it in this utter darkness, but of course, I saw nothing.

After a moment, I did see something. Several points of light. Reds, blues, yellows. Shapes flitted across my vision, as if darting, glowing fish circled my head. I couldn't understand where they had come from, these tiny fish. Were they inside the pack with me, swimming through hot, cloying air? Or maybe their light shone right through the bag's fabric? The rock in my left hand got heavier each moment, and despite my strength, I wouldn't be able to grasp it much longer. Maybe if I took a short rest, closed my eyes for a minute, I'd get my strength back. It was hard to relax with breaths rasping in and out, in and out, quickening. But I was so tired.

The rock slipped from my left hand and ricocheted off my freezing left thigh. Before I blacked out, all I could think of was the gemstone following that rock down the chute.

* * *

One of my first memories was of Master Thorn flinging me into the air and catching me. At the apex of each flight, I could see into the cart before falling back into the basket of his waiting arms. Master Thorn would coil himself for the next toss. He'd shout out something different each time I was airborne. "You can see the *entire world*," or "Look, a Vondabeast!" or maybe, "You're so big now, my arms are getting tired."

I could feel his wiry hands now, gripping me beneath each arm. I tried to speak, to tell him I was a big boy now, too heavy to be thrown about. But I also wanted him to shout out one more enthusiastic instruction. Maybe, "Grab the gem, Minimus, it's falling!"

But I was too sleepy to say anything. My lips were heavier than the boulders of Seven Rocks, and my tongue lay lifeless against my palate. Everything was cold except the bag that encased my head, smothering my face in air as thick as porridge.

I would rest a little. Relax here until I could figure everything out. Shrimple.

* * *

Cold air lapped over my face, and something pulled at me from behind. My arms and legs shook, partly from the cold water and partly from something else—jitters shooting from deep inside me. I blinked and saw a little light coming from below my nose. It took me a few moments and several blinks to figure out that I was floating on my back, the rope tied to my belt preventing me from drifting further downstream. Face-up, I realized there was water below but space above. I must have surfaced in a chamber beyond the fifth cave. I gasped, my lungs drinking in the cool air that flowed into the bag.

There were two immediate priorities. One was to get the pack off my head and see where the light was coming from. I wiggled my arms until one strap slipped loose, and I ripped my face free. The second was... something I couldn't remember.

A ray of wan sunlight lit the chamber, slanting down from a horizontal crack and reflecting from the stream's surface. A ledge supported a messy nest of sticks, feathers, and mud, the chamber's roof rising to a few hand spans above the current's eddies that ran more slowly than in the narrower chute.

I cleared my face of drips with my right hand and looked more closely at the nest. There should have been something in there. Part of my task.

A gem! That was the second priority. I'd had it in my hand, but now both palms were empty. I'd dropped it.

Ducking beneath the water, I looked down, searching for the fallen treasure. It was no use. The faint light above me cared little for penetrating the rippling water's surface. All below me was blackness. I bent double, so my hands could fumble at the invisible floor. Nothing.

A sharp pain in my heart stung me, knowing I'd come this far, had my hands on the fifth gem, the salvation of the Red Bean Queendom, and failed. Failed because of some strange dizziness. My plan didn't accommodate the hot air that had formed inside the upturned pack. Nor the complete darkness underwater; I should have expected that.

The pain wasn't exactly in my heart, though. It was lower and off to the right. It was where the taut rope pulled my belt against my waist in an oddly specific spot. I gave up scrabbling on the streambed and allowed my right hand to slip beneath the straining belt, massaging the painful spot.

My palm discovered a problem few people face. There was a gemstone the size of my fist wedged beneath my belt. Its point jabbed my icy hip, but I didn't care. This was the best pain I'd ever experienced—as my consciousness slipped away some instinct must have urged my hand to slot the gemstone safely away. Jing Jing would be proud of my ability to store treasures about my person. I eased the gem from beneath the belt and clutched it close to my chest. I had the gem, and now it was but a simple matter of putting my head back inside the pack's now cooler air and hauling myself back along the rope to the cave.

Without needing to feel for the nest, backtracking was quicker, and the air inside the pack didn't get so sludgy. My knees gripped the rope while my left hand snaked forward to pull me closer. It was like climbing a rope, except my journey was horizontal, working against the current. The same principles applied—pull, secure the rope with my legs, pull once again, repeat. My right hand remained clenched on the prize, and my strength didn't fade. Yes, my back scraped along the chute roof as the rope and the inflated pack pulled me upward, but nothing soothes perils of the flesh more than victory. Before I knew it, my head broke the waterline, and I felt the cave air whoosh into the pack.

"Guys! I did it! The gem is mine!" I shouted, voice muffled by the bag.

A familiar voice answered, but it was neither Apostle Dando nor the bard, Virgil Longspeaker.

"Not really," the voice said. "I think you'll find the gem is now *mine*."

Master Thorn and the Red Bean Princess

CHAPTER 28 - CAVE

The Same Day

With the pack over my head, my view of the cave included many feet but little else. My own were dripping. The wrinkled skin of hen's feet, where they scratched at the diffuse sand nearby. Dando and Virgil's sandals, standing almost on top of each other. A pair of black, scuffed riding boots a pace away from my friends. And were those scurrying monkey feet at the cave's margin?

It felt like an age as I struggled to free myself from the pack straps so I could see once again and identify the owner of the voice. The man bore a sour and pinched look, as if recently slapped by a wet carp. Mine no doubt took on the surprised expression the carp would have worn during the slap. It was Lord Vendark, beheader of donkeys and all-around unpleasant lackey of Queen Jada of Mossmarch. Had I never seen him again, it would have been too soon, and this was the last place I wanted to encounter him.

His cutlass was out, flat side level with the floor. The subtly curved blade had already drawn a rivulet of blood down Virgil's neck from where its point rested beneath the songsmith's chin. I noticed his bandages were off, and his speech was less slurred than the last time we met as he spoke. The donkey attack's effects had mostly worn off.

"It's over, you buffoon," he said in a voice that was too smooth to be a growl but too acid to be a pleasantry. At least he didn't call me a *buboon*, I thought, remembering the more creative admonishments Master Thorn had flung my way over the years. Or a *clonkey*.

I raised my right arm, letting the giant gemstone hang above the stream's current. If I dropped it, the rushing waters might wash it down the chute before Vendark could retrieve it.

"Hand it over, and we can all go our separate ways. You can exit the cave, admit defeat, and haul your greasy cart and threadbare master away from the shame. I'll see to it you are unharmed."

"What about my two…?" I began.

Apostle Dando shook his head a fraction, not wanting to move suddenly under threat of Vendark's blade. "You know he can't let me go. Or Virgil. He'd speak as much truth as I about what happened here. When this guy, whoever he is, snuck from that slot behind us, he told us he'd keep us alive only until you reappeared with the gem."

Virgil dared not nod with the cruel steel tip already scoring the flesh beneath his chin, but I could see the truth of the matter in his eyes. I realized the threat of dropping the gemstone into the stream was meaningless. Vendark didn't need the stone; he only required me to fail. I lowered my arm.

"There's a good boy," Vendark said. "I'm sure you'll spin a convincing story about how these two failed to survive the trial. You aren't even supposed to give out details of what happens in the cave, so you say nothing, or invent some old toot."

If I could get closer to Vendark, maybe I could overpower him. He was scrawny, and I was at least double his weight. Possibly, I could avoid his blade long enough to flatten and disarm him. I opened my palm and showed him the gem. It collected the dim light from the cave fungus and multiplied it, taking on a red glow of its own.

Vendark was no fool. He swiveled his hips and opened his stance so that Dando and Virgil huddled together at his left, backed off a pace, and transferred the blade to his left hand in a graceful move that I could not help but admire. Now he was far enough from the other two that he could retreat from any surprise attack, and he trained the pointy end of his cutlass on me, the biggest source of peril. The only solace I took from this maneuver was that the blade was now in his left—and likely less-skilled—hand. But I didn't see how I could close in on him without getting skewered. I considered goading the man, as Princess Tasha had on the barge, but facing an unhinged response wasn't something that seemed helpful.

Eying the gemstone seemed like a tactical error. Maybe it

was greed taking control, but he'd have been better off having me drop the gem into the stream and leave the cave. It seemed he wanted to pocket the gem. I tried to put Master Thorn's brain into Vendark's malevolent personality. What plan would emerge? It seemed the best outcome for him would be to kill us all and dump us down the underground stream, sending the gem along, too. If Vendark snuck in here, he could doubtless sneak out again. After a while, if I didn't reappear, the fifth trial would be treated as a failure.

He extended his right hand as I stepped closer. "Lob it over. Any closer, and by my father, I'll finish you."

It seemed likely he'd kill us all, despite his promise to spare me. Why risk my wagging tongue?

I moved my weight onto the balls of my feet and gripped the stony floor with damp toes. This was probably my only hope of a successful attack, so I needed to be ready.

I tossed the gemstone. High. Even in the gloom, I saw Vendark's eyes trace the stone's glittering flight, and his sword's tip rose the slightest bit.

As always, the capabilities of animals outstripped those of humankind. I shifted forward to launch myself at it, but the Meeran gem hen, previously uninterested and scratching near my feet, gave a furious screech before I could move. Maybe it was the idea of its gem being so casually treated, but I like to think it was the possibility of the ignoble Vendark touching the thing that set the hen off. With a fanfare of fluttering wings, the hen pecked Vendark's ankles in a blurring series of strikes. The pecking attack caused no actual damage, but it flustered for a moment.

Stepping back from the hen as he caught the gem, Vendark coughed violently, thumping at his chest, as if something had caught there. A puff of black, smoky air erupted from his mouth, redolent of coal rayvn dust. Vendark's inconvenient coughing attack puzzled me at the time, and it wasn't until much later that Rayne would discover the coal rayvns' protective role and cause me to reflect on what seemed like unbelievably good luck in the fifth cave.

Unbalanced, Vendark slipped on the wet rock at the stream's edge. Riding boots were not the best footwear in this damp space. His heel slid forward, and his blade's point shot up as he fell backward. He released the gem to fling a protective hand behind himself, and it bounced across the rocky floor, coming to rest by the rear wall. Dando's pack cushioned his landing a little, but Vendark still bit back a high-pitched shriek of pain as he slid his right hand along the floor to push himself upright again. Despite the fall, his cutlass slashed down to center on me once again.

I lashed up with my bare right foot, whacking the blade's butt with my big toe. The instant, throbbing pain was worth the result: my toe dislodged the sword from Vendark's grip, and it spun through the air between us.

The man's lank hair floated for a moment as he lunged at the airborne sword, but I got there first. My open palms found the flat of the blade, close to either end, and I slammed it down across my knee. The blade snapped in two, the pieces clattering to the floor.

Fortunately for my knee, but less ideal for Vendark's future palm readings, his reaching hand intervened between my knee and the breaking blade. The cutlass's edge left a deep, bleeding rut across his palm. I could see gristle and bone and had doubts about whether those fingers would ever move properly again. This grisly wound made the parallel but superficial cuts on my own palms seem inconsequential. I thanked the worms of the underworld that it hadn't been a Master Thorn blade; we'd probably both have suffered amputations.

Vendark howled in pain and defeat as I knocked him to the ground and stood over him, the sole of my foot pressing him to the cave floor as blood coursed from his wounded hand.

"That steel was poor quality, don't you think, Lord? Snapped in two by a mere *boy*?" I said.

I learned a lesson that day. Never consider a fight over until someone is running away, tied up, unconscious, or dead. With my calf and thigh open for attack, Vendark's good hand snatched a dagger from the sheath at his hip. His arm rose in a vicious stabbing motion intended to sever tendons and carve through flesh.

But there was no mortal wound that day. No future Minimus capable only of limping from bed to cart. Vendark's grasp fell not on his dagger, but on air alone.

A monkey laughed and the glint of dim light on the blade of the dagger Jing Jing held over his spiky hairdo followed soon after Vendark's clenched hand slapped my outer thigh. Once again, my sneak-thief animal friend's avarice had saved the day. I hadn't seen him slide the dagger from Vendark's sheath, but the dim cave light and monkey agility were in his favor.

My anger turned to the man pinned below me. "Did Queen Jada put you up to this, or is it your own devious plan?"

Vendark squirmed, closing his mangled palm to slow the bleeding, but could not get free. "I'd never tell you that, you worthless mongrel," he said, but then added, "Yes. Jada planned the whole thing."

His expression as his traitorous lips betrayed his brain will never leave me. Utter, stupendous surprise was written large. His eyes widened even more as he continued to speak.

"I threatened and bribed those fools at the gate and snuck in here last night, waiting for you back there in the shadows. If it wasn't for this stupid hen and my cough, I'd have killed you all and snuck back out again tonight. The gem is just a bonus. I wouldn't have even told Queen Jada about that."

Vendark's good hand clapped his mouth shut, although muffled words strained to get past. Dando chuckled, laughed a little louder, then doubled over, struggling to get any words out past his mirth.

"Look at my pack. See what he landed on? Sticking out there through the fabric? It's my land urchin quill. We always carry one during official duties in case we need to pass on the truthsayer's role to a fresh recruit. He must have stabbed himself on it as he fell, the stupid sod."

"I look forward to hearing this part immortalized in song," I said, smiling at Virgil.

"Already composing it in me head, now that there's not a

sword pointed at me throat!" he said.

Jing Jing was at my feet, offering up the gem. The hen and monkey were eye-to-eye, but she seemed much happier now that Vendark no longer held her creation. I wiped the seeping blood from my minor cuts on my tunic, accepted the gem from Jing Jing, and rolled Vendark over beneath my heel. I grabbed the back of his well-tailored riding jacket and lifted. His toes scraped along the ground, jerking with each of my steps as I dragged him. I wasn't at all worried about him wrestling free— one hand was useless, and the other seemed to be needed to block out any further admissions of guilt.

I turned to my two companions. "Dando, could you grab the birdcage, please? And thanks, Ezra. If your thunderbird link worked out, it's going to save a lot of explaining."

Virgil took an experimental strum of his lute, cleared his throat, and eased out two verses describing Vendark's barbarism and stupidity.

I strode ahead, heading for the sunlight. "Let's go, everyone. I'm sick of caves, and if I'm not wrong, there's a monumental feast awaiting us."

CHAPTER 29 - CAMP

The Same Day

The sounds of cheering increased in volume as we trod the passage toward the cave mouth, erupting in jubilation when the five of us strode forth. Well, the most furry among us shot forth on all fours, and Vendark was dragged out by the collar rather than striding, but these sights excited the crowd further. Trumpets and some other blaring instrument I couldn't identify punctuated the shouts.

The thunderbird must have been echoing Vendark's confrontation to the assembled crowd. A phalanx of Red Bean pikemen had swarmed up the causeway and were running along the ledge toward the cave as we emerged. I waved to them, signalling that everything was under control and they skidded to a stop, smiles as wide as greater scaly mudwaders' leathery bottoms.

Jing Jing took the thunderbird cage from Dando and sped up the rope to the balloon above, gripping the cage in one paw. When he reached the top, the gravelly voice of Ezra Longshanks, amplified by his thunderbird, boomed across the plain.

"Minimus Mu has passed the fifth and final trial! Here ends the thundercast."

My monkey friend slid down the rope just as the breeze picked up, and the balloon drifted over the crowd toward the Red Bean Queendom's border. I would see Ezra Longshanks again, far from here, but for now, he seemed content to poke his head over his basket's lip and absorb the panoply of rejoicing people below.

I shifted Vendark to my other hand as I bumped him along the ledge and down the zigzagging path to the guard house, flowing the troop of pikemen. He was still babbling away behind his hand when we reached the guardhouse.

None of the guards would meet my gaze. One muttered in a low voice, "He kidnapped Andre's family. We're really sorry."

Vendark swept his hand away from his mouth in a theatrical gesture. "I most certainly did not!" he shouted.

That was puzzling. Had the guards betrayed me, despite all the snacks and earlier well-wishing? Or had Lord Vendark's habitual lying overcome the urchin quill's magic?

Then Vendark continued. "I was in a rush after ordering the attack on Minimus's tent, and I only kidnapped Andre's children, not his whole family. I left the wife and sister in the house. Told them I'd—" I lost the rest as he slapped his hand over his lips once more.

At the causeway's base, the pikemen cleared a narrow slot through the still cheering crowd. Virgil, Dando, and I proceeded in single file. I dropped Vendark at the foot of a Golden Shores guardsman and forged along the narrow gap in the throng toward Princess Tasha, her parents, Rayne, and the incongruent Master Thorn at the far end. The guard dragged Vendark away on my behalf, and it was clear that the crowd had heard his every word in the cave. The guards tried to deflect any attacks on his grimy form, but there were so many kicks directed his way that Master Thorn would probably have called it a shoenami.

Everyone wanted to touch Dando, Virgil, and me as we passed. The smaller Red Bean citizens at the front brushed our legs while the taller second row patted shoulders and biceps. I'd never heard so many words of thanks, adulation, and encouragement. The pain of my sliced hands disappeared, and a warm flush crept from my feet to my ears. I held the final gem aloft as I raced the last few paces before kneeling to present it to Queen Violet.

Lord Alfred held a thunderbird in the crook of his arm, and the queen spoke to it, her voice booming forth under the bird's magic.

"Citizens of Red Bean and the lands of our sister queens!" she called out. It took a moment for the crowd to hush, and she paused before continuing. In that time, I'd knelt and gave in to the embraces that sped my way. Rayne had leapt at me, arms encircling my neck in the strongest clinch she could muster. Her face pressed against my neck, and her voice streamed a babble of relief and congratulations in my ear.

Master Thorn's longer arms encircled both Rayne and me. His normal eloquence melted away, and he repeated, "My boy! My boy!" For once, I felt like I was his child, a baby overwhelmed by the crowding adults. The pause in Violet's speech was long enough for Master Thorn to recover his composure. He released me and swept away a tear from his left eyebrow's substantial overhang. "Minimus, you are a phenomaly!"

"Umm... what's a—?"

"Silly salamander," he answered. "A phenomaly is something incredible that only happens once. That's you!"

Queen Violet cleared her throat and continued to speak to the quieting crowd.

"This is a momentous week we've been through. Our chosen champion, Minimus Mu, has accomplished more than we should have ever asked and completed all five of the champion's tasks. As you have all now heard and seen, the illegal attempt by Outer Pang's queen to treat us unfairly just because we are slight has proved to be nothing but overblown spite. And we've all heard her Lord outline a murderous plot that corrupts all our laws with no second thought. I call the other queens to confirm my position that Outer Pang should now face *transition*."

"What's transition?" I murmured to Rayne as her grip loosened, and she took up a tiptoed perch on my right knee.

Princess Tasha spoke in my other ear, answering for her handmaiden. "If a queen takes an unforgiveable action deemed so egregious by at least four other queens that it's no longer right for her to govern her land, they can confront her and take a stand. The result is a council, formed by her queen peers, that will rule her queendom for the next seven years."

Queen Violet turned to face the phalanx of queens and their guards behind her. Seelah of Meer gestured first, her lighter outfaced palm stark against her rich brown skin. Valance of Oceanplat followed, in tandem with the delicate hand of

Queen Liu of Inner Pang. Each raised her left hand and touched her tiara, acknowledging the grave proposed action.

At the end of the row, Queen Jada glowered, tiara-free, saying nothing but motioning her guardsmen to tighten their knot around her glittering black robes. I saw Sang of Seven Rocks was among the guards, their spears bristling as the accusations swirled.

The fourth vote needed came from Queen Angstaad of Golden Shores. She hardly needed to express her opinion of Queen Jada, and with a cursory raising of her hand to forehead, she swept her own guard out of her way and advanced on the cluster of Outer Pangan soldiers. Her sword snicked from its sheath, and she whirled it overhead, the air thrumming to its rhythm. Her mailed shoulder added a metallic accompaniment. Her guards' hands moved to their swords as Pangan soldiers leveled spears at Angstaad's approach, but she bid them keep their distance with a backhanded gesture.

"Get out of my way, or you'll *all* regret it," she growled. Her guards formed a semicircle behind her, their own weapons still sheathed but clearly ready to engage at a moment's notice.

The Outer Pangan guardsmen aimed their spears and braced for action.

"Guys, guys!" a voice called from beneath a golden Pangan helm among the tight pack of warriors. "You know they're right. Our queendom lies dishonored already. Don't make it any worse."

Sang of Seven Rocks threw his spear to the ground, followed by his helmet. Hand on the guardsman to his left's spear, he urged its point down. Relenting, that man, too, dropped his spear. Every other Outer Pangan soon followed. Sang swept a channel between the guards, exposing Jada to Queen Angstaad's direct wrath.

With a leap forward, Angstaad seized Jada by the hair, her sword pausing its deadly whirl to point, quivering, at the dark-haired queen's left eye, a hand's breadth away. Jada didn't even flinch.

"You can't hurt me," Jada spat, her neck pulsing where she

strained against Angstaad's grip. "You know as well as I that the code would then require your own death."

Angstaad growled, nostrils flaring. Despite the consequences, she raised her short sword high above her right shoulder and brought it down in a vicious slash. I expected to see a head bounce across the grass, but instead, Queen Angstaad wheeled on her heel and cast a hacked-off bundle of glossy blonde hair to the ground behind her. Queen Jada's face twisted into an ugly mask of apoplectic rage, framed by asymmetric tufts of short hair. She lunged for Angstaad's back, but her own troops restrained her before anything more dramatic could unfold. Angstaad didn't even bother turning—I couldn't imagine Jada's full fury was a match for the warrior queen's merest flick of a wrist.

Master Thorn and the Red Bean Princess

CHAPTER 30 - SOUTHERN MEER

The Same Day

Queen Violet asked *me* how many days of feasting should follow my success. I blurted out a week, but in hindsight, I probably could have requested a month or even a year. The first feast took place in the camp at the mountain's foot. We would decamp the next day and take the quick journey to Evermere, to continue the feasting there.

I thought I'd been eating the best food the queendom offered, but when confronted with the cornucopia the mobile kitchens mustered for the victory banquet, I knew the next six dinners would simmer in my memory forever. A chef rolled a basin roiling with gorge cod to my shoulder and asked me to select which fish he would prepare for me atop a sizzling iron hotplate his assistant wheeled alongside. There were salvers of buttery beans, salads with savory, bitter, and sweet leaves, and scallops smothered in a tangy sauce.

The desserts rivaled the pies from Seven Rocks, although I wouldn't have debated that with the Red Bean Queendom's newest citizen, who sat on Master Thorn's other side at the head table. Rayne feared Sang of Seven Rocks would face an uncertain future as a guardsman in Outer Pang after the favors he'd quietly provided throughout our recent adventures, and persuaded Tasha to enlist him in her mother's staff. He was now an honorary peer of the queendom, and could barely restrain his joy as he spoke about bringing his betrothed and her mother from Seven Rocks to live in Evermere.

As the servers slid the dessert course plates onto the head table and re-filled empty glasses, I looked past Rayne and Tasha on my right, to where Queen Violet stepped onto a platform and raised her thunderbird to address the diners and the myriad of feasting attendants beyond.

"My fellow queens, guests, and Beans! Outer Pang has fled the scene. The law is clear to everyone here. We are positioned to guide their queendom's transition from Jada's malaise into much better days. We'll supply a council of peers to be overseers, one member each from Oceanplat, Inner Pang, and Meer. Golden Shores will hold the throne. None shall wield the power alone. In Mossmarch, Red Bean will merely advise, and it should come as no surprise that Princess Tasha will there be my tongue and my eyes."

Queen Violet turned to her daughter and gave a brief bow. Alfred, on Violet's other side, beamed a smile so broad it almost left his face.

"You're ready for this, my darling," the queen concluded.

* * *

"Shall we snuggle under the cart one more time?" Rayne asked.

I wanted nothing more, and we ambled across the grass, casting contrasting shadows in the camp's flickering torchlight. With the fringed curtains drawn around the cart, Rayne and I leaned against the overstuffed cushions someone had left for us, arranging woolen blankets around our contours as if forming sand dunes of our own design. My stomach rumbled, embarking on its own five trials of over-feasting. I knew not how much time I would have with Rayne before Master Thorn's feet itched to peddle runcible sporks to new queendoms, or Rayne would return to Tasha's side in Mossmarch as her primary handmaiden. Neither of us had control over our destinies, but we could ignore that for a night, a week, or maybe a month.

Strains of a song struggled to pierce the fabric surrounding us. I recognized the singer's voice, a constant over the last five days.

"He's singing about you, Minimus. The biggest hero in Red Bean's history," Rayne murmured.

Somewhere outside, a coal rayvn hooted, a friendly call to the other denizens of the night.

CHAPTER 31 - EVERMERE

Milkday of Mountain, Year 127 (One Month Later)

"It's unbelievable," the minstrel Virgil Longspeaker said to his robed companion. "People follow me around, little and large. It's almost as if I'm a hero, too, basking in Minimus's glow. I'm only a singer!"

The truthsayer, Apostle Dando, nodded. "Me, too. And I can't even sing. All I do is say what happened, and fuel the waggling tongues with any parts I omit. But you must admit, we faced the sabreclaws, too, and you have a becoming scar under your chin to show from Lord Vendark's blade."

"That rotter," Virgil said. "Did you hear what Princess Tasha did to him? After the questioning—"

"—which would have been very interesting, what with that recent jab from my land urchin quill. It takes a month or two before you can prevent yourself from yammering out every suppressed truth in your brain," Dando said.

"Heh, yeah. Well, the princess assigned Vendark to the Council of Outer Pang. They force him to make weekly announcements in the square at Mossmarch. And take *questions* from the rabble. Now *that* would be a good laugh. Fancy a side journey?"

"Maybe," the apostle said. "I'll ask my guildmaster. I heard there's a company carrying Queen Jada's tiara that Minimus found at the Gorge of Razors. It's headed for safekeeping in Mossmarch until the transition is over and the next queen is selected. They might allow us to ride along."

"Might? How could they refuse the company of the queendom's most popular singer? And its best-looking truthsayer!"

Virgil clapped a friendly arm wrapped in tartan silk around his new friend's shoulder. "In the meantime, let's duck into this tavern here and see who'll show a couple of goat's teeth to buy us a round."

* * *

Mister Apples stamped his hooves under a snorted cloud of misty breath in the cool morning air. The horse seemed happy to be harnessed for a journey, and Minimus Mu, although reluctant to leave Evermere, would enjoy riding atop the cart instead of pulling it.

The cartwheels had been refashioned by the royal wainwright, and fresh springs fitted. Several other elements of the traveling cutlery business bore the fruits of unsolicited donations from across the queendom. The fold-up stall now had embroidered cloths and an umbrella bearing the Red Bean royal seal. The cart sported new hidden compartments, armored to protect the five gem hen gemstones that Queen Violet allowed Minimus Mu to keep. A fresh supply of metals for fabricating the finest implements and tablewares lay cached beneath the bench seat.

In the three weeks after the trials, Master Thorn had perfected the form and fabrication of the runcible spork. Its delicate curves, cunning serrated edge, and beautiful multifunctionality would surely prove an irresistible addition to every kitchen from Inner Pang to Far Inchaway.

Master Thorn regarded the strong-shouldered boy at his side. Minimus was cleaner and better dressed than before, with a haircut that almost tamed his thin and unruly mop, but it wasn't the trappings of luxury that moved the man's heart. The subtle lessons, the friendships, the puppet shows, the harping and carping that rolled off the boy's back like water from an otter—they'd all sunk in, as he'd proven. Five times. He considered telling Minimus the secret of his vanished mother, perhaps even introducing the boy to his father.

The cart groaned with all their worldly possessions, but Master Thorn realized they had no destination. All he knew was they needed to steer clear of Outer Pang. Who could predict what sympathizers of ex-Queen Jada they might encounter there? "Well, we can't go to Droz, can we, Minimus? Some of those barbarians haven't even *heard* of cutlery. And now that you fraternize with queens, I've heard that Queen Grizelda is one to avoid on account of her ever-gurning face. You choose our destination, my boy."

The boy opened and closed his mouth twice before responding. Minimus considered selecting Oceanplat, or even Wraithwatch across the Fading Sea. The spice merchants on the island of Del Carta would surely welcome fine cutlery. Those destinations would all entail the sea voyage he'd dreamed of, but risked a Masterly slap behind the ears and a retraction of the offer.

Still, Minimus liked it when Master Thorn called him *my boy*. It halved the impact of a mother that cast him aside and a father he'd never know.

"Golden Shores," he said. "I'm sure Queen Angstaad would welcome us into the Port of Yinti." The boy regarded Rayne and rubbed at the inner rim of his eye with a bent wrist. "Maybe the new ambassador to Outer Pang might need an official trip there? Say, in a month or two?"

With a wistful half-smile, the fine-featured redhead nodded. "Perhaps I could persuade the princess. Especially if the Champion of the Five Trials promises to be there."

* * *

The witch Alianthe felt the winds of peril ruffle her glossy rayvn feathers. The magic of all animals remained in jeopardy, and these two children of men must remain close. She flew beneath a slate sky, east, seaward, to make the required arrangements and pacts.

Last Words

Thank you for reading *Master Thorn and the Red Bean Princess*. If you enjoyed the story, leaving a review is a good way to let other readers know how to follow in your footsteps. I appreciate your feedback.

Minimus, Master Thorn, Rayne, and Jing Jing will return in *Master Thorn and the Mothers of Midnight*.

Minimus Mu, Master Thorn, and Jing Jing cross the Fading Sea and become entangled in an incursion into their world by the Mothers of Midnight, a frightening sect that threatens the liberty of children and the magic of every animal.

Join my mailing list and find more at
www.pattisontelford.com

Pattison Telford lives in Toronto, Canada, surrounded by non-magical people and animals that nevertheless possess certain charms.

The Calendar

Dates follow a pattern where the days of the month are named after foods, and the months after natural items. Years are counted from the great calendaring convention of Meer, which initiated Sugarday of Sun, Year 0. For example, this story begins on **Sugarday of Moon, Year 127.**

The months:

Spring:	Sun	Moon	
Summer:	River	Mountain	Tree
Autumn:	Stone	Lake	Rain
Winter:	Valley	Snow	

The days:

Each month consists of five weeks of five days each, with a three-day week from Cakeday to Spiceday. Some regions observe days of rest, feasting, or celebration during that short week.

Sugarday	Pepperday	Saltday	Milkday	Creamday
Beanday	Lentilday	Sproutday	Fishday	Cressday
Onionday	Lettuceday	Radishday	Lighningfruitday	Cheeseday
Yamday	Appleday	Lemonday	Limeday	Bunday
	Cakeday	Berryday	Spiceday	
Gingerday	Garlicday	Nutday	Hexrootday	Oatday

Animal Life

Although fish have no apparent magical powers, rich variety exists among the creatures that roam the land and skies. Animals mentioned in this story and their known magic are described here.

Abomination Bird: Capable of lifting a horse, this six-winged bird of prey is a powerful flyer and magically resistant to most forms of damage.

Coal Rayvn: This sooty black bird possesses both typical bird claws and a frontal pair of furry legs and paws. They emit puffs of dark dust as they flap, and have magical powers unknown to humans.

Donkey: The sure-footed but cantankerous cargo bearers can defend themselves with cones of intense noise.

Drift Goose: Albatross-like wingspan. Can remain airborne for days or weeks at a time to avoid danger.

Fanglimb: A non-magical and many-limbed sea creature whose ravaging tentacles are tipped with tooth-laden maws and searching eyestalks.

Golden Mountain Ram: The agile sheep that delight in cavorting on steep hillsides and rock faces can detonate themselves, forming a raging fireball if the herd is threatened.

Gongo Bird: Has long feathers like a peacock. Can soften itself to avoid damaging impacts. Discarded feathers are well-known tickling implements.

Gorge Cod: With scintillating rainbow scales and an enormous tail fin, this fish is caught only in the Gorge of Razors.

Hovering Goat: Capable and desirous of eating nearly anything, these goats are magically weightless and are a common sight wherever people gather. Their primary defense is to bring extreme bad luck upon anyone wishing them harm, which is a powerful enough deterrent for fortune seekers desiring their lighter-than-air teeth, used as currency across the queendoms.

Meeran Gem Hen: Fussy hens whose magical power is to produce finely-cut jewels, each enhanced with a unique geometric shape at its center.

Monkey: Exploration of their unquenchable curiosity is aided by their magic-assisted manual speed and dexterity.

Pangan Lemur: Nocturnal prowlers known for their inquisitive faces and co-operative communities. Their fur emits a dim glow at night, and they respond with shocks of lightning if threatened.

Ponykin: Tiny horses of a scale that Red Beaners can ride.

Sabreclaw: A feline apex predator, its razor-sharp claws can quell the magic of its prey animals.

Vondabeast: A shaggy, lumbering, hoofed grass-eater with threatening horns that can extend at speed in self-defense.